Drawing Freedom

Felicia Ketcheson

Lava Lake Books

Receive a Free Short Story

Receive an exclusive and free short story by subscribing to my newsletter at https://subscribepage.io/drawingreader. You'll also receive news about upcoming releases and exclusive content. Your email will never be shared.

If you only want to read the story, feel free to unsubscribe after downloading your copy.

Dedication

To Rocky, who brought so much joy to my life.

Author's Note

As a Canadian, I use Canadian spellings throughout.

Chapter One

Breel attempted to concentrate on reading an email, but the clunky old furnace running on the other side of the wall didn't make it easy. Then, without warning, clomping feet sounded overhead.

It had gotten easier to ignore the furnace but not footsteps from upstairs. Until a couple of weeks ago, no one had ever been in a house with a basement. But after Breel and her allies escaped Lexum after President Tatem tried to kill them at Mortae, they moved into a house in the desert with a basement.

The footsteps shook the building and jiggled the mouse and printer on Breel's birch table-turned desk. Dust rained down from the ceiling's exposed beams and wooden boards.

"Emergency meeting! Emergency meeting!" shouted Manum.

Breel's heart rate doubled. Her limbs shook as she turned to her boyfriend, Cafrec, who stared back with wide crystal-blue eyes hidden behind a lock of sandy-coloured hair. For once, Cafrec's presence didn't calm Breel. This was the second emergency meeting Manum had called. The first had been when the Department of Enforcement scheduled officers to search the area.

At first, the DOE's searches for them had been within Lexum. But when the officers didn't find them within the city, they turned to the old Lexum suburbs.

Every DOE search brought Breel back to when she and Cafrec fled Lexum to Intercludae—the now extinct secret society underneath Lexum, which was home to one hundred and fifty ex-Lexum citizens working to overthrow Tatem. DOE officers had chased them as they escaped via a pipe in the wall. When they returned to Lexum to apprehend Tatem with some Intercludae residents, everything went wrong.

Someone had tipped off Tatem that a small group had gone to his estate to take him down, so he arrested them. After Samit Tucap helped them escape Mortae, they lived as fugitives. Everyone else on their side lived in Lexum, pretending to be pro-Tatem while assisting their cause in secret.

Tatem often called for searches; however, Breel's group had enough DOE contacts to influence most of them and avoid capture. Their people either ensured the DOE searched elsewhere in the desert or assigned their own people as search leader. But impromptu searches didn't always give enough time to do that. They had gotten lucky during the previous emergency because at the last minute, a DOE contact had changed the search leader to an ally.

What are the chances of the DOE not finding us again?

Breel's legs shook as she climbed the creaking wooden stairs. She gathered with the others in the kitchen, congregating between the hallway and the kitchen's L-shaped counter. Vectus, who had taught Breel and Cafrec programming; Manum, a weight training teacher; and Breel's mother, Criba, a secretary, arrived first. Ex-DOE officers Lexo and Praxa; and Breel's brother, Trafis followed Breel and Cafrec upstairs. It was a sea of black pants and belts with various coloured sweaters—reds, oranges, and navy blues.

Though it was a sunny day, someone had turned on the kitchen light as, otherwise, the room would've been dark because of the semi-closed blinds. They had learned to keep them open enough to allow for some natural light, but not enough for someone outside to see inside.

Breel leaned against the warped wooden countertop, Cafrec beside her, then looked at Manum. His face and muscular arms glistened from a workout. Wiping sweat from his brow, he noticed Samit sitting at the small table he used for a desk behind the dining table in the adjoining room. Samit's fingers flew over his laptop's keyboard.

"Stop working for once, Samit," Manum said.

Samit turned, light reflecting off his bald head, then did a double take upon seeing everyone.

One month ago, Breel and Cafrec had called Samit "Mr. Tucap" because, as the Head of Computer Programmers in the Department of Education, he'd been their boss. After moving into the house, they'd voted no-nonsense Samit as their leader since he had management experience.

I just can't get away from this guy as my superior.

Samit walked over, then draped his long body onto the counter, avoiding one of the many stains they'd been unable to remove.

Manum cleared his throat. "The DOE is about to search the area again."

Breel's stomach dropped.

Again?

"Were they tipped off?" she asked, pushing her glasses up her nose.

Manum shook his head. "It doesn't sound like it."

It wasn't much consolation. Regardless of whether it was random, the DOE would find them.

Vectus scratched his head, his short, red hair clashing with his scarlet sweater. "How much time?"

"We got this info late, so maximum half an hour," said Manum. "Let's get moving like last time, everyone."

They didn't waste time. Manum turned off the generator. They shut down their laptops, then placed them into the kitchen cabinets, being careful when opening and closing the cracked and misaligned doors. Samit wedged inside the two monitors he insisted he needed. Lexo and Vectus moved the dining room birch spindle chairs to the basement's storage room. Criba ensured they had locked the front door while Manum, Lexo, and Praxa retrieved weapons from the hall closet across from it. The same dart guns used by the DOE, they'd knock someone out for an hour or two.

Everyone descended the stairs into the basement, then passed by Breel and Cafrec's desks to enter the furnace room. No one wasted time finding a spot without cobwebs or rust stains from the furnace. Breel and Cafrec sat next to a bend in a sagging pipe, which was home to thick cobwebs. Manum pulled a string to turn off the flickering lightbulb hanging from the ceiling. The basement's musty smell was even thicker with the door closed, hitting everyone like an inescapable infinite loop.

If the DOE find us, it'll be my fault that Mother and Trafis die.

Breel's stomach dropped at the thought. Criba and Trafis were only there because they'd followed Breel after her failed Mortae. If she hadn't agreed to go to Intercludae with Cafrec, they'd be in Lexum and, arguably, safer.

Five minutes.

Her body shook even though the room wasn't cold. A dry throat made swallowing difficult.

Don't cough, don't cough.

The sound of everyone's breathing, including her own, was audible. She tried not to think about Criba and Trafis being with her because when she did, her breath caught, and she had to bite her tongue to keep from crying. Concentrating on the warm feel of Cafrec's arm around her shoulders eased some of the panic coursing through her.

Ten minutes.

The DOE officers would be closer. Travelling in a group of five, loaded with guns and a stash of darts, it was hard to know if they'd search every building they came across or just within a particular area.

Searching everything would take time. The lower class had lived in the suburbs until fifty years ago when Tatem became president and moved everyone within Lexum's walls. The first group of houses and warehouses the DOE would've come across were parallel to and five miles from Lexum's walls, with desert separating them from Lexum. It had warehouses and dilapidated and claustrophobic rowhouses. Roofs, broken glass, leaves, and other debris cluttered the roads. Searching in every corner was an impossible task.

Next, there were two more groups of housing two miles away from and perpendicular to the first group. Nestled in between the houses were the factories where most of the lower class had worked. Beside every factory stood a well constructed, oversized bungalow which had housed the factory supervisor. One of the bungalows now housed Breel and her group. Searching each factory and house would take the officers hours.

Twenty minutes.

Voices sounded from outside.

Someone (*Mother?*) gasped.

Cafrec's nails dug into Breel's arm. She removed one of his fingers, her movements jerky from the adrenaline pumping through her. Taking the hint, he loosened his grip.

"Looks as abandoned as everything else," said a baritone voice. "Leaf piles, wrecked roof, weathered walls..."

Thank goodness we left the exterior as damaged as when we got here.

"Yeah, no one could live here," said another. He sounded younger. "Let's head back and get out of this chilly wind. I wish we brought jackets."

Is he making excuses because he's on our side? If he isn't...

Breel shuddered at the thought of the officers coming inside.

"Officer!" shouted a woman. Her voice could've carried a mile. "You'll do your job."

"Excuse me, I'm the search leader." It was the baritone voiced man.

Silence. Breel imagined the three officers facing off with the leader glaring as the others stayed quiet. Tatem prohibited disobedience, so if either officer continued, the search leader was within his right to report it, leading to their Mortae. The arguing stopped.

Perhaps one of them is on our side and wondering what to do?

The woman spoke. "Will we search? If I was a horrid President Tatem hater, I'd pick this house over those rowhouses."

"But there are no footprints," said somebody else. "If they were here, wouldn't there be footprints?"

Criba gasped. Footprints weren't something anyone had thought about. However, it was windy enough for sand to cover any footprints within hours.

"The bungalows beside the other factories were empty," said the leader. "But yes, we must search. To save time, the rest of you search the factory, and I'll meet you there after searching the house."

Breel gasped. Her muscles seized as Cafrec's arm tightened.

It'll be fine, it'll be fine. We have ex-DOE with us. It'll be fine.

"Is splitting up wise?" asked the woman.

"I gave you an order, officer."

"Yes, sir."

Bile threatened to rise in her throat.

There'll only be one of them. We'll be okay, we'll be okay...

But despite what she told herself, Breel didn't think they'd be okay at all.

Chapter Two

The next few minutes were some of the longest of Breel's life.

Silence, then a squeak as the front door opened. Though Breel and the others had hidden their things, the lack of dust, dirt, and grime would be a clear sign they lived in the house.

Footsteps sounded (louder than Manum's because of the officer's government-issued boots) as the officer walked through the dining room and kitchen.

Someone muffled a sneezed then gasped.

Trafis. The dust must've triggered his allergies.

But it didn't matter. The DOE had found them.

Manum whispered, "Lexo, Praxa. Let's go."

Someone opened the door, then, moments later, shut it.

This time, Breel ignored Cafrec's nails digging into her. The odds were good with Manum, Lexo, and Praxa against one officer, but there were also the four other officers to deal with later.

Please be careful, please be careful.

"Lexo?"

Breel gasped at the baritone voice of the search leader. But instead of sounding aggressive, he sounded curious.

"Luap?" Lexo's voice was small.

"Yeah, man. I've dropped my weapon. Can you drop yours?"

"Why should we trust you?" Manum asked.

Luap's laugh was a deep rumble. "I was Lexo's partner during his stint as a patrol officer. Lexo, you can trust me."

No one spoke. Manum would've been out front to protect Lexo and Praxa. But after Luap called to Lexo, Lexo would've stepped in front, weapon pointed at him. As for Praxa, she didn't seem DOE officer material at all.

I bet she's standing behind them, hoping she won't have to use her weapon.

Breel's hand ached from Cafrec clenching it.

"Why didn't you tell me?" Lexo asked.

"That I'm anti-Tatem?" said Luap. "You didn't tell me either, man. I only knew when I saw your face plastered on all those posters and the news. You did a good job of hiding—ahh! What was that for?! You trying to blind me?"

"Making sure you had dropped your gun," said Manum. "Couldn't tell without a light, so I used my flashlight."

"You can all come out," said Lexo. "His gun's down."

It was as if someone had lifted a fifty-pound weight from Breel's shoulders.

We'll live to see another day.

Someone flicked on a flashlight, illuminating everyone in an eerie glow as they got to their feet. Cafrec eased his grip on Breel's hand as they exited, her jelly legs regaining strength.

Luap descended the stairs. He had the same wide shoulders, thick arms, and crew cut as Manum. Like all Leaders of Today, he wore black dress pants and a white dress shirt underneath his department sweater. It was the Department of Enforcement's sunshine yellow with the DOE officer Career Group's two thick neon yellow stripes around his biceps.

Strange that seeing career stripes is weird.

She'd seen them all her life—except on Leaders of Tomorrow who wore thicker dress shirts rather than sweaters. Breel and the others had snagged black pants and sweaters of various colours—without career striping—from Intercludae, so it'd been three weeks since seeing stripes in person.

Luap observed everyone. "Yep, I recognize you from the posters and news, except you..." He pointed to Vectus, then turned back to Lexo, slapping him on the back. Somehow, slender Lexo didn't fly across the room. "Good to see you again, my man."

Lexo blinked in confusion and scratched his blonde head. "You, too. I didn't know you were on our side."

"You're the first people to know."

Manum patted his arm. "We're grateful."

Breel's heart slowed to its normal rhythm. If Luap could continue leading searches and preventing officers from entering the house, it'd keep them safe.

"When'd you become anti-Tater?" asked Manum, using his nickname for Tatem.

Luap's gaze drifted to the ceiling. His expression faltered, frowning as he noticed the ceiling.

Not used to seeing exposed wooden beams and floorboards and a low ceiling.

"Uh...a year or two, I guess. Started when the retirement home sucked my parents' vitality dry. Then I watched the Mortae of a close friend."

Breel shuddered. She was lucky to have never witnessed the Mortae of somebody close to her, but many had. Since Tatem punished Leaders of Tomorrow with Mortae after receiving their third warning, and Leaders of Today had no warnings, it meant most weeks had at least one Mortae.

It was a relief to no longer attend them in person—watching the replay on the evening news was enough. Seeing everyone in the Quaddro (the public square in the centre of Lexum) with Tatem standing on a raised platform, pumping up the crowd. The DOE escorting the Vucapi to the platform to receive their punishment while their family watched from the front row and the crowd demanded punishment. The Deliverer (dressed in brown robes and a mask to conceal their identity) injecting the lethal needle into the arm of the Vucapi. Tatem reminding citizens of the societal importance of Mortae.

The most sickening part was Tatem convincing citizens about the importance of Mortae. Seeing the death of a close friend had been enough to make Luap reconsider his beliefs—but that was unusual.

Luap turned to Lexo. "How about you, Lexo man?"

"Similar. I was ten when the government forced my grandparents to retire and move to the retirement home. When they refused, my parents believed they deserved their Mortae. I turned to the only person I thought would understand."

He motioned to Manum who had taught weight training to Lexo, Praxa, and most of the other younger DOE officers.

Manum clapped a hand on Lexo's shoulder and smiled. "I knew Lexo was anti-Tater at heart even though he didn't yet know it." Turning to Luap, he asked, "Are you willing to work with us?"

Luap's eyes lit up. "Of course! I've volunteered to lead many searches, hoping to find and help you. I'm happy to do whatever you need."

Breel and Cafrec grinned. Luap had influence as a DOE search leader, which gave them an enormous advantage.

Manum shook Luap's hand. "Excellent. I'll be in touch once Samit gets you an email to contact us and our other sources. He's created an email system to communicate with our allies."

Luap frowned. "How does President Tatem not find out?"

"Because of me," Samit said.

Oh, here he goes speaking as if Luap asked the colour of the sky.

Samit puffed out his chest. "Tatem himself called me Lexum's best hacker. I can get around any firewall or encryption his people throw at me. Our use of Lexum's network is undetectable, thanks to me."

"Oh," said Luap, unfazed. "Okay."

"It's imperative you keep our whereabouts a secret," said Samit. "You understand?"

"Not even to others on our side," said Lexo.

Luap moved his thumb and forefinger across his lips. "Your location stays with me. Now, I need to go before those idiots return."

They bid Luap farewell and hoped he'd lead the next search.

***

Everyone returned to their rickety birch table-turned desks which they had gotten from the factory one hundred feet away. Breel's muscles relaxed as she sat then swept the dust on her desk onto the floor, adding to the piles of dust and sand—an ever-present reminder of the surrounding desert. Some slipped into the jagged cracks in the concrete floor.

Amazing how quickly it's collected since we cleaned one month ago.

Cleaning had been a priority after moving in. It hadn't been easy as not only had the house sat vacant for fifty years, but nobody had ever cleaned. They contacted an anti-Tatem housekeeper for tips, then spent a day washing the windowpanes, dusting, and cleaning the wooden floorboards, bathrooms, and kitchen with hand soap and the few towels available. The house wasn't spotless like the houses in Lexum, which professionals cleaned daily; however, it was a tremendous improvement.

Cafrec sat at his desk beside Breel's then wiped it, too. "That was lucky with Luap."

Yeah. But for how long will we keep getting lucky?

Working close together was like the handful of days they had worked in the same office at the Department of Education after Breel finished school and before they left for Intercludae. The only downside wasn't having a window.

Sometimes, Breel couldn't believe she'd known Cafrec for little more than one month. A lot had happened since meeting. Decoding Samit's instructions to escape to Intercludae via a drainage pipe in Lexum's walls. Learning her uncle Famut—who had dated Cafrec's cousin, Centia—hadn't died five years before but was leader of Intercludae's residents. Invading Lexum to apprehend Tatem. Tatem murdering Famut, then arresting and sentencing everyone to Mortae. Escaping execution with the other Vucapi. Criba and Trafis coming with them. Following Samit to a safe house. Waiting for Praxa and Lexo to find a house in the suburbs to live in. Leaving Lexum one week later.

Breel didn't know what she'd do without Cafrec. She certainly wouldn't be living as a fugitive. Though Famut had encouraged her to think for herself, he hadn't been around to give her the final push. That had been Cafrec.

As Cafrec gazed at his screen, hair obscuring his view, Breel's heart fluttered. She used to think such sensations only happened when someone first had a crush on someone, but after dating Cafrec for over a month, looking at him still made her heart forget how to beat a steady rhythm.

Breel's laptop pinged, distracting her. She checked her inbox to find an email from Evad—a Department of Health doctor.

Evad was one of over eight hundred and fifty known allies living in Lexum. Only those with reason to believe the DOE knew they were anti-Tatem or had a specific skill set had left for Intercludae. The underground society had been big enough to house few people, and most could make bigger contributions recruiting others and passing information within Lexum.

"Hi, Breel," Evad had written. "Something good happened today."

Breel grinned. Evad had first emailed her two weeks ago, thrilled to speak with Famut's niece as they'd worked together until Famut began working as a geneticist at the fertility clinic. Breel and Evad emailed to swap stories and memories of Famut.

Evad said, "A patient said we had a few classes together as Leaders of Tomorrow then asked if I knew Famut. I could tell that he sensed I share Famut's beliefs, as he smiled and said, 'I knew him, too.' His mannerisms and anecdotes suggest he's on our side. Many people remember Famut and, when it's safe, speak about him with respect. I know things seem bleak, but more and more people join our side every day. We will get there...Evad."

Breel smiled, grateful that Evad told her this. Reading his emails lifted her spirits not just because he reminisced about Famut, but because he was always positive.

Cafrec was no different. Despite their situation, he was a font of optimism. His outlook gave her the will to continue what they were doing.

Chapter Three

The evening news played after supper. Electricity was thanks to an electrician from the Department of Utilities talking them through how to get the generator running.

Most of the group brought their kitchen chairs into the living room to watch the television as only three could fit on the couch, which Breel, Cafrec, and Trafis had snagged. Time had worn and faded the brown couch. Cleaning it had been impossible, so sitting on it sent a cloud of dust and sand flying into the air, causing Trafis to sneeze three times.

As usual, Samit joined late as he insisted on squeezing in as much work as possible.

The living room was a good size at thirteen by seventeen feet; however, one couch, six chairs, a television, and Criba's desk in the corner filled it. They had replaced the broken windows with garbage bags taped to the warped wooden frames. The wooden wall behind the television had a big enough chunk missing to reveal the frame.

An unseen newscaster droned on about the day's events. It was typical news: changes to mandatory Department of Expansion course curriculums certain Career Groups took as Leaders of Today, a farmer singing his praises to President Tatem, and a man from the Department of Enforcement saying he had no updates on the whereabouts of the missing Vucapi or those who fled with them. There was also a Mortae.

Since Breel and the others had escaped their own Mortae (at which non-lethal darts had rained onto the crowd and citizens stormed the platform) Tatem had made changes.

He no longer trusted citizens, so his four security officers flanked him during all times, including during Mortae. The Deliverer killed multiple Vucapi ("victims" Famut had called them) as there were too many to dedicate one Mortae per victim.

The news panned the Quaddro while highlighting the Mortae, which took place on a long platform. Behind it was a wall with a door from which The Deliverer, Tatem, and his security would emerge. During her Mortae, Breel had learned the door led to a staircase which descended to where the DOE held Vucapi until bringing them onto the platform as Tatem announced their name.

Leaders of Tomorrow sat on the platform's wooden benches, each with a DOE officer standing behind them, hands on their shoulders. Tatem stood in the middle behind a microphone, flanked by his four personal security guards. Breel counted eight Vucapi before the video switched to President Hargam Tatem's daily address from his office.

Standing in front of his oak desk which overflowed the screen, Tatem ran a hand over his slicked back salt-and-pepper hair. One month before, the same hand had shot Famut with a gun. Hatred bubbled in Breel's stomach as she pushed away the image of her uncle crumpling to the ground.

Tatem smoothed his characteristic tailored ash gray suit into which he'd tucked his cherry-red tie. He shook his head at the camera, eyes downcast. "Today's Mortae included fourteen Leaders of Tomorrow. It disheartens me to see so many citizens turned into Vucapi. It seems it took but one small group to turn against us then somehow manipulate dozens of citizens. If we are to keep our way of life, we must act now. Thankfully, as you know, we have caught many of the insurrectionists."

Cafrec snorted. "Because someone turned them in."

Tatem gestured to the camera. "But we have yet to catch the Vucapi who escaped their Mortae, nor those who joined forces with them."

The screen split down the middle, with Tatem on the right. Breel's heart skipped a beat when her picture and some text appeared on the left. It was the picture taken for her ID on orientation day during the first day of work. She wore the Department of Education navy-blue sweater with computer programmer stripings—a thick scarlet stripe sandwiched between thin white stripes. Underneath was a white dress shirt, its collar over the sweater. She had her curly black hair tucked behind her ears.

Breel lowered her glasses to avoid seeing herself.

"Breel Sorep," said Tatem. "Computer programmer and new Leader of Today."

Cafrec placed his hand on Breel's, startling her. He squeezed as the picture changed to himself. "Cafrec Masna. Computer programmer."

"Manum, Lexo, and Praxa, all rebels who betrayed us years ago." Their pictures appeared.

I guess having lived in Intercludae for longer than Cafrec and me means they don't warrant last names or having their Career Group listed.

Manum looked around five years younger in his picture. When Breel and Cafrec arrived in Intercludae, he was their second-in-command training their military force (all ex-DOE) as he had taught most of them.

Lexo and Praxa, not much older than Breel, were more muscular in their orientation day picture. Praxa's smile was tentative, but Lexo's was wide, his green eyes glowing with excitement.

Tatem spoke again. "There's also Criba Sorep, secretary and mother of Breel; and Trafis Sorep, future English teacher one year away from becoming a Leader of Today, who's the son of Criba and brother of Breel."

Their pictures flashed on the screen. Trafis had black hair which, like Criba's, was straight without a curl in sight. Criba was the odd one out in the family with brown hair.

"Last, Samit Tucap," said Tatem. "Head of Computer Programmers for the Department of Education. Breel and Cafrec had worked under him."

In Samit's picture, he wore the same uniform as Breel and Cafrec and held his head high with his chest out and chin up.

Wow, he even looks pompous in a picture.

Once Tatem finished, all eight pictures filled the screen.

The only unmentioned person was Vectus, who had arrived in Intercludae not long before Breel and Cafrec, as the DOE presumed him dead during the tunnel attack. Tatem had called for the attack after somebody told him that people living in Intercludae would infiltrate Lexum via tunnels connecting it to Intercludae. Among the dead was Ragula, Breel's Intercludae roommate. As far as they knew, Vectus was the sole survivor.

It had been only in the past few days that Breel's muscles didn't seize whenever she saw or heard Vectus as he'd been the most intimidating teacher she and Cafrec ever had. Everyday Mr. Vectus Progrio raised his voice—often yelling, his face turning as red as his hair. Mr. Progrio never took questions well, saying they insinuated he didn't know how to teach, and didn't tolerate antics. Questions or antics were a guaranteed, inches-from-your-face Mr. Progrio towering above the offending student. But it had all been an act to portray himself as a Hargamite—a Tatem worshipper.

Everyone knew they had a Hargamite within their ranks—Tatem had said as much when he captured them in his house. Intercludae residents had posted on a wall the pictures of the hundreds of people on their side living in Lexum as Famut and others believed putting faces to names would help Intercludae residents feel more connected to them. However, though the DOE hadn't approached even half of the citizens on the wall, they'd killed enough for them to believe that the spy had lived in Intercludae.

The photos disappeared from the television, leaving only Tatem. "Now, more than ever, it is imperative to contact the Department of Enforcement if you even suspect someone is against our way of life. We have no punishment for reporting anyone who turns out to be a true citizen. If you have *any* reason to suspect someone, it is your duty to report them. It does not matter whether they are your spouse, child, parent, teacher, colleague, or department head. I expect an enormous increase in calls as citizens inform us about suspected activities. We have officers on standby ready to investigate the increased number of reports we expect to receive. No—demand we receive.

"I commend those citizens who have been reporting others. You are the true citizens of Lexum, and we value your continued reports. Thanks to you reporting others during this critical time, we have kept Lexum running smoothly and will be back to normal soon. But a return to normal can only happen if citizens report rebellious acts. Report citizens even if you have a shred of doubt, as it is the Department of Enforcement's job, not yours, to determine if they are a loyal citizen. As for those who are engaging in unlawful activities, make no mistake—we will find out. That is all for today, citizens. Until tomorrow, good night."

The moment Criba turned off the television, Breel began to relax as just thinking about Tatem got her back up. She wasn't alone.

"He sucks all the warmth out of the room," Famut had once said.

Criba placed the remote on the couch's arm. "What a horrible, horrible man."

Vectus shuddered. "He gives me the creeps."

Breel pressed her lips together, preventing herself from laughing at the irony.

I used to think you were creepy, Mr. Progrio.

Criba smiled. "This is so nice and weird."

No one had to ask to know she was referring to talking to people in other Career Groups. Other than a couple of warnings and her brief stint in Intercludae, it was the first time Breel had had conversations with people who'd been in the DOE officer Career Group.

At first, only those who'd been to Intercludae for any length of time (Manum, Lexo, and, the rare time she talked, Praxa) spoke to everyone with ease. It took a couple of weeks for the others to not feel anxious when someone in a different Career Group spoke or asked them a question. Breel would ignore or glare before remembering the DOE wasn't around to police them and sentence them to Mortae for breaking a law.

Everyone returned to the dining room table for their meeting. They met after breakfast, lunch, and the post-supper news to discuss progress and their plan. Other than Samit's desk, the only items in the dining room were the warped birch wood table and matching chairs. Several early splinter incidents in unfortunate places meant everyone sat on towels.

The group took their usual spots. Breel sat beside Cafrec, who took her hand under the table. Across from them sat Criba and Trafis. At the table's head, adjacent to Breel and Criba, was Samit. Manum sat across from him at the other end. Vectus sat beside Cafrec, an empty space beside him, with Lexo and Praxa across the table.

Days ago, they had learned the DOE was torturing people. Breel's stomach churned whenever she thought about what their allies were experiencing. Samit had countered such thinking, saying everyone understood what they were getting into when they joined the anti-Tatem side.

Trafis placed his head in his hand. "I still can't believe he's doing this."

Samit (as usual, the only one standing during the meeting) blinked as if he was deciphering hundreds of lines of uncommented spaghetti code. "It's President Tatem. Anything is on the table."

He has a point.

Most murmured in agreement that torture had only been a matter of time.

"Couldn't this make it easier?" Trafis asked. "I mean, if Tatem's torturing people, why would anyone stay a Hargamite?"

Breel restrained the urge to roll her eyes at her naive brother. "They were on his side even when it was 'just' public execution."

Including you.

Samit nodded. "Also, I hear Tatem's trying to keep it secret as telling anyone about being tortured is grounds for Mortae for you and your entire family. For example, listen to this email I received from a fellow programmer."

Everyone kept in contact with their sources in one to three departments, depending on size. Breel's was the Department of Health. Only Trafis didn't have a department as having escaped as a Leader of Tomorrow, he didn't feel comfortable emailing Leaders of Today.

Samit reached for a paper on his desk behind him. It looked no different from his Department of Education desk with papers stacked in so many places they hid the surface underneath. But somehow, Samit found what he was looking for without issue.

Holding it up, Samit said, "This man's been anti-Tatem for a year and keeps begging me to tell him our location so he and his girlfriend can escape. He said, 'Samit, I understand needing to keep yourself safe. But can't you meet me halfway? I assume you're living outside Lexum, so can't you tell me how to leave, then meet me outside Lexum's walls? You don't know what it's like here now. Since my girlfriend was friends with someone who died in the tunnel attack, the DOE won't stop interrogating her. One day, her face was bloody and bruised. She cried and shook all evening. Even though it was obvious, she refused to tell me they tortured her. Please, please, please let us come.'"

Breel's heart ached at his words.

What a horrific situation. And the poor guy's reaching out to Samit who won't show him one ounce of compassion.

Criba's lower lip quivered. "Can't we help?"

Samit placed the paper back on his desk. "No. We agreed we'd only share our location in extraordinary or pertinent circumstances."

"But..." Criba's voice quavered. "That was before we knew Tatem's torturing people."

"Makes no difference."

Samit's inside contact wasn't the first person to beg, but he was the first to mention torture, making their "no" a harder decision to make.

To keep themselves as safe as possible, they had only told two groups of people they lived in the desert. The first group resupplied them by placing what they needed in the tunnels twice per week. The second were several contacts higher in the DOE who knew their exact location to aid in scheduling searches away from the area. Nobody else needed to know.

Manum stood then began doing one-handed push-ups behind his chair. "Tater won't be able to hide the torture for long."

Tatem's mandatory daily exercises did nothing more than get citizens toned and, unlike Manum and DOE officers, other citizens didn't have time to gain more muscle even if they wanted or if Tatem allowed it.

"I'm sure we'll hear more about it," said Samit. "But people being tortured makes no difference. Now, let's have your reports."

Breel scoffed. *Typical Samit.*

Samit turned to her, his lips pursed. "Is there a problem?"

"Well, yeah. Torture's a big deal, and you're pushing it under the rug. Do you even care about this programmer and his girlfriend?"

When Samit glanced at the others for their reactions, Criba's nod made him frown.

Samit sighed. "Listen, we already agreed we can't bring people here."

"Yeah, but shouldn't we discuss whether torture's an extraordinary circumstance?" asked Breel.

"Breel," said Manum, "for once, I agree with Samit."

"Words no one ever thought they'd hear!" said Cafrec.

Manum switched arms then continued his push-ups. "We cannot bend our rule for torture. Things will only worsen. If we allow all torture victims to come, we'll need more housing, food, and supplies which creates a higher risk of the DOE finding us."

Breel sighed, knowing he was right especially with Tatem's double agent—who they assumed was alive. Famut had also considered it risky which is why he only told certain people Intercludae's location.

Manum returned to his seat then looked at Samit. "We can only sympathize."

Samit's eyes narrowed as he pursed his lips once more.

Before either of them could speak, Vectus said, "Samit will provide our sympathies and help this man understand our perspective."

Samit nodded without complaint.

I guess he listens to Vectus because he's a fellow experienced programmer.

Clearing his throat, Samit said. "Onto today's assignments. Breel?"

They received tons of information from their Lexum contacts, such as copies of department reports. Breel's main role was building databases to collate data and make it readable for everyone.

It'd been the last role Breel had wanted. Her job under Samit at the Department of Education had been designing and programming databases. Her parents had been so proud of her scoring the highest mark on the Demna Exam among the other computer programmers. That achievement got her into the highest prestige department, but Breel hadn't cared. Now, she no longer wanted to care about databases. For her, the biggest benefit of escaping Lexum had been drawing.

When living in Lexum, she'd study someone's face, draw it, compare her drawing to their face the next time she saw them, then improve her picture. But it brought significant risk. A housekeeper had found her drawing notebook before she wrote the Demna Exam, leading to her second warning for drawing. A third would've meant Mortae.

What nobody except Famut had understood was that drawing provided an escape from Tatem's grip. It relaxed and calmed her after school, improving her concentration for homework. Unlike Tatem claimed, a hobby didn't distract from learning. Instead, it was self care.

Famut had said Intercludae was a place where she could draw whenever and wherever she wanted. But she'd had little opportunity to draw in her short time there. Now they were so busy trying to overthrow Tatem, she had no time between meetings, creating and maintaining databases, and leaving the house for walks, target practice, and retrieving supplies.

I might as well still be in Lexum...

Breel pulled herself out of her head and back to the meeting. "I've finished reviewing our DOE data. Tatem himself recruited the elite force members who're all DOE officers meeting several requirements. They just started training."

Two weeks prior, Tatem had announced implementing a trained elite force as he no longer believed his DOE officers were enough to maintain order. Unlike regular DOE officers (who carried tranquilizing darts so Tatem could execute lawbreakers by Mortae) they would carry guns with bullets like Tatem's personal security guards.

"The requirements we assumed?" Lexo asked.

As an ex-DOE officer, Lexo had provided a list of traits Tatem would want in an elite force member. As he read, Praxa nodded along, her brown hair falling in front of her shoulders.

"Yes," said Breel. "Spotless records, flawless work performance, and outstanding grades in the Demna Exam's practical portion. The records of all immediate family members must also be clean—not a single warning."

It was common for children to receive one warning, but somehow, some children never broke the law ("Never get caught," Famut would've said).

But now, things were different. Tatem had abolished warnings. As with Leaders of Today, any transgression made by a Leader of Tomorrow meant automatic Mortae.

Samit tapped a pen against the table. "How many in the elite force?"

"Thirty-two."

"What else do we know about them?" Samit asked.

"Nothing yet," said Breel. "I'll look them up."

Samit nodded. "Good. Cafrec, assist her."

Cafrec grinned. "Yes, sir, Mr. Tucap, sir!"

Breel smirked. When he was their boss, Samit had demanded they call him "sir" or "Mr. Tucap"—a ploy to appear as a Hargamite. After working under Samit for a year, Cafrec found calling him Samit difficult. He and Breel had had the same job working with databases, but now he worked with Samit hacking into Lexum's systems and maintaining their computer security. Cafrec loved any excuse to do something else.

"Manum," said Samit, "ask our DOE sources what they know about the new elite force members."

Samit had assigned the Department of Enforcement to Manum since many of the younger DOE officers knew him. Manum spent most of his time receiving, organizing, and reading their reports.

Samit turned to Lexo and Praxa. "Assist Manum if he needs it. Criba and Trafis, go through the information Breel has on the anniversary party to see what's useful."

In three weeks, Tatem was hosting a celebration to commemorate the fiftieth anniversary of the end of the civil war between the lower and upper classes and his elevation to president. It had come as a shock since Tatem had disallowed celebrations. Breel's group kept tabs on the planning to determine if they could use it to overthrow Tatem. She had automated keyword searches on departmental reports with words such as "fifty," "fiftieth," "50," "anniversary," and "party" to flag them as potentially relevant. It was a lot of data to filter through so Lexo and Praxa verified the database flagged all relevant reports while Criba and Trafis read flagged items.

While working with databases rather than drawing wasn't what Breel wanted to do, she was grateful to have escaped Lexum. Especially now. Tatem was going all out to crush his opposition. An elite force and the end of warnings for Leaders of Tomorrow were just the beginning.

Chapter Four

After their meeting, Manum (finished his daily one hundred push-ups) jumped to his feet. "Target practice time."

Breel wanted to work, but it'd been a few days since their last practice, and she didn't hate it. Target practice meant spending time outdoors and getting to know everyone in a more relaxed setting. The only person who didn't join was Samit who'd already turned around to work at his desk.

Manum frowned. "Samit, you've yet to join us."

Everyone else had given up convincing Samit of the importance in becoming comfortable with and gaining skills in using a dart gun.

"Shooting the DOE is what you, Lexo, and Praxa are for," said Samit to his monitor.

Though Manum had been a weight training teacher, Famut put him in charge of training the ex-DOE in Intercludae. As such, he'd done a lot of target practice.

Manum rolled his eyes. "And if we're killed? Or you're alone? How will you defend yourself?"

But Samit said nothing as he clicked his mouse

Lexo had already retrieved the guns and two wooden doors (which they had brought from Intercludae) from the hall closet opposite the front door. Cafrec and Trafis grinned as Lexo passed them each a gun. The weapons and one hundred darts had arrived in their first resupply shipment.

They opened the front door, which hung on an angle, then avoided the holes and loose cement on the crumbling front steps. The sun, an orange ball low in the horizon, would disappear within an hour behind the rowhouses one mile away. During the first few weeks, after every evening meeting, everyone except Samit had sat outside watching the sunset. They'd never witnessed it in Lexum, given the height of the walls.

The flat desert had little vegetation. The only other nearby building was the factory. Like the house, time and abandonment had warped and cracked its wooden siding. Whereas the house's shingles were curled but intact, the factory roof had holes. Both buildings had sand piled against their west wall along with debris—shingles, pieces of wood, leaves from the treeline one mile away, and who knew what else.

Lexo and Praxa rested the two splintering doors against the side of the house. Two or three times per week everyone tried to improve their aim at the bullseyes drawn on the doors. Lexo and Praxa said it was like what they'd done in school except without mandatory improvement and fierce competition.

Cafrec and Trafis shot first, standing fifteen feet away from the targets.

Cafrec aimed then pulled the trigger. He missed the bullseye by half a foot. "Shoot!"

Trafis patted his back. "Yeah, you did. Badly."

Cafrec laughed. He'd yet to get a bullseye. Even Vectus had gotten one despite recoiling every time the dart flew from his weapon.

"Lemme show you how it's done, Mr. Programmer." Trafis took one second to aim then fired a dart which landed a hair away from the centre.

"Well done!" Manum said.

Trafis grinned at Cafrec. "That's what you need to do."

Cafrec stroked his chin. "Hmm. I give you credit for walking the talk."

Trafis fired again. "Yeah, bullseye!"

He danced on the spot. The corners of Cafrec's mouth formed a smile. It was the first time in which Trafis had ever gloated about anything. Cafrec had his joking and Breel had her drawing, perhaps Trafis had shooting—the first thing he seemed to enjoy and be skilled in.

He could be an officer after we overthrow Tatem. Breel laughed to herself. *That's as unlikely as a database's code working the first time it's run.*

"Try standing farther back, Trafis," Lexo suggested.

Trafis shot from twenty feet—bullseye. Then from twenty-five feet—bullseye. Even thirty feet away, he was only a few inches off.

Trafis grinned from ear to ear. "Wow!"

Lexo stared in awe. "You may be a better shot than Praxa was as a beginner!"

Trafis turned to Praxa, standing off to the side with Lexo and drawing in the sand with her foot. "Oh? You were good?" he asked.

She nodded but, in true Praxa form, said nothing as her face reddened.

Lexo put an arm around her. "Good doesn't cut it! She was in the top ten of all time for moving target practice during the practical portion of the DOE officer Demna Exam."

Breel gaped at unassuming Praxa—toned, average height, with straight shoulder-length brown hair, she didn't appear like a DOE officer let alone a prodigy with a gun.

Impressive.

"Ooh, can we try moving targets?" Trafis asked.

Lexo shook his head. "We don't have that technology here, unfortunately. All right, next pairing."

Breel and Criba stepped forward. They were both better than Cafrec, but nothing like Trafis, Lexo, and Praxa. Breel had improved each time before stagnating, her darts never getting closer than a couple of inches from the centre.

When they finished, Breel dragged herself to the sidelines beside Cafrec. Her shoulders slumped as she tried to push her poor performance out of her mind.

Lexo interrupted his conversation with Praxa to flash an encouraging smile. "You're consistent, at least, which is great. More practice and you'll hit the bullseye again."

"Thanks," Breel said.

Whenever someone thought they did a terrible job, Lexo could always pick out something they did well.

Lexo should be a teacher. He and Trafis should've swapped Career Groups.

Criba's performance had been far worse than even Cafrec's, but she'd made incremental improvements and now aimed better than Breel. Vectus wasn't much better than Cafrec. Beside him, Manum did a decent job.

Lexo and Praxa practiced last. They started at forty feet away then increased the distance five feet at a time, taking turns firing at each distance until they got a bullseye or missed three attempts.

After half an hour, they covered their footprints as a precaution, removed the darts from the boards, then returned to work. Samit didn't acknowledge them, but that wasn't out of the ordinary. Breel and Cafrec followed Trafis, Lexo and Praxa downstairs. Lexo and Praxa worked in the storage room and Trafis in the bedroom he shared with Cafrec.

Getting and transporting laptops and other supplies to work had been difficult. But after going through the same resupplying process multiple times per week, things were smoother. First, a programmer from the storage facilities adjusted a database listing the number of each needed item in storage so there wouldn't be discrepancies. Next, someone smuggled the items to a van for a driver to take them to a house with a tunnel leading to Intercludae. Samit planted previous video feeds on a loop, so if the DOE watched cameras, they'd see previous footage and not the live feed. Finally, people from Breel's group walked two miles to the rowhouses then another five miles through the tunnel from Intercludae to retrieve the supplies.

Once they had their initial equipment, Samit had upgraded their security to ensure they could continue emailing contacts and viewing network information without Tatem's detection.

Cafrec descended the stairs with a bounce in his step, his energy causing Breel to smile.

"I'm so glad Samit asked me to help you with your database!" he said.

"Me, too. I'm sorry Samit gave you the security and hacking jobs."

Half the time, Cafrec's eyes glazed over. But Samit insisted on the arrangement because school records showed Cafrec was better at computer security and Breel at database creation. She'd never tell Cafrec, but it was a relief as security hadn't been her favourite subject.

Cafrec took her arm then pulled her close. Her heart fluttered as he kissed her. "Not your fault."

"You should remind him he has plenty of other programmers to rely on."

Cafrec shrugged. "It won't last forever."

At least he has a good attitude.

They fired up their computers then opened Breel's database. It worked by users searching for a keyword or search term to see all relevant emails and reports. They could also enter a citizen's name to see all their email threads and any reports written by or about them.

Breel instructed Cafrec on how to find the section listing the elite force officers. "I'll read the first sixteen and you do the last sixteen?"

"Sure."

She selected the first name, opening a new window. The picture of a twenty-three-year-old woman with dark, pupilless eyes stared back. Below was a list of information pulled from a Lexum citizen database.

Mother: Department of Enforcement; DOE officer for the Quaddro Section (deceased)

Father: Department of Enforcement; DOE officer for the Governmental Offices (deceased)

Brother: Department of Enforcement; DOE Officer; for Wall Security (Head)

Spouse: Department of Enforcement; DOE officer; for Wall Security
Children: None

Demna Exam practical grade: 99%

Elite force recommendation from Career Group Head: One of our best officers ranking in the top five percent across all metrics. Her grades in Department of Expansion courses are always perfect or near perfect. When I told her I'll recommend her for the elite force, she said "Good. I wanna kill those President Tatem haters!" A few years ago, being shortlisted as one of President Tatem's new personal security officers disappointed her. The elite force is the next best career for someone who values our way of life.

Elite force training rank: 5/32

Breel whistled.

Cafrec winked. "Trying to catch my attention?"

"Ha. I already did that, didn't I?"

Meeting Cafrec had been thanks to Famut and Cafrec's cousin, Centia, who'd dated each other while leading the rebellion against Tatem. Though Famut never told Breel he was priming her to become a rebel,

Centia told Cafrec that he'd one day have Breel as an officemate. Even though Cafrec had thought of her for years before they met, the pedestal he'd put her on wasn't so high that she failed to meet his expectations.

"Pretty wow," Cafrec said, a twinkle in his eye.

Breel rolled her eyes. "Wow" had been her response when Cafrec had told her he loved her.

At least we can laugh about it now.

Getting serious, Breel said, "I whistled because this person came from a family of DOE officers and just missed becoming one of Tatem's new security."

"Sounds like a fanatic. My guy claims to have killed several citizens attempting to escape."

Reading everything took the rest of the evening. Before turning in for the night, they discussed their findings. Cafrec moved his chair to sit side-by-side, their legs entwined and holding hands.

These moments are the best part of the day.

She allowed herself to enjoy it before talking about what she had read. "None of the people I read about have children."

Cafrec's eyes drifted upward. "You know, neither did mine."

"It had to have been on purpose, so they have little to lose."

Cafrec nodded. "Yep. Makes sense. Mine were in their late teens and early twenties."

"Same. All top performers."

Cafrec leaned forward then took Breel's hands in his. "I'm so grateful we're both safe and no longer in Lexum."

Safe? No one's safe. He must mean safer.

She wrapped her fingers around his hands. "I'm not sure I could've gone through life as a Leader of Today without causing my own Mortae."

It was the first time she'd admitted this to anyone.

Cafrec frowned. "Sure, you would've."

"No, I doubt it."

He tightened his grip on her hands. "I would've fought the DOE off you."

Breel raised an eyebrow. "But Tatem would execute you, too."

"At least I wouldn't have to live in that horrid place without you."

Ohhh!

Her heart nearly burst. "That's both the sweetest and stupidest thing anyone's ever said to me."

He laughed then tucked a lock of curls behind her ear. "I was going for the first one. I love you."

She threw herself into his arms, nuzzling her face into his neck. Cafrec stroked her back, her body tingling at his touch.

What'd I ever do to deserve him?

"I love you, too, Cafrec."

He kissed her once more before extracting himself from her arms. Leaning back into his chair, he asked, "Have you heard about your father lately?"

Criba and others had asked Breel to pull information about family members from her database. Breel's father could've fled with them after Breel's failed Mortae. However, ever the rule follower, he had stayed.

"Nothing new," said Breel. "I guess that's good news."

The DOE had questioned every one of their family members, of course. Since her father's entire family had fled, they had questioned him more frequently. One DOE report had stood out.

"This is the third time this week we've interrogated Duknum," the DOE officer had written. "I've interrogated him several times myself and he's a rock. The only information he has is things we already know. In sum, during childhood, his brother, Famut Sorep, had often done not quite illegal things. Years later, Duknum believed Famut was a bad influence on his children, especially his daughter, Breel. As a Leader of Tomorrow, the DOE gave her two warnings for drawing—the last one days before she became a Leader of Today. His daughter defecting didn't surprise Duknum, but it shocked him when his wife (Criba) and son (Trafis) did. When they begged him to follow, he refused. When asked, he says they haven't contacted him. I believe him because if he knew anything, we'd have gotten it out of him by this point. Given his innocence, I recommend we stop interrogating Duknum Sorep."

Reading those words had lifted a weight from Breel's shoulders. Her father was safe—for now.

"Do you ever look up your parents?" she asked Cafrec.

Cafrec made a face. "Those Hargamites? No way."

They must be horrible people if he doesn't care about how they're doing...

That made him the only one not keeping tabs on his family. She ached for Cafrec but would never tell him that.

Chapter Five

Breel kissed Cafrec good night then walked upstairs to her bedroom.

The sleeping arrangements for nine people were less than adequate. Samit and Vectus shared the bedroom off the kitchen which was also where Vectus worked. Next to the living room was Manum and Lexo's bedroom which Manum used as his office. Breel shared the middle bedroom with Criba and Praxa as it was a couple of inches wider than the others, giving them enough space for a few feet between each bed. The bedframes were the standard metal frames which they had carried, along with box springs, from Lexum. No one wanted the burden of carrying heavy mattresses, so they made do with light sleeping mats overtop the box springs.

The lack of privacy sometimes caused Breel to go into the bathroom for a moment to herself. However, Criba and Praxa weren't terrible roommates. Praxa may as well have been invisible as she hadn't spoken more than a handful of sentences to anyone other than Manum and Lexo. She and Criba were both quiet sleepers. When they first moved in, Criba's crying often woke Breel. Knowing it'd embarrass her mother, Breel never told her. The crying had stopped after a couple of weeks.

As Breel pulled on her navy-blue pyjamas (which had come from Intercludae) her thoughts drifted to Duknum. Lexum provided everything, even housing, for citizens. Her family had lived in a three-bedroom house since her parents had two children. The Department of

Households' mandatory move to a two-bedroom would've happened two weeks after Breel moved out. Instead, with his entire family gone, they moved Duknum to a one-bedroom.

He hadn't lived alone since marrying Criba, so the change would've been hard. Waking alone. Exercising by himself in the mornings. Eating breakfast in silence. Not having Criba accompanying him on the bus to and from the Governmental Offices. Spending the evening eating by himself. Having no one to speak to after the news in the precious few moments when Leaders of Today weren't working on their Department of Expansion courses.

Breel would've given anything to know how he was coping.

***

As usual, the next morning Breel waited to use one of the two bathrooms. Manum, Lexo, and Praxa did their morning workout in the living room and Samit worked at his computer. She slipped into the hall unseen before Manum could berate her for not joining.

By the time Breel dressed, Criba had warmed breakfast, and everyone was at the table. The group had outvoted Breel when she said she wanted to learn how to cook. It ended up being a good thing because they found it hard enough to toast bread and heat prepared food from Lexum after a life of having pre-warmed meals delivered to their front doors. There'd been some failures with burnt toast, rock-hard eggs and boiled over soup. After everyone had taken several turns, Criba and Lexo offered to heat all the meals as, unlike most of the others, they made food edible.

Having spent long enough in Intercludae, Manum, Lexo, and Praxa knew the importance of washing dishes and utensils after every meal. However, it was new for those who had spent mere days in Intercludae

(Vectus, Breel and Cafrec) and for Samit, Criba, and Trafis who'd never lived there. In Lexum where everyone had a specialized job, dishwashing wasn't something most citizens thought about.

Just as surprising was how quickly the kitchen got dirty. But by the time they realized hardened food covered the counters, cleaning them was impossible. Even if it wasn't, they didn't know how to fix it as nobody had lived in a house with a kitchen. The only kitchen Breel had ever seen in Lexum was during a class trip to the Department of Food. They now cleaned the countertops and table after every meal while doing their best to ignore stubborn stains.

"Pass the butter," Samit said.

It was a phrase never uttered in Lexum where toast came pre-buttered.

Cafrec stabbed a sausage with one hand while handing Samit the butter with the other. Breel sipped her coffee then grimaced. No one had yet to brew a decent cup but, needing the coffee Lexum had always provided at breakfast, everyone drank it. No longer having their intake limited, Samit and Lexo had taken to drinking two cups each morning.

Some day, one of us will brew it right.

"I have an addition to our meeting agenda," Manum said.

Samit sighed, shoulders sagging. He put his knife on his plate, the butter forgotten, then looked at Manum across the table. "Lemme guess, your son?"

Breel interrupted shovelling scrambled eggs into her mouth to watch the exchange.

"Yes."

Samit dropped his hand onto the table. Vectus jumped at the bang. "Again?"

"You don't understand," said Manum.

"No, *you* don't understand. We agreed to only give our location in extenuating circumstances. Your son isn't in immediate danger."

Samit returned to buttering his bread.

Breel agreed but would've welcomed Manum's son, Mr. Gaimster. He had taught Breel and Cafrec discrete mathematics and was a favourite teacher of many. Mr. Gaimster was involved in recruiting Leaders of Tomorrow, so it was natural for Manum to worry despite assurances that he took precautions.

"Your brother and his family aren't in immediate danger either," Manum said. "For once you should think about other people instead of yourself."

Samit's knife clattered onto his plate as he leapt to his feet. "You take that back!"

"My son's risking more than most," Manum said.

Samit pursed his lips. His brother Sanctus and Sanctus's wife Vida had risked a lot to find them shelter after their failed Mortae. Thanks to Samit, Sanctus, and other programmers planting fake feeds, they had remained undetected. Sanctus was involved in security and Samit kept begging him to leave Lexum. It was unlikely that Mr. Gaimster risked more than Sanctus and Vida had.

"Fine," said Samit. "But you shouldn't disrespect me, our leader."

"Oooh," said Cafrec.

Samit's face reddened and his nostrils flared. "Something to add, Cafrec?"

Cafrec hesitated. "Well, you sound...like Tatem."

"What!?" shouted Samit.

He looked around the table, waiting for somebody to step in.

Criba lowered her gaze. Trafis, who once told Breel he felt awkward being the only Leader of Today in the house, did the same. Lexo and

Praxa said nothing. Though they'd be on Manum's side, they had yet to stick up to Samit. Vectus and Breel were the only ones who didn't shift their gaze. The last person Breel stared down had been Tatem when he had inspected her and the others whom he'd sentenced to Mortae.

"You did sound like him," Breel said. "The whole 'disrespecting me' thing."

"Well, he did."

"Enough." Vectus's booming voice silenced the room. "There's no disrespecting *anyone*. Samit and Manum, grow up. We can't accomplish our goals with you arguing all the time."

Thank goodness for Vectus.

Cafrec placed his cutlery on his empty plate then leaned back, running a hand through his hair. "Oh yes, I used the perfect amount of gel this morning—an entire bottle!"

Grateful that he cut the tension, Breel snickered at his mockery of Tatem, as did Trafis, Lexo, and Vectus. Samit and Manum ignored him ("I guess they expect us to be serious all the time," Cafrec had once said to Breel) while Praxa glared at Cafrec.

Geesh, what's her problem?

After breakfast, they cleared the table for their meeting. Like most everything else, it was an unfamiliar task as in Lexum they had house-keepers to do it.

Samit stood then turned to Criba to start the meeting. "What can you tell us about the anniversary party?"

Criba sat up straighter. "During that weekend, Tatem will give citizens who normally work each weekend one of the two days off, so everyone can celebrate."

Whoa, he's letting citizens take time off of work?

It was unprecedented. What made it even stranger was that it was for something fun. Tatem had outlawed fun fifty years ago, and now, to celebrate, he was allowing it for two days.

"He thinks people know how to celebrate?" asked Cafrec.

The only celebration I've ever had was the cake the Department of Food sent after I received my Demna Exam results.

"Everything will take place in the Quaddro since being the city square, it's the only space big enough," said Trafis.

"President Tatem's planning a speech," said Criba. "It'll only be during the first day, so he'll broadcast it to citizens who can't leave work. Some reports hint he'll make a big announcement during the speech, but he's keeping it hushed."

Big shock.

Tatem made sure that everyone worked in silos with citizens only learning things required for their career or future career—no more, no less.

"Any ideas of what the announcement could be?" Lexo asked.

Trafis shrugged. "Not sure, but based on what we read, we think it's about education."

Breel gasped but only Cafrec, staring back at her with wide eyes, heard.

He also thinks it's about abolishing the Nito Test.

The Department of Education administered the Nito Test to five-year-olds to determine their aptitude then assign an appropriate Career Group. The test was approaching obsolescence thanks to genetic engineering. When a couple went to the fertility clinic (Tatem ensured no one could conceive naturally) geneticists secretly examined their embryos' DNA to determine which Career Group made the most sense. Then the geneticists re-engineered their genes, if needed, to make them an exact match for the Career Group's required innate abilities.

Now genetic engineering was more accurate than the Nito Test in determining someone's optimal Career Group. But of course, Tatem hadn't stopped at that. He also demanded turning off and on certain genes—such as turning off those which increase the likelihood of rebelling and turning on those making someone more loyal. Tatem had pulled Famut and Centia from treating patients to work as geneticists for the project. Only they, Breel, Cafrec, and the few other citizens part of the genetic engineering experiments knew about it.

Breel and Cafrec knew because Famut had told them before explaining about his and Centia's meddling with genetics. Behind the backs of Cafrec and Breel's parents, he had made Cafrec biologically Tatem's son, and Breel biologically the daughter of Xorem, Tatem's wife. As only biological relations could enter anyone's home, it was part of Famut's grand plan to get into Tatem's house to apprehend Tatem.

As far as Breel and Cafrec knew, the only other person whom Famut had told was Manum. So far, he'd yet to betray Breel's trust by telling Criba and Trafis.

"Brainstorm what the announcement could be," said Samit. "No matter how crazy it is. Go."

Breel gripped both Cafrec's hand and the table, releasing the latter when a splinter of wood poked her palm.

If they mention the Nito Test...but if they don't...should we say something?

"A more intense Department of Expansion program for Leaders of Today," said Manum.

Phew, not the Nito Test.

"A way to speed up Leader of Tomorrow education," said Trafis.

"Maybe it's not related to education," said Lexo. "It could be more laws."

The tension in Breel's body released. No one was close. The danger had passed.

Cafrec's blue eyes twinkled. "Tatem's retiring!"

That got a few laughs.

"Only on his deathbed," muttered Manum.

Beside him, Praxa stared at the table.

Ugh, why doesn't she ever contribute?

Despite having seen Praxa in action during target practice, it was times like this that made it impossible to picture her taciturn self laying down Tatem's laws as a DOE officer.

Samit stroked his chin. "I'm sure the answer will reveal itself soon. We'll all keep our eyes out. Breel and Cafrec, what can you tell us about the elite force?"

They summarized the trends they found—near perfect grades, young, excellent performance, no children, and spotless records.

"Oh yeah," said Cafrec, "and they're fanatics who all begged to be on the force. Many wanted a chance to kill rather than tranquillize citizens."

"Not surprising," said Manum. "Do you have the list of names?"

Breel pushed a sheet of paper toward him and the ex-DOE. "We thought you might ask."

Manum kept nodding as he, Lexo, and Praxa reviewed the list. "Yeah, I taught most of them. None of these names surprise me. One had a life goal of being on Tater's personal security team, as it meant carrying a lethal weapon. Another hoped to one day strangle a man with..."

Manum trailed off as his face paled. On the day of their failed Mortae, Manum had strangled a DOE officer with a chain in a fit of rage over the tunnel attack killing most of the ex-DOE officers he'd trained.

Rescuing him, Breel asked, "Is there any chance some are anti-Tatem but not in contact with us?"

Manum snorted. "Not a chance for anyone I know."

"I agree," said Lexo. "I know about one-third of the list, and I never felt comfortable around any of them."

Praxa cleared her throat. "Me too. They were unbearable. True Hargamites."

Criba sighed. "If they're all President Tatem fanatics, what hope do we have?"

Hearing Criba have such an attitude felt like a stab in the chest.

It's all because Father refused to join us.

Before Breel could reassure her mother, to say there was hope in the hundreds of people on their side and countless more who had yet to make themselves known, Samit spoke.

"We'll have none of that," he said. "We can't win with that attitude."

Criba's shoulders drooped then she stood, her arms hanging as she turned away.

"Mother," said Breel.

"Sorry," Criba muttered as she walked through the kitchen toward her bedroom.

"Where're you going?" Samit asked. "Criba, get back here!"

"Leave her alone," Vectus said.

Despite the urge to follow, Breel stayed. The meeting wasn't over, and she didn't want Samit's wrath for leaving early, too.

I hope the rest of the meeting is quick.

Chapter Six

"It's imperative that we don't become discouraged," Samit said after Criba left the meeting. "We're in a better place than one month ago."

Cafrec laughed. "That's because one month ago, we were in Lexum."

"You know that's not what I meant," said Samit. "I was referring to learning of more people on our side and the increased security I put in place. Thanks to my skills, it's even safer for us to use Lexum's network."

Manum groaned.

Oh, not again.

Breel rested her head on her hand, waiting for the impending argument to end. But Samit didn't hear him and Manum said nothing else.

When Samit ended the meeting, Breel left to find Criba. She was in their bedroom sitting on the bed closest to the door with her elbows on her knees, head in her hands. Breel sat on her own bed across from her, their knees inches from touching.

"Mother," she said to get her attention.

She's not your mother, not really...

She is too your mother! It wasn't Xorem who raised you, looked after you, and loved you.

Breel pushed the horrible knowledge of what Famut did out of her mind. "Walk?"

Manum encouraged everyone to walk at least once per day if there were no scheduled DOE searches in the area. They walked in groups of two or three to decompress or discuss things in a new environment. Only Samit never took part, ignoring Manum's lectures on the negative health consequences of never leaving his desk.

After checking with Manum that the DOE had no searches scheduled, they each took a loaded dart gun, then left the house. Walls of dark clouds dimmed the daylight as the sun attempted to peek through with limited success.

"Might rain," said Breel.

"Let's stick close to the house."

They walked toward the treeline, away from Lexum. Unless she was retrieving supplies, Breel avoided walking closer to Lexum as seeing the city walls grow bigger on the skyline gave her the chills.

Unlike the treeline alongside Lexum's walls, the foliage Breel and Criba walked toward was abundant. Breel's theory was that someone had planted the birch trees to provide wood to build the suburb's houses, warehouses, and factories. There would have to be a water source for their roots somewhere but, needing to keep near the house, they had never investigated. Beyond the trees was a sharp drop-off anyway, littered with rocks, dead branches, and other debris.

Criba kicked a leaf. "It all feels so hopeless but..."

"My father."

"Yes."

Breel ached for Criba who had joined her children rather than stay with her husband. It was unclear whether she regretted her choice, but Breel would never ask.

Criba moved the gun to her other hand. "I told myself to avoid reading the information you found on him, but I can't. At least the DOE isn't interrogating him anymore."

We assume they aren't.

Breel patted her mother's arm but stopped when the wind blew, sending sand into the air. Shutting her eyes, Breel held her hair. When it was over, Criba removed the sand from her own hair with a shake then waited for Breel to do the same.

"Oh, Breel," she said once they continued walking. "Not only did he lose us he lost the house! I wish I knew if he regrets not joining us. Maybe he does but can't find us. We should contact him."

Criba's eyes pleaded for her to agree.

"I don't think we should," said Breel. "It's not an extenuating circumstance. Also, it may endanger him because if he's interrogated again, he'll have information. Or he could act differently, causing the DOE to re-target him. Plus, the DOE monitors everyone they interrogate—especially Father since his entire family left."

Criba stopped to touch a two-foot-high bush growing in the middle of nowhere. "I know. I feel so bad for him...he had no time to choose."

While it was true (they had run as bullets flew and a hoard of citizens attempted to overtake them) it was hard to know whether he'd have joined them even if he had all day to consider his options.

"He was always about safety and following the rules," said Breel. "But coming with us would've gone against that."

"You're talking in the past tense again."

"Sorry, I..." Having no explanation, Breel trailed off.

Criba sighed. "If he had more time, if it was a different situation, he would've chosen his family."

If you say so.

Hiding her true feelings was best, so Breel said nothing. At any rate, it was possible Duknum had done such a good job of hiding himself to his children that Criba was right.

Another gust of wind churned up a cloud of sand. They spent a moment coughing and spitting out the grains. Breel's glasses saved her eyes from the worst of it, but Criba needed a minute to blink hers clean.

All her life, Breel had imagined the world outside Lexum's walls. She'd hated them for imprisoning her and hiding what lay beyond. Some thought Tatem had built the walls during the civil war; however, Breel knew they'd been there long before. She'd believed it was to separate the lower and higher classes.

It also keeps out the sand.

They walked in silence. Breel resisted asking Criba what she was thinking about. Prior to leaving Lexum, Criba rarely told Breel her thoughts, but she'd shared a lot since leaving Lexum. It was hard to say whether it was because she no longer had Duknum to confide in, or whether she now felt safe being transparent.

"Do you..." Criba bit her lower lip. "Do you think the group would allow me to enter Lexum and talk to him?"

"No. Mother, no way. The DOE circulated our pictures everywhere."

"I know, I know." Criba dragged her feet, stirring up sand. "What if Samit plants fake feeds in the house so the DOE can't see me?"

Breel couldn't blame Criba for her desperation. However, while Samit planted fake video feeds to move supplies, this would be different. As per a Department of Households report, Duknum's new house was far from a tunnel or pipe to the desert, which meant Samit would need to plant fake feeds in every security camera along a lengthy route.

After mentioning this, Breel said, "Even if Samit did, someone will probably see you and if they recognize you, it's over..."

The question was whether "over" meant Mortae or life imprisonment.

Knowing Tatem, it'd be some new Mortae more horrific than lethal injection.

Her mother sighed. "I know, I know. I'm just..."

Criba stopped to hug Breel—a rare show of affection in their family.

"I wish he came, too," said Breel.

Criba released her. "I hope he'll see our perspective soon."

Me, too, but I doubt it.

Even if Duknum had changed sides, there'd be a battle raging in his mind as he'd want to find them without compromising their safety. His only chance was knowing an ally he trusted enough to reveal he's anti-Tatem. Breel had gone through that when meeting Cafrec; however, trusting him hadn't been too difficult since he'd been close to Famut. Duknum wouldn't get that lucky.

Criba looked toward the house half a mile away. "We should get back. I need to help Trafis read through the mounds of anniversary information."

As they turned around, Criba's words *then what hope do we have* crossed Breel's mind.

It *did* seem hopeless. Their numbers were low because of the tunnel attack, inside sources feared exposure, and recruitment was difficult. With the DOE watching and interrogating allies, many refused to do anything suspicious.

To recruit more citizens to their cause, they'd have to use new methods.

Chapter Seven

Breel returned from her walk to find Cafrec at his desk and talking to Trafis. Breel smiled at the sight of their budding friendship.

After Trafis left, Cafrec stood to kiss Breel but stopped short. He smirked. "Your face is gritty from sand."

"Oh."

She left for the bathroom, squeezing into the space between the toilet, shower, and counter, while being careful of where she stepped on the warped linoleum. It curled so much in places that it revealed the subfloor. Water stains from the shower had seeped into and under the linoleum long ago.

The shower was a walk-in with a rusting metal base and yellowed acrylic walls. Mould had grown near the bottom where the wall had cracked but they had removed most of it. The original door had been so brittle that it broke the first time someone closed it, so they replaced it with a blue curtain. A bottle of communal vanilla shampoo sat on a skinny shelf next to a bar of unscented soap.

The condition of the toilet wasn't any better. The porcelain had cracked and the bowl and bolts fastening the seat and lid had rusted. Rust covered the tank parts, too, but not so much that the toilet didn't flush.

Breel stood at the counter. Wooden and rotting, it wasn't large enough to hold one person's toiletries let alone nine people, so they put everything in the medicine cabinet after removing the rust and caked on dust.

Breel looked in the mirror which also functioned as the medicine cabinet's misaligned door then moved herself to see her face past the mirror's black patches. Sure enough, sand had stuck to her face. Breel turned on the taps, wincing as they squeaked. The water didn't have the same fast flow as Lexum, so she cupped her hands to catch every drop.

"Better?" she asked, returning to Cafrec a couple of minutes later.

He smiled then hugged her, fingers digging into her sides. "Much. How's your mother?"

Breel shrugged. "Okay, I guess."

She wasn't comfortable telling Cafrec everything they'd discussed. If Criba wanted him to know, Criba would tell him. However, Breel was grateful that he cared enough to ask.

She got to work on designing a new database to review the elite force data. But instead of concentrating on lines of code, her mind drifted to drawing. Someday (*if Tatem doesn't slaughter us first*) they'd reform Lexum then she'd draw as Famut had promised.

The afternoon was long, but the hope of drawing kept her motivated. Suppertime (spaghetti and meatballs) was a welcomed break.

While everyone else ate, Samit remained at his desk, hands flying across the keyboard.

Breel tapped his shoulder from her seat. He jumped, minimized the email he'd been composing, then frowned upon seeing everyone. "When'd you get here?"

"I came in to heat the food over five minutes ago," said Criba.

"Oh. Okay. And um...Criba, about earlier...I'm sorry."

Vectus must've told him to apologize.

Supper was quiet as Samit and Manum seemed to have an unspoken agreement to ignore each other.

When Cafrec finished eating, he held his spoon to his mouth. "Citizens of Lexum!" He ran a hand through his hair. "It is I, your diabolical leader, about to tell you the ways I'll make your life even more horrible."

Breel, Trafis, and Lexo laughed. Samit rolled his eyes but said nothing. The others smiled—except for Praxa, who kept her head down.

That girl needs a sense of humour.

Cafrec pointed at Trafis. "It's now illegal for people to fall asleep in less than five minutes!"

"Well, I'm screwed," muttered Breel.

Samit soaked up the remaining sauce on his plate with some garlic bread. "Must you do this? Listening to the actual thing is enough."

"Oh, let him have his fun," said Vectus.

Samit groaned then popped the bread into his mouth. "I'll be working until the news."

Breel glanced at her watch. It was six-fifty—he had ten minutes.

Cafrec frowned. "We're not under Tatem anymore. You're allowed to do nothing sometimes."

"I know, but there's lots to do."

He turned to face his desk behind his place at the table then began typing out an email. Cafrec continued his Tatem impersonation until they moved to the living room. As always, Samit arrived last, sitting on a chair beside Breel who sat at the end of the couch with Cafrec.

The unseen news anchor spoke of the day's Mortae. "As you know, it was for twelve Leaders of Tomorrow who engaged in grievous acts."

Criba gasped, a hand over her mouth. "Oh, those poor children and parents!"

Breel looked away as they replayed it.

Twelve children...Glad I didn't have to see that in person.

Tatem listed their "crimes"—being late for class, engaging in hobbies, and picking fights.

The next story was something Tatem would've kept hushed one month ago. "Today, a DOE officer questioned two citizens for speaking to nonrelations and non-coworkers. One of these citizens strangled the officer but, thankfully, a passerby intervened before it was too late. The Mortae for both citizens will be in two days."

Breel shook her head. Tatem had always frowned upon talking to people you had no business speaking; however, now it was outright illegal.

Why'd they think they'd get away with trying to kill an officer?

Next was Tatem's address. He stood in front of his desk, as usual, with a sombre expression as he smoothed his suit jacket. "Citizens, some of you continue disobeying our laws. Attacking anyone is a disgrace and automatic Mortae."

"What isn't an automatic Mortae," Cafrec muttered.

They all chuckled despite it not being funny.

"Then," continued Tatem, "there is the issue of what caused this incident. There is no need to talk to nonrelations and citizens with whom you do not work or attend classes. If you do, I assume you're passing rebellious information. As such, you must report any such discussions you overhear. Not doing so makes you as bad as the perpetrators because it shows you condone their act. You know about the generous rewards I will give you for reporting anyone. New, enticing rewards include a personal gardener, allowing you fresh fruit and vegetables whenever you want; dessert at every supper; and receiving a year-long break from Department of Expansion courses every five years."

Tatem sipped water from a glass then paused, allowing the rewards to sink in.

Breel's jaw dropped. After struggling to get citizens to report others using his usual tactics, Tatem had resorted to things he'd never considered. A non-prescribed amount of food at a non-prescribed time? Dessert every day? A year of no courses? Enticing wasn't a strong enough word to describe it.

He's doing it because he knows how irresistible citizens will find the rewards.

"He's awful!" said Cafrec. "They're going to get so many stupid reports. 'Oh, my neighbour came home five minutes late' or 'my son won't eat his vegetables.' Tatem's going to regret bribing citizens."

Samit shook his head. "Using bribes to get people arrested and killed is sickening."

Tatem continued. "The number of required Mortae has grown from around one per week to several per week. This saddens and disappoints me."

Cafrec gestured at the television. "What'd you expect when you make everything illegal and abolish warnings!"

Breel patted his leg. "Shh."

But he was right. There were far more Leaders of Tomorrow Vucapi now because of the lack of warnings.

Tatem touched his hair. "To minimize the disruption to work and school, we will have one Mortae per day, no matter the number of Vucapi. But parents, you must improve. Your children cannot continue breaking our laws. You must make them understand the importance of embracing the collective. Do not force me to enact a law in which the illegal actions of children result in Mortae for them and their parents."

"Whoa," Breel muttered.

"He's gone waaaay too far," said Trafis.

Breel smiled. One month ago, Trafis was pro-Tatem and, like their parents, begging Breel to obey. Now, not only did Tatem disgust him, but he was ashamed for having ever thought Tatem was a "good man" (to quote Duknum) who wanted the best for everyone.

As Tatem's blue eyes sparkled, a shiver raced down Breel's spine.

He can't wait to punish parents.

"Leaders of Tomorrow are our future," Tatem said. "In twelve years, our society cannot function without them. You must do better if we are to continue our way of life."

Samit tsked. "Who in their right mind wants that way of life?"

Everyone murmured in agreement.

"I am ending tonight's speech early so you can use these extra minutes to speak to your children. Make them understand for their own sake—and yours. Until tomorrow, good night."

Samit turned off the television then everybody spoke at once. It was impossible to parse out anything other than the words "monster," "murderer," and various expletives.

"That's enough," Samit said. Everyone quieted as he stood then faced the group in front of the television. "Tatem's desperate which means he hasn't found us or gotten information out of our sources, not that they have much to provide."

"But these new laws make it harder for our people to work," said Lexo. "How can we recruit anyone?"

Breel nodded. Increasing their numbers had been difficult. Now it was nearly impossible.

Famut had said they recruited people from as many departments, sections, and Career Groups as possible. Then it came to her—that was the solution.

Breel stood beside Samit, who did a double take. "I know what we should do," she said. "We have sources everywhere, so don't we have enough departments and Career Groups covered that nobody needs to talk to anyone illegally?"

Samit nodded. "Yes! They can each focus their recruitment on people they're allowed to talk to."

"Exactly," said Breel. "Then the people they recruit can talk to their family members, who can then talk to their coworkers...and so on. That's how we spread."

"Right," said Samit. "Why don't we talk about our findings from the afternoon then return to this?"

"I'd like to speak to the Soreps for a moment," said Vectus as everyone headed to the dining room.

Breel's heart lurched.

Vectus smiled. "Don't worry, it's nothing bad."

He motioned to the couch. Criba and Trafis sat with Breel.

Vectus handed Criba a sheet of paper. "I know you cover Duknum's department, Criba, but a programmer told me something, and I wanted to show you in case you hadn't heard yet."

Even though he said it wasn't bad news, a vice squeezed Breel's heart as Vectus left the room then the three of them leaned in to read what he'd handed them. It was email sent earlier that day from the Director of the Department of Occupation to Duknum's boss.

"You're to retire in a couple of weeks and have only brought forward Duknum Sorep as a possible new Department of Occupation's Head of Computer Programmers. I spoke with others and the consensus is he's one of our department's best programmers—skilled, dedicated, and hardworking. Many mentioned his faltering after his family escaped, which made me doubt promoting him. However, the interrogation led to nothing and now he's working harder than ever. Therefore, I accept Duknum Sorep as your replacement. Start training immediately."

Tears pricked at the corners of Breel's eyes.

He's fine. Father is fine.

Duknum had never said he aspired to become head, but he didn't have to. He had always worked hard on his Department of Expansion courses and would often mention going above and beyond at work to encourage his children to do so, too. A promotion to department head was a badge of honour and pride.

Criba dabbed her eyes with her sleeve. "Good for him." Her expression faltered. "I wish I could tell him how proud I am."

Breel patted her hand. "Me, too."

Chapter Eight

All eyes were on Breel, Trafis, and Criba as they joined everyone at the kitchen table. Breel eased herself onto her chair with care to avoid splinters.

Cafrec leaned into her. "Everything okay?"

"My father's boss promoted him to head."

He whistled. "Good for him."

Even Samit smiled. "I figured that'd happen, eventually. Your father was always a go-getter, Breel."

The meeting started with Manum saying that he'd learned more about the elite force from their DOE sources. "Everyone I spoke to said that the elite force members they know were born for the assignment. Most have reported countless citizens, even their own family."

What terrible people for showing more loyalty to Tatem than their loved ones.

"What?" said Criba, her voice high.

Manum nodded. "It's awful. We all know that housekeepers are the biggest reporters. The second biggest? Family members. One reported his nephews many times, leading to their Mortae. He said they deserved it for breaking the law—as did their parents."

That's awful! I was so, so lucky that my strict parents never considered reporting me. Sad that so many parents have told the DOE about their own children.

"So, nothing we don't know," Samit said.

"That these people are fanatical?" said Cafrec. "Yeah."

"I have some good news," said Samit. "A source from the Department of Education said when she left yesterday's Mortae, a man spoke to her husband. The man—a DOE officer, like her husband—said he was always uncertain about Tatem and after learning Manum is anti-Tatem, is now anti-Tatem, too."

Manum leaned forward. "Who was it?"

Samit shrugged. "Didn't give a name."

Manum sat back in his chair. "Oh. I hope he stays safe."

While this was only one person who had joined them, one undecided person doing so without direct influence meant there had to be more like him.

Finally, a smidgen of hope.

Samit showed everyone a piece of paper. "The last bit of news is about Manum's son."

Manum gasped like a programmer finding a critical error moments before submitting their work. "Why didn't you tell me?"

"I got it right before the news."

Still should've told him in private like Vectus did about my father.

But Breel didn't dare speak her thoughts as getting Manum even angrier at Samit was a terrible idea.

"It's good news," Samit said added, then read. "'My students know my father's an escaped Vucapi. While I fear for him, in a twisted way, his near-Mortae has been beneficial. More and more students have realized I share his beliefs, so they ask for extra help to have the opportunity to say they want to join us in private. I encourage them but also ensure they know the importance of being careful. Four of my students' entire families are anti-Tatem. I know of over two dozen people on our side between students, their family members, and a handful of teachers. There'll be more in the coming days and weeks. Tell my father I'm cautious. I know how valued those of us are on the inside. Gaimster.'"

Breel grinned. "Sounds like he's doing all he can for our cause."

Manum's nostrils flared. "Are you kidding me? I told him to stop this!"

"He said he's being careful," said Vectus.

"If he was careful, he wouldn't be doing this!" Manum banged a fist on the table. "Samit, work on getting my son here—now."

Samit blinked. "Excuse me?"

"Either you bring him here, or I get him myself."

"He's being safe," Criba said. "The DOE doesn't suspect him, so I'm sure he'll be fine."

Manum pointed a finger at her. "Easy for you to say. Your children are right here with you. And you," he added, looking at Samit, "you don't even have kids. Just like the rest of you! You don't know what it's like to worry day and night about your child."

Silence echoed throughout the room.

"I know," said Criba. "When Breel disappeared to Intercludae, I worried for days not knowing whether she was dead or alive. You know where your son is, and sure, he's doing something you don't want him to do. But he's made his choice, just like you and all our allies, because he feels it's right."

Manum bit his lip as his shoulders dropped. "I know you're right, but it's eating me alive. I recruited him to our cause! It's my fault."

"Mr. Gaimster?" said Praxa. As she put a hand on his arm, you could've heard a pin drop. "Even if you never recruited him, don't you think seeing you as a Vucapi would've converted him?"

She has a point.

If Manum and his son were as close as he claimed, seeing his father like that would've made Mr. Gaimster reconsider his beliefs—just like Criba and Trafis had.

Manum patted her hand. "It's possible. I...I need to be alone."

Samit tsked, muttering something under his breath, as Manum left the room.

Vectus cleared his throat. "Samit, it'd do you good to be a bit more sensitive."

"Oooh," Cafrec said.

Samit's expression was unreadable as he stared at Vectus. Then, he smiled—*smiled*! "You sound like Sanctus. Hmm, I'm overdue for sending him an email. Meeting over."

He sat then turned to his computer.

Everyone exchanged baffled glances—*Glad that didn't erupt*—then left the table. Trafis joined Breel and Cafrec at their desks, sitting in the birch spindle chair they kept for visitors.

"Samit must've been fun to work for," Trafis said.

"Oh yeah," said Cafrec. "Great boss!"

Trafis cocked his head then, realizing Cafrec had been sarcastic, laughed. "I can't believe Uncle Famut was friends with him!"

"You aren't the first."

The three whipped their heads around to find Samit standing at the bottom of the stairs. Trafis's face turned the colour of a beet.

"Listen," said Samit. "Sanctus had plenty of sensitivity for both of us. He's always been the people person—like Famut. The three of us were close even though you'd be more likely to find me working at a computer. But Sanctus and Famut needed people. Maybe that's where the sensitivity comes in. I was happier by myself. Manum claims that's why my first and only girlfriend dumped me for him when I know he stole her from me."

Breel blinked in confusion. Samit and Manum never said that they knew each other let alone that Manum had stolen his girlfriend.

Samit continued before anyone could ask questions. "We were around your age. What made it even harder was her dying not long after."

"What happened?" Breel asked.

And why have you not gotten over her? That must've been over twenty years ago!

"An accident after their son was born." He waved a hand, dismissing the conversation. "What I'm here for is to request another database, Breel."

Another database to create!

Excitement jolted through her at the prospect of a new project followed by dread. The database tracking reports was already high maintenance with the constant influx of new information bringing with it new ways to categorize the data. Now he wanted a second...

"We're sending and receiving hundreds of emails every day. Like with department reports, I want all these emails captured in a searchable database. I also want you to create categories to pull keywords of interest."

It was far simpler than the other database since the email server was one source, rather than the report server with one source per department. However, the massive number of emails meant the file size would increase fast, so it was key to ensure efficiency and responsiveness to user commands.

"I'll get started right away."

***

When Breel walked upstairs to turn in for the night, Cafrec followed to ask Samit a question. Voices sounded from the living room, so they went to investigate, finding everyone standing around chatting, some in sweaters and others in navy-blue pyjamas.

"Where's Samit?" asked Cafrec.

Manum raised an eyebrow. "Where'd you think?"

Cafrec put a finger to his lips, walked into the dining room, then peeked at Samit's monitor. "Whatcha doing?"

Samit jumped, sending a pile of papers falling to the floor. He minimized his screen before picking them up. "Get out of here, Cafrec!"

Cafrec returned to the others with a smirk.

"What's he doing?" Breel asked.

"Typing an email."

When Breel had gotten Samit's attention earlier, he'd also hidden an email.

What's he hiding?

Cafrec lowered his voice. "Has Samit ever been part of anything that wasn't a meal, meeting, or news watching?"

It was a rhetorical question.

Criba nudged Lexo. "Continue what you were saying."

Lexo nodded. "We should think about what things will look like after Tatem."

Breel had yet to consider it, but Lexo was right. They were putting all their efforts into how to overthrow Tatem. They knew they wanted things to be different, but they'd yet to think through all the changes they'd make.

"We discussed that in Intercludae," said Manum. "We planned on having a city council like they had fifty years ago. Citizens will elect government officials to sit on the council for two-year terms. We created guidance documents for the council, but they're in draft as we want more people deciding our future. Everyone in Lexum deserves a say."

Lexo nodded. "Good. That's good."

Cafrec clapped him on the back. Praxa, beside Lexo, glared at Cafrec.

Geesh, what's her problem?

"Do you mention it because you wanna be part of all those decisions?" Cafrec asked.

Lexo made a face. "No way. You?"

"Nah."

Breel was with Lexo and Cafrec. Figuring all those things out was for others to do. Once Tatem was gone, she wanted to spend her time drawing for Lexum, not sitting on a council.

Chapter Nine

Breel woke in a cold sweat. Her heart tried to burst from its cage as her lungs took in as much air as possible.

Breath, breath.

She took deep breaths to slow her erratic breathing.

Cafrec, Cafrec.

She pictured his floppy hair and wide grin to rid herself of the horrific image of Tatem pointing a gun at Famut.

It took a minute for her breathing and heartbeat to return to normal, doing so much faster than a couple of weeks ago.

Breel rolled over to check the clock. It was only six thirty—half an hour before her alarm. Not wanting to go back to sleep in case the nightmare resumed, she got dressed. As usual, she found Samit at his desk and typing as if he had to pound out one million words by the end of the day.

Does the man ever sleep?

Cafrec was there, too, wearing one of their few russet-brown sweaters.

Breel slipped into her chair then kissed him. "Couldn't sleep?"

Samit jumped. He turned, saw them at the table, then sighed before returning to his work.

As Cafrec shrugged, Breel recalled Samit minimizing his emails.

Does he have something else to hide but is annoyed we're here so he can't do it?

"I couldn't sleep," said Cafrec.

"Me neither," she whispered. "Nightmare."

"Me too," Cafrec said.

The only other people who knew about their nightmares were Criba and Trafis since they shared rooms. Praxa was too deep a sleeper to wake and didn't seem to have the same issue. If nightmares plagued the others, they kept it to themselves.

Since they were awake, Breel and Cafrec heated scrambled eggs and sausage, toasted bread, and brewed coffee as the others got up one by one. Some, such as Praxa, sauntered in wearing their navy-blue pyjamas whereas Manum and others greeted everyone with a chipper "hello," already dressed in black pants and various coloured sweaters.

Samit, of course, continued working. This time he wasn't composing or reading an email and when Breel tapped his shoulder for breakfast, he didn't jump or minimize anything.

So, he only cares about us reading his emails?

Samit turned to the table then yawned while looking at his plate. His eyes drooped like when he was Breel's department head and doing hers and Cafrec's work on top of his own as they prepped to leave for Intercludae.

"You should work less and sleep more," Breel suggested.

Samit stabbed eggs with his fork then shovelled them into his mouth. "Can't. Lots to do."

Criba frowned. "You have Breel, Cafrec, and Vectus who are capable programmers. Can't you give them some more to do?"

"Cafrec already assists me." He spoke with a mouth full of egg. "Breel and Vectus have their own jobs."

Criba bit her sausage. "You look exhausted."

Samit smiled. "Is that concern, Criba?"

Criba frowned. "None of us should burn ourselves out this early."

Samit's smile didn't disappear. "You didn't answer my question. But yes, I'll delegate better."

During breakfast, Breel kept thinking about Samit hiding things. It probably didn't mean anything but that wasn't a guarantee. If the others had noticed, they'd yet to say anything.

I guess it's up to me, then. Everyone needs to know because what if he's the spy?

Swallowing hard, Breel asked, "Samit, why do you keep minimizing emails when someone's looking at your screen?"

The silence was deafening. Samit froze, eyes narrowing into a glare. Breel didn't break eye contact.

Hold your ground, Breel. You have every right to question him about the safety of you and everyone else opposing Tatem.

Samit broke off first, blinking as his gaze faltered. "What...what're you implying?"

He'd gone from sleepy to wide awake and defensive.

"Nothing," said Breel.

Not yet anyway.

Samit looked at his plate. "I don't like people reading behind my back, that's all."

While understandable, Samit was so hasty to hide his emails, it stuck out like a red flag.

But would he ask me to create an email database if he was hiding emails?

Samit didn't *seem* like a spy; however, he was someone to monitor.

By some miracle, no one else said anything about it. Lexo poured Samit and himself a second cup of coffee as their post-breakfast meeting began. Breel talked about how the new database was coming along and that she hoped to finish coding by noon. When it was ready, it'd import all new emails from the Lexum server twice per day.

After returning to work, Breel was well into her flow when Manum and Lexo appeared.

"Can we talk?" Manum asked.

Lexo pointed upstairs. "Praxa's at the top of the stairs keeping watch."

Breel frowned as she exchanged glances with Cafrec, whose brow furrowed.

"I don't understand," Breel said.

Manum motioned for Lexo to sit in the chair. They both wore blood-red sweaters like Tragpraev (Tatem's previous housekeeper and double agent) had worn working in the Department of Households.

We could use a Tragpraev around here...

Dust and sand covered everything no matter how careful they were. It collected in the corners of the floor and whenever Breel and Cafrec moved their chairs, they disturbed a thin layer of sand.

Manum stood beside Lexo. "We question Samit's loyalties."

Cafrec laughed then shot Breel an incredulous look. Manum's serious expression didn't falter. Lexo frowned.

Why's Cafrec laughing?

"That's ridiculous," said Cafrec.

"Why's he working all hours of the day?" Manum asked. "Even worse, as you said Breel, he hides his emails. Whether or not you were accusing him, it seems a strong case for him being a spy. We know there's a spy somewhere."

They thought the spy had been Tragpraev. After Tatem killed Famut, Tragpraev revealed himself as a Hargamite. However, he appeared at their failed Mortae to reveal the truth when he attempted to murder Tatem. But Tatem's security killed Tragpraev first.

"I know we believe the spy was likely an Intercludae resident," said Lexo, "but—"

Cafrec cut him off. "Yeah, and Mr. Tu—Samit was never there."

Manum sighed. "Think about it, Cafrec. Samit was friends with Famut. That he rescued us from our failed Mortae means he knew more than most about what was happening. What if Famut told him more than he should've? What if Samit betrayed Famut? What if begging Sanctus to come here is so we think he's on our side? You heard him brag that Tatem said he's Lexum's most skilled hacker. That means he's met the tyrant. Plus, Sanctus's picture was on the wall in Intercludae along with all our other internal Lexum contacts, which means Samit must be a spy or else Sanctus wouldn't be alive."

Breel resisted the urge to tell Manum most of this made little sense. Famut had also met Tatem, and he didn't work for the man. Vectus said Intercludae residents had destroyed the pictures of Lexum contacts before the DOE saw them. But even if they hadn't destroyed them, Sanctus was far from the only anti-Tatem citizen the DOE hadn't arrested.

If Samit, or whoever the spy was, had memorized even half of the identities of those in the pictures, Tatem would've ordered Mortae for far more Lexum contacts. But most lived. The spy had either forgotten most of the identities or didn't memorize them.

As Breel attempted to explain this, Manum kept shaking his head. Lexo, too, frowned at some of what they said.

"I'm not saying I don't think he's a spy," Breel said. "If I was, I wouldn't have brought up him being so secretive. I'm saying there's evidence he could be but there's also evidence he's not."

Cafrec said, "Sure, Samit's a little...you know. But he's one of us. Plus—"

Manum raised a hand. "All I ask is that, as programmers, you see what he's doing. He sends many emails. Does he email people he shouldn't? He's also hidden an email from me, so I wonder."

Cafrec pointed to Breel's laptop. "He wouldn't ask Breel to build an email database if he was hiding them."

"He could have done some hacking thing to hide specific ones," said Lexo.

Cafrec laughed at the words "hacking thing."

"All right," said Breel. "If Cafrec's okay with it, we'll do it."

He nodded. "We can't promise anything, though. Samit's taught me some things, but I'm still learning."

Manum nodded with a strange little smirk as he looked from Cafrec to Breel.

Geesh, we haven't even started, and he's convinced we'll find something.

The moment Manum and Lexo returned upstairs, Breel and Cafrec moved their chairs closer to discuss.

"I guess I see where they're coming from," said Cafrec. "I mean, yeah, not wanting us to see his emails is suspect. And with the security set up and me to maintain the systems put in place, he only leads us and contacts his surveillance people. So, I agree that I'm not sure why he works such long hours. But I don't think he's a spy, he simply doesn't want his screens read. But I agree that we should check to be sure."

If all went well, if they proved his actions weren't suspicious, Manum would go easy on Samit.

***

Once Breel finished coding, she began importing the emails into her database. It'd finish around the time they returned from lunch. Before heading upstairs, she checked her inbox for Department of Health up-dates. The subject line "I found someone important" jumped out.

She clicked the email. "Breel Sorep—You don't know me, but my name is Breh. An anti-Tatem colleague gave me your email. After a promotion to head nurse on a floor of the retirement home last month, I learned an interesting secret—there's a man named Clonis isolated from everyone else. They don't allow Clonis to integrate with other residents and only select staff know he exists. The moment I met him, I knew he must be Tatem's brother."

Breel's jaw dropped.

Tatem has a brother?

If that was news to her, it'd be news to everyone except those he grew up with. Tatem had never mentioned family, so Breel had assumed he was an only child. She shuddered at the thought of having Tatem for a sibling. He'd have laughed at others' misfortunes (perhaps even causing them), injuring his siblings every chance he got, and been an all-around scary child.

Breh's email continued. "Clonis doesn't hide his dislike for Tatem. He said if it's for a good cause, he can provide useful information. What'd you recommend?"

Breel couldn't believe their luck. Talking to Clonis could be the event that'd turn things in their favour. It could mean the end of Tatem.

Breh's email ended with a postscript. "I worked with your uncle years ago. Famut was a great colleague and doctor who cared about people. Looking forward to hearing from you. Breh."

Breel hit print. The printer between her and Cafrec clicked on, chug-ging as it churned out the printed email. She slapped the paper it spat out onto Cafrec's desk. "Read this!"

He jumped, having been engrossed in reading a report. "Okay…" He picked it up, eyes moving back and forth and widening the more he read. "Wow!"

"Amazing, right?"

Cafrec turned to her. "Very! This Breh guy knows Tatem's brother? I didn't even know he had a sibling."

"Me neither. This could change everything!"

His smiled widened. "Oh Breel, I love seeing you get excited."

Breel's cheeks burned. "Thanks.

He kissed her. "When all this is done, I look forward to you getting excited more often."

How'd I get so lucky to find someone so sweet? And to think Tatem's his biological father…

She pushed the last thought out of her mind. Cafrec continued claiming it didn't bother him. But if being biologically Xorem's daughter bothered her, being related to Tatem must bother Cafrec. When he was ready, Breel was prepared to help him through it.

***

Lunch was long. Breel concentrated on her bacon, lettuce, and tomato sandwich to contain her excitement about Breh's email. But eating faster didn't make the meeting happen quicker.

When Samit called the meeting to order, Breel shot her hand into the air. "May I start?"

Samit smiled—a rare event. "The way you've been fidgeting and scarfing down your food quicker than Cafrec, I figured you had something to share."

"I do! First, the boring update is I finished the email database, and it's importing everything. Second, I received an email from a new retirement home head nurse named Breh."

"Ah, yes," said Samit. "I just set him up to email us."

Breel read Breh's message, pausing when she got to the sentence about Clonis being Tatem's brother. There was a collective gasp. Everyone's eyes lit up as they talked over each other.

"His *brother*?"

"He still has family?"

"I'd love to hear what he has to say about Tatem!"

Once the chattering dissipated, Breel finished reading the email then, placing the paper on the table, she said, "We must make an exception to our rule and bring him here."

She cringed, preparing herself for the chorus of "no's." But even Samit agreed.

"Allow my son to come with him," Manum said.

Oh no, not another Samit and Manum argument.

Samit groaned. "Manum, we've been over this. It sounds like he doesn't even want to come."

"No, not really," Manum admitted.

Samit rolled his eyes. "Then why're we having this conversation?"

"If we had a plan to bring him here, he'd come. Then I can stop worrying about his safety."

"That's not happening," said Samit.

Breel agreed. The Mr. Gaimster she knew was too dedicated to his work and students to abandon them. However, she stayed out of it.

Manum stared at the table. "I guess you're right."

Trafis caught Breel's eye as he mouthed the word "Whoa."

Samit returned to their meeting. "Tatem must have Clonis well secured, so how do we get him here?"

It wouldn't be easy. Far more people than Breh would need to be in on it. They'd need to plant fake video feeds, get Clonis out of the building without coming across other staff or residents, then drive him to the pipe in the Lexum walls. Clonis would need to crawl through the pipe to the desert. There were also the DOE officers on the walls who'd see Clonis unless he escaped through a tunnel leading to Intercludae.

"We need more information before making a plan," said Criba. "It's seven miles to Lexum. Tatem's around seventy, right? I assume Clonis is around the same age. Can he even walk that far?"

"Good question," Samit said.

Breel scribbled "Capability?" on the email.

"Also," said Cafrec, "does he want to help? Breh said he's willing to give us information but is he willing to come here and do more if needed?"

Another good point which Breel jotted down.

Samit leaned forward, spreading both hands onto the table. "In the meantime, I want everyone brainstorming how to get Clonis here. We'll discuss once we hear back."

When Breel returned to her desk, she emailed Breh their questions. By the time she got to her database, Cafrec had confirmed with Lexum's email server that Samit had sent no emails using his original Lexum email address. He'd only emailed within the server he'd created for the anti-Tatem group. So far, according to Breel's database, he'd sent and received over nine hundred emails since leaving Lexum.

Cafrec whistled. "Geesh, the guy emails more than I thought."

They figured that if Samit was a spy, he'd have safeguards preventing certain emails from importing into the database, so Cafrec searched the server Samit had created for emails that didn't make it into Breel's database.

Meanwhile, Breel wrote quick and dirty code for the database to count, for each correspondent, the total emails Samit had sent and received, the average sent and received per day, and the date of the last message. By far, Samit corresponded with Sanctus the most with a few hundred emails between them.

She read some of his emails with Sanctus. In earlier ones, Samit wrote things such as, "Sanctus, I beg you to reconsider. You and Vida will be safer here than in Lexum. We'll bring a doctor to help with the birth. Anything you need or want to get you here. Please."

After a few days of this, Sanctus sent a terse email. "Samit, we have more important things to discuss than you hounding me. Please stop. Yes, it's dangerous. However, Vida and I believe it's more dangerous for her and our child to have no access to the hospital. I have vital work to do. You know that."

The messages didn't seem out of the ordinary.

"He's sent or received one thousand one hundred and thirty-nine emails," Cafrec said.

He turned to face her, leaning forward, waiting to hear what her database said. As Breel checked, her stomach dropped as if the internet cut out while studying for the Demna Exam. Only nine hundred and forty-five emails had imported.

Samit's hiding emails...

"What's wrong?" Cafrec asked. When she told him, his jaw dropped as he stared at Breel's screen with wide eyes. "I...I can't believe it."

The database was missing one hundred and ninety-four emails. They investigated it further, comparing the number of messages sent between Samit and each of his correspondents in the server and database. It didn't take long to find that all the missing emails were encrypted and to and from a hidden email address.

There was only one explanation. Samit and this mystery person were spies.

Chapter Ten

Cafrec worked on accessing the encrypted emails between Samit and the unknown person.

There had to be an explanation. This mystery person was—*or claimed to be*—anti-Tatem otherwise they wouldn't be part of Samit's email server which meant there was no reason for Samit to encrypt them. But it seemed he had something to hide.

"How dare you!"

They jumped at the shout. A moment later, feet clomped on the stairs then Samit appeared. Breel tensed as he glared at Cafrec, face red and just as intimidating as when he was their head.

Even though Samit hadn't directed his anger at Breel, her entire body had seized. If Samit was a spy, who knows what he'd do. If by some miracle Samit wasn't a spy, they may have ruined their relationship with him.

"How dare you, Cafrec!" A vein pulsed above Samit's left eye.

Cafrec shrunk into his chair. For once, he had no words.

Samit towered over Cafrec like Vectus had when teaching. "You think I wouldn't find out? I was the head of the computer programmers in the top department! You better believe I'm Lexum's best programmer. I told you my hacking skills are second-to-none—even Tatem said so. You're a poor and stupid hacker for thinking you can hack me without detection."

Samit's yelling attracted the attention of the others.

Vectus pushed through to stand between Samit and Breel and Cafrec. "Why're you yelling?" His voice stayed level.

"They spied on me!" Samit's breathing was audible, his jaw set.

"What?" Criba looked at Breel and Cafrec in shock.

Breel lowered her gaze.

Awkward.

Manum groaned then threw his arms into the air. "Oh, give them a break. I put them up to it. Blame me."

"You?!" Samit yelled.

Samit took one step toward Manum then, before anyone could stop him, threw a punch. Manum shouted in pain as he staggered back, hand on his bleeding nose.

Breel's heart rate had increased not because it scared her but because it was new. Assault didn't happen in Lexum as such an offense resulted in Mortae. Everyone kept back, exchanging glances, unsure what to do.

When Samit attacked him again, Manum was ready. He ducked Samit's fist before throwing his own punch. Samit screamed, falling to the floor like a deadweight. Manum stepped closer, but Lexo and Praxa pulled him back, begging him to stop.

Manum assured them he was done then wiped his face on a handkerchief, staining it with blood. Criba leaned over Samit, who moaned on the ground while holding his bleeding face. As Criba helped him sit, he glared at Manum through tearing eyes.

"You started it," said Manum, the fabric of his handkerchief muffling his voice.

Samit gritted his teeth as he snatched the handkerchief Vectus handed him.

Samit glared at Manum. "Why were they spying on me?"

"I'm suspicious."

Samit's eyes widened. "Of *me*? I'm the least suspicious person here! Famut was my friend."

Manum laughed. "That proves nothing. Breel asked why you hide your work and instead of explaining, you got defensive. Plus, you're always working. No one can convince you to leave for a walk or target practice. You only talk to us if it's about work. You're working before breakfast and after everyone else is in bed. We need to drag you away from your computer to eat and watch the news. Why? Do you work for Tatem?"

Samit gasped then winced. "This is ridiculous! No, I don't work for him. I'm not a spy."

Manum turned to Breel and Cafrec. "What'd you two find?"

Awkward again.

Breel dropped her gaze then noticed the stairwell. Samit stood then cleared his throat before demanding they answer. Her fingers twitched.

I wish I could disappear.

Swallowing hard, Breel said, "Samit sends many emails. All his correspondence is with our sources but—"

Manum's face fell. "It is?"

He's disappointed to hear that one bit of good news?

"Yeah," said Cafrec. "However, he's encrypted his emails with someone so we can't even see who they're with let alone what they're emailing about. He also blocked them from importing into Breel's database."

"How dare you!" Samit said. His face was red, his hands balled into fists. "How dare you attempt to read my private emails! I'm not a spy!"

Criba and Praxa shuffled their feet then backed up a step. Lexo, near the stairs beside Praxa, had his eyes glued on Manum, ready to jump in and assist, if needed. The only person who looked amused was Trafis who suppressed a smile, his eyes darting between Samit and Manum.

How can he find this exciting?

Breel shifted her weight as Samit yelled. As he insisted his innocence, saying the emails are personal and nobody's business, a sense of guilt overcame Breel.

What if we're wrong? What if his anger's because we attempted to violate his privacy by reading them?

Manum crossed his arms. "For someone claiming to not be a spy, you sure are defensive."

Samit gestured with the hand not holding the handkerchief against his face. "Of course I'm defensive! You're accusing me of things that aren't true!"

Manum backed out of Samit's range. "Think of it from our perspective. The encrypted emails suggest you and the other person are spies feeding each other information."

If he wasn't a spy, Samit's only option was to decrypt the emails. Someone would read them, determine everything was fine, then they could return to normal.

Sweat beaded across Samit's forehead. "We aren't spies! We're done here."

Samit started for the stairs, but Lexo and Praxa blocked his way.

Lexo raised a hand, stopping him. "Not so fast. You haven't convinced me you're not a spy."

"What!?" Samit turned to everyone else. "Surely you all don't think that!?"

Manum and Praxa dropped their gazes. Trafis took interest in a pile of sand in the corner. Breel looked at anything and anyone but Samit, wrestling with her uncertainty.

"Cafrec, Breel, I was your head!!" Samit said. "You worked under me for a year, Cafrec!"

Cafrec glanced at him then averted his gaze to the ground. "I don't know what to think. If you're not a spy, I don't understand why you encrypted those emails."

Samit turned to Criba. "Tell them I'm not a spy."

Criba bit her lower lip. "I don't know that for sure."

His jaw dropped. "I was friends with Famut and one of his first recruits! Why would I turn on my friend?"

"That's a good question," said Manum. "Why did you?"

"I'm not a spy!"

Breel winced as Samit's voice echoed throughout the basement. "Samit, all you need to do is decrypt those emails. We'll read some, prove you're not a spy, then pretend this never happened."

Samit's jaw set. "I can't pretend it never happened. This is ridiculous! Me, a spy...I'm the least likely spy here! As head of my Career Group, I'm used to working long hours. We have nothing to do other than work, anyway. And you know what? I like my work!"

What's he talking about? We have far more to do than just work!

"You can join us for walks and target practice," Lexo said.

Samit groaned. "I hate it when people think introversion's a crime. No one's giving Praxa a hard time, and she's the biggest introvert here! Perhaps I should speak to Tatem, you know, the person I work for, and tell him he has everything wrong! After all, citizens should talk to each other instead of working in silence."

Manum raised a hand, palm out. "Calm down."

Samit made a rude gesture. "Don't tell me to calm down. You could've talked to me, but you didn't."

"Asking someone you think may be a spy whether they're a spy is a terrible idea," Manum said. "What about the emails we can't read? That's the biggest issue and you haven't explained why they're encrypted."

"Because they're private! That doesn't make me a spy."

Cafrec stood then motioned to his chair. "Then prove it by showing us the emails."

"No."

Manum sighed. "Then you leave us no choice."

Samit forced a laugh. "What, killing me?"

Breel chuckled but Samit didn't crack a smile.

Oh, he's serious!

"And bring ourselves to Tatem's level?" Manum asked. "Are you crazy? No. You're confined to your bedroom with someone guarding the door."

"What?!" Samit shouted.

It was the only thing they could do. Samit had far too much access to everyone and everything. While Vectus and Cafrec worked on decrypting his emails, everyone agreed to deny Samit computer access until they accessed the emails, and they proved he wasn't a spy.

Samit laughed. "I'm never going to let you read those emails, so good luck! It's a sixteen-digit encryption. You'll never break it even if you had one thousand years."

"Let's get going," said Manum.

Breel's heart sank as Manum and Lexo walked Samit upstairs.

This is awful. Our leader...possibly a spy.

There was a Lexum-sized pit in Breel's stomach. If Samit was a spy, Tatem would know where they were hiding and waiting for the best moment to strike.

Vectus's leaned against the wall, shaking his head. "I never would've expected Samit...he can't possibly be a spy..."

Breel noticed Trafis frowning. "Why doesn't he give us access to the emails if he isn't a spy?" he asked.

"The only explanation is he *is* a spy," said Cafrec, slumped in his chair. "Guess my intuition is off."

Criba patted his shoulder. "Don't be so hard on yourself. We all found it hard to believe until you said he's hiding emails from us. I hope it's not true..."

The five of them brainstormed possibilities. The emails could be to a family member with whom he complained about everyone in the house. Or hassling Mr. Gaimster, the child of his ex-girlfriend. Or intimate emails with a new girlfriend.

Those reasons can't possibly be worth the isolation...which means he must be a spy. If he wasn't, he'd do the reasonable thing.

Things were grim and didn't look like they'd improve.

Chapter Eleven

They put Samit in the room he shared with Vectus off the kitchen. Vectus had moved from working in their bedroom to Samit's desk. He had stacked Samit's sea of papers—nothing suspicious there—in the corner. Unlike Samit with his two monitors, Vectus only used a laptop and mouse.

Manum joined the others for supper while watching the bedroom door. The meal was sombre with nobody speaking except Manum who moaned and grimaced during every bite due to his bruised and colourful nose. Nobody mentioned what had happened.

The moment Cafrec finished eating, he jumped to his feet then ran his hand over his hair. "My fellow citizens! Today brings a new law: everyone must slick back their hair. Hair gel for all!"

Everyone but Praxa laughed, relieving the tension.

"You don't think I'm funny, Praxa?" Cafrec asked.

Praxa eyed her plate as Lexo patted her arm. "Please don't bother her."

"Yes, let it go," said Manum.

Cafrec glanced at Breel who shrugged. It wasn't hard to believe Praxa was devoid of humour. After all, humour was scant and close to being illegal in Lexum.

After the evening news, Vectus called the meeting to order from his seat. It was strange without Samit chairing from the head of the table.

As Vectus praised Breel's email database, her cheeks burned. Next, she read the latest update from Breh. "'Breel, don't have long. Talked to Clonis who's ecstatic about assisting. He's a year older than Pres. Tatem but we agree that he's capable of the journey. Best way to get him to you is faking a medical event. When that happens, drivers and a nurse bring the resident to the hospital. We can ensure one of our nurses and drivers do that job and they can take him to a tunnel instead of the hospital. The nurse can work with one of our doctors to put paperwork through saying he died on the drive so there's no search. Breh.'"

It all sounded promising and soon, they'd put the plan into action. The room buzzed as the group expressed how much they looked forward to meeting Tatem's brother. But nonetheless, meeting Clonis would be nerve-wracking. Breh recognizing Clonis meant he looked like Tatem. There was a good chance he had the same salt-and-pepper hair and blue eyes, so his presence would be a constant reminder of Tatem's face.

However, those downsides were minor inconveniences. Everyone wanted to meet Clonis and know why Tatem kept him alive all these years since at any point Clonis could tell tales from their childhood that Tatem would want kept quiet.

Most of all, Breel wanted to know what Tatem had been like at her age. He'd only been eighteen, a year younger than her, when he achieved the highest mark in his graduating class, awarding him the scholarship to go to postsecondary school in Lexum. It also gave him the sole lower-class citizen seat on the Lexum council. Not long after, he elevated himself to president as the last living government official.

Manum frowned at the conversation then crossed his arms. "Every-thing Breh says seems too good to be true."

Everyone stopped speaking, some even mid-sentence. Manum wasn't wrong, but bringing Clonis was worth the risk. He agreed but said he couldn't help being suspicious. Vectus tasked Lexo and Praxa with meeting Clonis in the tunnel. Once he arrived, they'd watch him and not allow him to use the computers.

"Breel," said Vectus, "tell Breh I'll contact him to assist with arranging the right people and surveillance. I'm sure Samit's people can do that without him."

As their leader—*ex-leader?*—Samit liked the control of coordinating multiple departments, when needed.

Next, Vectus said he and Cafrec had gotten nowhere in decrypting Samit's emails. "We'll keep trying, but there's a better chance of Tatem putting an end to Mortae than us decrypting those emails."

After the meeting, Breel stopped in Cafrec and Trafis's bedroom to talk to her brother. A small room, the two beds had little space between them because of Trafis's desk in the corner. On it sat his laptop, mouse, and a printer. Being in the corner of the basement and farthest from the front door, it had the least amount of sand and dirt which was why Trafis, with his allergies, had taken it.

Breel sat on the end of Cafrec's bed as Trafis turned in his desk chair.

He leaned forward. "So, d'you think he's a spy?"

Breel shrugged. "I really don't know. I'd hoped not but maybe he is?"

"Scary. We thought we could trust him but perhaps not." He sighed. "What is it?"

"Oh, I miss Lexum."

Breel's jaw fell, and her heart constricted.

He does? Oh no!

Trafis added, "Oh, not what you think at all! I don't regret coming."

He'd finally said the words she'd been wanting to hear. Until that moment, she hadn't known whether Trafis came to be with her or because he believed in the cause.

"Of course," Trafis added, "I miss things like fresh food and not being in a desert. But this is so much better than studying something I'm not interested in or good at."

Destined to be an English teacher, Trafis had had mediocre grades and subpar teaching skills.

"Once we overthrow him, everyone can do what they want with their lives," said Trafis.

"What d'you want to do?" she asked.

If technology existed to detect whether citizens thought about their wants versus society's needs, thinking about one's preferred career would be illegal. Since Trafis had never considered his wants, he never would've broken that law.

Trafis sighed then rested his feet on the edge of the bed. "I don't know. You're lucky you know what you'd like to do."

Breel patted his leg. "Don't worry. I bet most people don't know."

"That's what Lexo said. He hates being an officer, but when he considered other Career Groups, he couldn't decide which he'd prefer. I guess I feel I should know since you and Mother do."

Criba had been a secretary for the Department of Occupation's Computer Programming Career Group; however, she dreamed of being a writer. But, as far as Breel knew, she had never written for fun.

Breel nodded. "I understand. But remember, Tatem ensures we only think about what we can do for society, not ourselves. Anyway, you're an excellent shot with a dart gun. You could be an officer."

Trafis' eyes widened then he shook his head. "No way."

Yeah, I can't see it either.

Trafis had been another brainwashed citizen doing everything Tatem had wanted him to do. Yet, he'd chosen to come to the other side because of Tatem's actions. It gave hope that Duknum, and countless others, would one day do the same.

Chapter Twelve

The next morning, Samit still refused to decrypt his emails. Manum, Lexo, and Praxa had had many hushed and impassioned conversations about not enjoying working on their laptops while in the hallway guarding him. As the hours ticked by, and Samit's refusal continued, the likelihood of him being a spy seemed more and more certain.

Vectus, Criba, and Lexo had all talked to Samit without luck. Breel and Cafrec took their turn after their post-lunch meeting.

Samit was sitting on his bed, back against the wall, glaring at Vectus's empty desk in the corner. Manum's punch had half shut one eye. A bruise (an array of blues, purples, yellows, and reds) extended halfway down the left side of his face.

"I'm not doing it," he said the moment Breel closed the door. She stood with Cafrec at the foot of the bed.

"Mr.—Samit," said Cafrec, "I want to believe you're on our side. I find it hard to believe you're a spy. But if you're not one, why can't you show us the emails?"

Samit smacked the bed with a hand. "I'm sick of this! They're private! How many times do I have to tell everyone that?"

"Let's assume you're anti-Tatem," said Breel. "Is keeping them private worth being imprisoned?"

Samit groaned. "I should shoot a video of myself answering that question then put it on repeat. Yes, I've made that clear."

It was obvious that they weren't going to get anywhere, so they left. The moment they stepped into the dining room, Vectus turned from Samit's desk with a raised eyebrow. When Breel shook her head, he threw his hands into the air.

Back at her desk, Breel found a message from Sanctus in her inbox. "Breel: Samit and I keep in touch, but I haven't heard from him since the day before yesterday. We email at least once per day. Is everything okay? Sanctus."

Breel called an emergency meeting. Everyone, except Lexo who was guarding Samit, crowded around her computer.

After reading the email, the group agreed to tell Sanctus they believe Samit's a spy for encrypting emails. They wouldn't provide more detail in case both Samit and Sanctus were spies and Samit had only encrypted some of their messages.

Breel refreshed her email every few minutes, but Sanctus had yet to message her by suppertime.

The evening news spoke more about the harsh realities of Lexum. Breel kept finding herself drumming her fingers on her legs, her mind on her whether she had a new email from Sanctus.

"Citizens," said Tatem, standing in front of his desk, "as you know, today's Vucapi were twelve Leaders of Tomorrow and three Leaders of Today."

Yikes, twelve more Leaders of Tomorrow...

Breel's stomach churned. It seemed far worse than the fourteen from the other day. One Mortae with so many was an anomaly, but more than that could be the start of a new reality.

Watching would've been awful. Families of the Vucapi were always at the front to have a prime view of the Mortae. They stood in the coveted Platinum Section of the Quaddro rewarded to citizens for embracing the collective and to punish victims' families. DOE officers would've held family members back, preventing them from rushing the platform. But Tatem would let the chaos play out—the cries of anguish from parents, their feeble attempts to rescue their children, the crowd's cheers as the DOE subdued them.

The television showed the platform during the Mortae. Despite looking away, the brief image of the dozen crying children seared into Breel's mind. Their white dress shirts caught the sun's rays while tears streamed down their faces, and they kicked and punched the officers holding them in place.

Before long, the news showed Tatem in his office. "I do not desire to have citizens perish." Though his voice cracked with feigned emotion, his eyes glowed.

Sickening. He used to be more skilled at hiding his sadistic glee.

Tatem raised a finger. "But these citizens were not true, loyal citizens of Lexum. If you don't follow our laws, you are a danger to our way of life and too risky to remain a citizen."

"Remain a citizen?" Cafrec whispered to Breel. "Funny way to say, 'let live.'"

"We all must do our duty to protect our society. Review the flyers showing the names and faces of those at large. I've ordered all Department of Enforcement officers to shoot them on sight—regardless of whether they're regular force carrying tranquilizing dart guns or the new elite force carrying pistols. If you see any fugitives, learn of their whereabouts, or have information which assists in their capture, you must report it. Just as important is reporting anyone engaging or likely engaging in illegal activities. Remember, I will give you glorious rewards for reporting a citizen who is not embracing the collective. Until tomorrow, good night."

He had said nothing new.

But while Tatem never had good news, Vectus did during their meeting. Everyone involved with getting Clonis to them had agreed to the plan. Next was putting it into action. But faking a medical emergency and death then ensuring the right citizens drove Clonis took a lot of coordination. They expected it'd take several days to set up everything.

After the meeting, Breel asked Criba and Trafis to come to her desk to share an update on Duknum. They rushed to the basement, thundering down the stairs before Breel could even get to the staircase.

Breel handed them two printed emails. The first was from Duknum's head, whom he was replacing, which said, "Duknum, you'll be a fine head."

Criba relaxed her hand, colour returned to her knuckles. "He will."

The next email was from a DOE officer to his own section head. "I said in my report Duknum Sorep is a rock, so I'm glad you agree to end the interrogations. Yes, we'll keep tabs on him. We've learned he's the incoming head of his section. Impressive given the stress he's been under."

Breel and her family were grateful to get this bit of news as it meant that, at least for the moment, Duknum was okay. He was safer now and proven trustworthy enough to be promoted.

However, Breel didn't show Criba and Trafis the email she had found from Duknum to a colleague and soon-to-be subordinate. "Thanks," Duknum had written. "I appreciate your concern. But I don't think about my family. They're traitors to President Tatem and Lexum's citizens. Not sure why you assume I'd think about people like that. They're dead to me."

Breel had read that email over and over, but his words never changed.

Recalling the devastation and shock on Duknum's face when Criba and Trafis fled with Breel made his words hard to believe. She could only hope he said them to protect himself as Tatem would suspect anyone who says they miss their traitorous family.

When Criba and Trafis left, Breel checked her inbox to find that Sanctus had emailed her minutes before.

"Breel," he wrote, "I have a gut feeling. Is Samit only encrypting emails with one person?"

"Yes," replied Breel.

She drummed her fingers on the desk, waiting for a response. It took ten minutes.

"Breel: Oh, Samit...He'll kill me for saying this, but clearly, I must. Before he left Lexum, he told Vida and me he was back in contact with a programming friend from school who'd just joined our anti-Tatem rebellion. I'd never seen him so happy when he said they talked back and forth for hours after setting her up with a safe email address. I checked the email server, and she's not listed as a person he's emailed, so I suspect he's hiding his emails with her. But it's not because they're spies—it's because he loves her, and their email content is likely not work-friendly. Tell Samit to talk to me and I'll set him straight. Sanctus."

Breel groaned. They could've avoided all of this if Samit had been open.

Why does he feel the need to hide this? Is being in love embarrassing to him? Or is he wanting to hide that he isn't always working?

She called Cafrec over. He leaned over her shoulder, laughing through most of the email. "All this because he didn't want us to know he's interested in someone? Come on!"

He plunked into his chair, shaking his head.

"At least he's not a spy," said Breel. "We should tell the others."

They printed the email thread then gathered everyone in the dining room. After Breel read the messages, Manum threw his head back in disbelief. "That's why he refused to tell us anything? Are you kidding me?"

Vectus stepped in. "Now, as ridiculous as it is, I'm sure it makes sense to Samit. Please don't give him a hard time."

Manum was two steps closer to the room Samit was in before Vectus asked where he was going.

"To talk to the idiot," Manum said without turning around.

Criba frowned. "I'm not sure that's a good idea."

Manum groaned but returned to the table. "Yeah, probably shouldn't be me. What'd you want to do?"

Criba pointed to Cafrec. "Cafrec knows him best, so I suggest he talk to Samit."

Cafrec's face fell but then he nodded. His gaze went beyond the kitchen to the hallway as his expression hardened into determination. "Okay."

"Show him the emails with Sanctus first," said Vectus. "If it makes him feel better, he can pick who reads a sample of emails to verify what Sanctus said."

Breel patted Cafrec's arm as he rose from the table. "Good luck."

***

Everyone waited in the living room as Cafrec tried convincing Samit to let them read his personal emails. Trafis played with his hands while beside him, Breel drummed her fingers on the couch's arm.

While waiting, Criba spoke with Praxa who, for once, said more than a few words. Criba said how lucky she felt to have met Duknum on her first day of work at the Department of Occupation. For most citizens, if they didn't meet their spouse in school or within the first few years of work, the chances of finding someone was low.

I never realized how lucky I am to have found Cafrec at my age.

Praxa stretched her legs. "I've dated a little, but the first guy was super pro-Tatem and the second, in Intercludae, was killed in the tunnel attacks."

Breel gasped. "I'm so sorry. I didn't know."

"Thanks. Yeah, we'd only been dating a week. But still..." She trailed off.

"You could always date Lexo."

Breel laughed since Lexo had been the one to say it. He grinned as he patted Praxa's back.

"Uh, no," said Praxa. To the others, she added, "Lexo and I went to school together. He's more like an annoying brother."

Breel laughed then looked at Trafis. "I know all about annoying brothers."

Criba smiled. "Now, now, children."

Before Trafis could quip back, Cafrec returned, flashing a smile and two thumbs-up. Behind him, Samit, face bruised and multicoloured, stared at his feet.

Samit cleared his throat. "Sorry for scaring you all. I guess..."

"Go on," said Criba, not unkindly.

He sighed. "I didn't want you to know I'm spending so much time talking with her. Plus, people have wondered what she sees in me, and I didn't want to hear it."

Vectus frowned. "You think that little of us?"

"I wish Sanctus kept his mouth shut..." said Samit, avoiding the question.

Breel stopped herself from laughing. "He's just looking out for you."

Vectus stood. "Let's see those emails."

The moment they disappeared, everyone turned to Cafrec. Sitting between Criba and Manum, he said, "It took a while to convince him to show us the emails, but I got him to realize that staying in that room is no way to live and that if he isn't a spy, we need him for the cause."

Criba patted his leg. "Good job."

Fifteen minutes later, Vectus returned without Samit.

"All is fine," said Vectus before the questions could begin. "Just the typical emails you'd expect along with the occasional programming talk."

As if by selecting "Run" on some code, there was a collective sigh of relief.

Vectus sat in the chair he had vacated near the dining room. "He's emailing her then heading to bed."

Bed? Not staying up working? That's different...

As everyone started talking in smaller groups, the atmosphere felt lighter knowing that Samit—and Sanctus—weren't spies.

But that meant someone else *was* a spy.

The worst part was not being any closer to figuring out their identity.

Chapter Thirteen

The group was talkative during lunch the next day. Only Samit and Praxa concentrated on eating their chicken noodle soup and Cobb salad.

Partway through the meal, Criba said to Samit, "Tell us about her."

Samit froze. "You want to know about her?"

He glanced at the others, who nodded.

Samit's eyebrows raised in surprise then he stared at the wall to avoid eye contact. "We were friends in school. Since she's in the Department of Logistics, we didn't talk much as Leaders of Today except if we saw each other at Mortae and things like that. A couple of months ago, one of our contacts in that department emailed me that someone anti-Tatem wants to help. When I set up an email address so they could talk with us without Tatem knowing, I learned it was her. We emailed every day and even saw each other a few times before I came here."

Hmm not anything about her, *but at least he's opening up.*

For the rest of the meal Samit had a starry-eyed look about him as he sat in a daze. But the biggest lunch topic was Clonis's impending arrival. Even Cafrec's meal lay forgotten while discussing what Clonis might be like.

"I wonder if he has Tatem's eyes," said Criba. Noticing Cafrec, she said, "Yours are similar, Cafrec."

Breel's heart constricted, but Cafrec didn't flinch.

"Maybe Clonis loves his hair, too." Cafrec ran his hand over his head. "Or he's bald because Tatem got all the hair."

Samit pulled himself from his daydreaming to say, "I'm looking forward to what he'll say about Tatem."

Everyone fell silent as they finished eating. As usual, Cafrec finished first. He stood then stared into Breel's eyes while holding a fork to his mouth. "Citizens! Bow to your master!"

Even Samit laughed.

Wow, thinking about this woman sure put him in a good mood.

"Citizens," said Cafrec, "to ensure Lexum has the best workers possible, Leaders of Tomorrow must now achieve perfect grades or else their punishment will be Mortae."

"Very accurate," Vectus said as Cafrec touched his hair.

Cafrec sat then took Breel's hand. She squeezed his back, but her attention was on Vectus chuckling at Cafrec's antics.

So strange seeing him being human.

Curious, she asked, "Vectus, how'd you manage pretending to be pro-Tatem?"

He flushed but answered. "Not easily. The hardest part was being so strict instead of toning things way down to help my students. But I decided that was the best persona. It's hard to suspect someone's anti-Tatem when they're strict and touting his greatness. After a time, it became easier, though it was never easy."

"You did it for self-protection," said Cafrec.

Vectus rested his fork onto his empty plate. "Yes. But Famut also told me to be hard on you both, to push you to learn. I couldn't single out students, so was hard on everyone."

"It worked," said Breel. "You were the most intimidating and difficult teacher I had."

She regretted blurting out those words before Vectus's jaw had even dropped, his hand frozen over his plate. "Oh, Breel...I'm sorry."

He's such a nice guy. Why'd I say that?

Breel's gut wrenched. She tried backpedaling. "No, it was a good thing."

Well, maybe...He made me a better programmer.

Cafrec grinned. "Yeah, you prepared us for Mr. Tucap."

Samit's fork clattered onto his plate. "Excuse me? I, too, put on an act."

Vectus bit his lip, worry lines on his forehead. "Was I everyone's least favourite teacher?"

Breel hesitated because telling the truth was the last thing she wanted to do. But Vectus caught on.

"Ah." Vectus pursed his lips. "I see. I'm very sorry I made things so difficult. Aren't most teachers like that, though?"

"They are," Breel assured him.

"But I was...extreme?"

"On the extreme side, yes," said Cafrec. "But we understand."

Breel was desperate to make things right. "Please don't feel bad. You were doing your job. I'm sure lots of students benefitted from your pushing. I did."

Vectus shrugged. He sighed, eyes downcast. "Perhaps. But I feel awful. I should've realized how bad I was when I told another programming teacher that I made yet another student cry, and he said he'd never done that."

Manum scoffed. Even Lexo's brow furrowed but, before he could say anything, Manum said, "You can't base that off one teacher."

"Even when they were my strictest colleague?"

"Nope," said Manum. "I know of plenty of teachers who did the same thing."

Everyone nodded.

Breel's most memorable had been in an advanced algebra class. After a student got the lowest mark on a test for the third time in a row, the teacher called him a myriad of insulting things then said he'd never pass the Demna Exam. It had been heartbreaking, especially since the student got good marks in his other classes. He wasn't in Breel's Career Group, so she never learned what became of him.

"Mine was an act, too," Samit said. "Best way to protect yourself is to act like you love Tatem and be strict with your underlings."

Yeah, but warm and fuzzy will never be your style, even post-Tatem.

Cafrec smirked—undoubtedly thinking the same thing—but didn't comment.

***

The evening news was nothing to speak of—another Tatem speech espousing his new laws and saying citizens must obey to avoid being tomorrow's Vucapi.

Afterward, Samit opened their meeting by asking for updates.

"Trafis and I have one," said Criba.

Samit motioned for them to continue.

Trafis cleared his throat. "We found an email Tatem sent two days ago about the anniversary, asking about preparations for his announcement. He was vague, but it was something about the Nito Test."

Breel looked to Cafrec, whose gaze was already on her with eyes that were anything but sparkling. Without warning, her sweater felt too warm.

It is *about using genetics to choose Career Groups.*

"We wondered if it's changing the type of questions or the exam format," Criba said.

Samit nodded. "Could be."

Or abolishing the Nito Test.

But Breel didn't dare suggest that. If she did, everyone would ask for her reasoning behind such a preposterous idea. That was a mess of spaghetti code she didn't want to get into—it hit too close to home.

She sunk into her chair when Samit asked her to filter emails by the Nito Test for Criba and Trafis to read. They were bound to find something which could mean stumbling upon emails about genetics. That was one step away from learning that Famut and Centia had been the geneticists involved and Breel's true biological origins.

Breel's thoughts drifted back to the meeting when Samit spoke about Clonis. "Breh said transportation is set and they're working on logistics for faking his death. We can expect him within three or four days."

The thought of meeting someone who'd been so close to Tatem caused Breel to quiver. With luck, the information Clonis had would be useful. If not, they'd have to gain the upper hand some other way.

Chapter Fourteen

Before returning to work, Breel went for a walk with Criba and Trafis. The dart gun in a holster at her hip still felt like a foreign object.

I really hope I'll only ever have to use it again in target practice.

Unlike yesterday, there was no wind. The setting sun beamed, undeterred by the wisps of clouds. Breel wiped sweat off her brow.

Three weeks had passed since Criba and Trafis joined Breel and neither had explained why. Breel hesitated to ask—until now.

Swallowing hard, she said, "What made you two come with me on...that day?"

She followed me even though she's not my biological mother.

No, stop thinking about that.

Breel pulled herself away from those thoughts. In the end, it didn't matter that Criba wasn't her biological mother. For Breel, it didn't change their relationship or how she felt about Criba.

Criba threw Breel a confused sideways glance. "I thought it was obvious."

It was?

Breel shrugged as she pushed up her sleeves in the hopes of cooling down.

"I've known Tatem's an evil man since my sister's Mortae," Criba said.

Trafis tripped over his feet. "Since what!?"

It wasn't news to Breel. Trying to scare her into quitting drawing, her parents had told her how Criba's sister was killed when they were Leaders of Tomorrow.

"Sorry for never telling you about her, Trafis," said Criba. "I don't enjoy talking about it. Our parents favoured her, and her death was hard. That day, I realized Tatem's a horrible person for killing children. Then, Breel, when we were at your...your..."

Yeah, my Mortae.

She nodded then motioned for Criba to go on.

Criba swallowed hard. When she spoke, her voice cracked. "When I saw you on the platform, I realized I hadn't protected you enough. I hadn't wanted to stifle your dreams, but I wanted to keep you safe. Both of you. That day, when the DOE started shooting, I only cared about getting to you. Then, when Trafis joined you, my decision was straightforward."

Criba had left everything she knew, including her husband, to be with her children.

Maybe she will *have to give her life for Trafis and me.*

Pushing that unwelcomed thought from her mind, Breel wiped her forehead. "Why was it easy?"

Criba stopped then reached for their hands, pulling them close. Trafis's eyebrows shot up.

"Because," said Criba, "you two mean the world to me. I want to work toward a better future for you."

Breel squeezed her mother's hand before letting go. "Oh."

She was speechless. Criba had always been a rule follower—another citizen doing Tatem's bidding because she feared the consequences of doing anything else. But Criba wasn't weak. She had kept in line to avoid punishment and protect her family until, one day, protecting her family meant being disobedient. For her own children, she'd made one of the biggest sacrifices imaginable.

Criba patted Breel's shoulder. "If you have children one day, you'll understand."

Children...

If they achieved a post-Tatem world, for the first time becoming a mother didn't seem like a bad idea. Breel pictured a little boy and girl with glasses and blue sparkling eyes. Perhaps they'd have Breel's drawing skills or share Cafrec's love of making others laugh.

Stop it, Breel. That's years away.

"What about you, Trafis?" Breel asked.

Trafis shrugged as he kicked a pile of sand.

"There had to be a reason," Breel said. "I mean, you joined me before Mother!"

"Well..." Trafis glanced at Breel, his cheeks red. "In part, I wanted to protect you. Stupid, I know."

They'd always been close, but Breel had never felt such love for him as she did in that moment. He startled when she hugged him.

"That's not stupid," Breel said.

"Not at all," Criba agreed.

Trafis returned the hug. "Like Mother with her sister, when I saw you on the platform, I realized how wrong Father's been. Tatem's not a 'good man.' I don't have ideas about how I want things to be after Tatem, but I know I don't want people fearing death."

Beaming, Breel put her arm around him again. It was a complete turn from his prior opinion.

"That's what Uncle Famut was advocating and fighting for, right?" said Trafis. "A free society without threat of execution?"

Trafis finally gets it.

Breel squeezed his shoulder before letting go. "I'm proud of you."

They had reached the treeline. Like the trees in Lexum, they were birch with gorgeous cream coloured bark and branches reaching for the sun. Breel caught a dark green leaf bigger than her hand as it danced to the ground. The veins running through the leaf were like secondary roads extending from Main Street.

As Trafis took an interest in the leaf, they discussed how they'd paid little attention to nature. Lexum had plenty of birch trees and chrysanthemums but forbade slowing down to examine and admire them. More than once, Breel had witnessed the DOE scolding Leaders of Tomorrow for staring at a blade of grass or playing with flowers. Such unproductive activities didn't contribute to society.

Criba touched the leaf as if it were made of glass. "It's beautiful. We missed so much."

Everyone had. But if they achieved their goal, no one would miss such simple pleasures again. If a single Mortae could change the views of Criba and Trafis, it meant others could be affected, too.

There could be hundreds of citizens turned anti-Tatem after witnessing a loved one's Mortae. They just don't know what to do about it.

Rowhouses loomed in the distance. They looked like the ones closer to Lexum with caved in roofs, smashed windows, and crumbling bricks. Various building materials and leaves littered the ground, piled beside the buildings.

They passed four streets before realizing they'd walked one mile to the treeline plus an extra mile to the rowhouses—the farthest they'd walked yet.

"Should we head back?" Breel asked. It was cooler with the treeline blocking the sun; however, she was thirsty, and they didn't have water.

The sun was setting, so Criba and Trafis agreed. But as they approached the next street a sound stopped them in their tracks—voices!

Chapter Fifteen

Breel froze mid-step. She went from enjoying a pleasant walk with her family to having a racing heart. Every sound from the wind to the leaves blowing on the ground and creaking metal was as loud as the gun Tatem used to shoot Famut. The person talking wasn't in view.

They must be on the next street.

Trafis pointed to the gun in his hand, indicating Criba and Breel should hold theirs, too. Breel's stomach churned at the thought of using her weapon, but she retrieved it from its holster, the metal cold against her hand. Seeing Criba and Trafis holding their guns brought her back to Tatem's house. Her breath caught as once again, the visual of Famut falling to the ground entered her mind.

No, no, no. Don't go there.

Hearing her own raspy breath in the terrifying present situation brought her back. Trafis had already stepped forward, body against the last house in the row as he creeped toward the intersection. He held his gun straight out like a DOE officer.

Criba was steps behind, gun shaking in her hand. Breel found herself beside Criba, her lungs fighting for every breath.

Please be our own people. Please be our own people.

No, that's impossible...no one else went for a walk.

The only explanation was DOE officers on an unscheduled search.

The voices were closer. If it was like most searches, there'd be five of them. Five trained officers versus three non-officers learning how to use weapons.

"Doesn't look like they're here," said a young sounding woman.

Another woman said, "I agree but let's continue down this row then check the remaining ones before calling it a day."

She must be their leader.

Breel and her family exchanged worried glances—the DOE would find them within moments. Trafis aimed his gun then waited for the officers to round the corner. Breel forced herself a couple of steps forward for a clear shot.

Shooting someone is the best course of action right now.

The thought made her shudder. Even though the dart wasn't lethal, she didn't want to shoot someone. But the alternative was them shooting her and her family then Tatem sentencing them to die.

Unless they're the elite force carrying weapons with bullets. Our best bet is for them to be elite officers who'll kill us. Anything's better than the officers bringing us to Tatem.

Breel lowered her weapon before remembering Criba and Trafis right beside her and Cafrec and the others back at the house. If Breel did nothing, everyone could die.

She raised her gun then tried clearing her mind to concentrate on what she had to do but images of the Quaddro's platform forced their way in. Breel blinked, desperate to stop them. Focus was essential to act the moment the officers were visible.

"I can't believe we're still looking for them," said a man.

Just like that, black pants and a sunshine yellow sweater with neon yellow Career Group stripings came into view. Breel's heart leapt into her throat as her pointer finger froze on the trigger.

You must do it! Do it!

While wrestling with herself, something whizzed near her ear then another a second later. Criba and Trafis had fired their guns. Criba's went wide, but Trafis's hit an officer. The woman was on the ground in moments. The remaining four officers froze then retrieved their guns within seconds before looking for the source of the darts. Before they could find it, Trafis and Criba shot two more officers.

"It's them!"

As the remaining two aimed their weapons, Breel, Trafis, and Criba stepped back to shelter beside the rowhouses. Breel's heart sounded like it was 100 decibels as she waited for someone to appear. The moment she saw a body, she pulled the trigger. Her target yelped then dropped to the ground.

The last officer didn't move into view. Before Breel thought of a plan, Trafis peered around the corner then jumped back as a dart whizzed past where he'd been standing. He peeked his head out again then pulled the trigger. A *thump* sounded moments later.

Breel's hand shook. "Oh wow...We got them all."

Criba patted Trafis's arm. "Thanks to your brother."

Trafis grinned as he returned the gun to the holster. His entire body shook but his smile was genuine.

"Helps that they have little opportunity to use their weapons," he said.

Breel wrapped her arms around him. "Don't be modest. They put you in the wrong Career Group! I'm so glad you were with us on this walk, otherwise Mother and I would've been..."

Dead or the next Vucapi.

The question now was what to do with the officers. They only had an hour or two before they regained consciousness. Leaving them wasn't an option as they'd return to Lexum to tell their section head who'd send numerous officers out to search the area. It wouldn't take long for them to find the safe house.

There was but one choice—imprisoning them.

Since Trafis was the best with a weapon and Breel was far better than Criba, they agreed Criba would get others to help escort the officers back, though Breel and Trafis had to do some convincing that leaving them was the best choice. Before Criba left, they collected the officers' guns and ID card scanners.

Breel and Trafis sat, guns in hand, waiting. Having prisoners would be a whole new complexity. Like when they thought Samit might be a spy, they'd need guarding. Sloppiness would get people killed. They'd need more food which meant more supply runs and more opportunities for capture. There was also the risk of the officers overhearing plans then using it against them if they escaped.

Criba returned half an hour later with Manum, Lexo, Vectus, a backpack, and five lengths of rope. She sighed with relief seeing Breel and Trafis safe.

While waiting for the officers to regain consciousness, Vectus and Criba put the officers' guns and scanners in the backpack while Manum and Lexo tied their hands behind their backs.

Not long after Lexo tied the last officer, a middle-aged woman woke. She glared while attempting to pull apart her hands, demanding they release her because she's the search leader. The ropes held despite her muscles. She said nothing but didn't have to—she'd kill them at the first opportunity.

The next DOE officer who woke—a woman no older than Breel—had wide, tearing eyes and shoulder-length black hair flecked with sand. Her chest heaved with each breath. "Please...please don't kill me!"

Manum's smile caused her panicked expression to falter. "We won't stoop to Tatem's level."

Her lower lip trembled. "So...so you won't kill us?"

"We don't plan on it," said Manum.

She dried her eyes with her shoulders as best she could without use of her hands.

Over the next fifteen minutes, the other three officers woke. There was another young woman and a young man both with the same short brown hair and piercing green eyes. They also needed assurance that Breel and the others wouldn't harm them. The last was a middle-aged man who blinked in surprise, sat, then startled upon seeing everyone.

"I can't believe you didn't kill us," he muttered.

They got the officers standing then instructed them to walk single file. Lexo and Trafis followed with Breel and Criba on either side and Vectus leading the way. The search leader shook the sand out of her short blonde hair as she muttered under her breath, saying things like "oh, when I get my hands on you," and "Tatem will make you pay."

Eyeing Breel and the others, the three young officers walked stiffly.

They don't believe Manum about not killing them. But why should they when they're used to Tatem?

Breel kept expecting the officers to run or take their weapons. But except for the search leader's mutters, the walk was uneventful.

Before long, they were back at the house. Cafrec and Praxa had cleaned the furnace room to hold the officers, sweeping the floor and removing as many cobwebs as possible. They hadn't cleaned the room when they first arrived since they hadn't plan on using it.

"You can't keep us locked forever," said the search leader. She glared at Manum as he gripped her upper arm to steer her into the room.

Once all the officers were inside, Manum closed the door then propped a chair against the door handle. Lexo offered to sit outside the room and guard while the others discussed the situation.

The moment they were upstairs, Cafrec wrapped his arms around Breel, burying his nose in her hair. "I was so, so worried. You must've been terrified."

Her body shook against his as she recounted what happened. For a few minutes, they said nothing as he held her. As he did, her pulse slowed, and her limbs stopped shaking.

It took a few minutes for everyone to reconvene in the dining room. Manum said how sorry he was that this had happened. His hands trembled as he explained it had been a last-minute search, so he'd only received the news from Luap minutes before Criba arrived for reinforcements.

"It's not your fault," said Criba. "We always knew this might happen. We're lucky we had Trafis with us."

Trafis grinned as Manum's eyes widened in surprise. "Well done, Trafis," he said. "Sounds like you could've done better on the practical part of the Demna Exam than some Leaders of Tomorrow in the DOE officer Career Group!"

Trafis's grin disappeared. "I don't know why I'm good at it. Don't think I enjoyed shooting them, because I didn't."

"I'm sure that's the case for any normal officer," said Breel.

"Exactly," said Manum. "You did what you had to do and with luck, will never have to do it again."

Samit clapped his hands. "Okay, we need to discuss what to do with them. Obviously, we can't let the officers go. When you were all gone, I suggested Lexo and Praxa switch desks with Breel and Cafrec so that Lexo and Praxa work outside the furnace room and Breel and Cafrec in the storage room."

Breel agreed it made sense. With Lexo and Praxa working at the bottom of the stairs beside the furnace room door, they could work and guard at the same time. They'd only need a dedicated guard for meals, meetings, and nighttime. Breel and Cafrec were happy about moving to the storage room as it provided more privacy.

"But," said Samit, "as we discussed, unless the furnace is running, which is uncommon this time of year, they're going to hear every word that you say."

Trafis frowned. "Does that matter if we're keeping them here?"

"Of course," said Breel. "What if they escape? Not only would they know where we are, but they'd know our plans and other information. I agree, we need to do something so they can't hear us."

Vectus had already contacted someone from the Department of Households who agreed to add sound machines to the next supply run. Placing them outside the furnace room would create enough white noise to mask their conversations.

Manum frowned. "That's a decent temporary solution. But will we detain them for weeks or months? We'll need a lot more food and guarding will get tiresome. It'll also mean less work gets done since night guards will need to sleep during the day."

Samit sighed. "Then why don't you suggest an idea?"

Nobody had one.

"What about bringing people to guard?" Trafis asked.

Samit shook his head. "No way should we risk that."

"While I agree," said Manum, "no one's mentioned the biggest immediate risk is that these officers aren't returning to Lexum. I'll let our people in the DOE know the situation, but it's only a matter of hours before they send a search party. When they do, they'll look in the area these officers were scheduled to search."

The hair on Breel's arms stood on end.

Oh no, he's right! If our inside people can't manipulate the information, we'll be done for.

Everyone stayed up late to wait for a response to Manum's email but after an hour of nothing, they went to bed. Lexo offered to guard the officers throughout the night and keep tabs on Manum's email to alert the group if a search party was imminent.

Knowing that five DOE officers were in the house made sleep difficult. Breel's mind spun as she thought about the day's events—especially freezing at a critical moment. If she crossed paths with the DOE again, she vowed to act as quickly as Trafis. The life of everyone in the house depended upon it.

Chapter Sixteen

Breel opened her eyes. Not only was she alive, but she was in one piece which could only mean one thing—their people in the DOE had performed a miracle.

Manum wasn't at breakfast, having relieved Lexo of guard duty.

Breel grimaced at the bitter taste of her coffee. Across the table, Lexo chugged his. "Whoa, that doesn't hurt?" she asked.

Lexo laughed. "It's water. Don't want to have trouble sleeping."

After breakfast and before going to bed, Lexo gave his update. The night had been uneventful except for the search leader yelling threats and profanities through the door which stopped after an hour of Lexo ignoring her. A DOE contact had responded to Manum's email, saying it was, of course, impossible to hide the fact that five officers were missing. However, in the night, a small group of officers had planted evidence in the far corner of the rowhouses and warehouses closest to Lexum. They chose this area as it was four miles from where they'd found the officers and a place in which the officers had likely walked through. They shot a few darts into some buildings and left a shredded DOE uniform and scanner. Luap led the search party and was due back anytime from their investigation.

Not perfect, but good enough for the DOE to concentrate their search a few miles away.

It was supply retrieval day which meant getting more food and the sound machines. Two days earlier, they had sent a supply list to their Department of Households contact who'd ensure delivery to a tunnel connecting Intercludae to the backyard of a source. They had managed to add both the sound machines and some food last minute. Before finalizing the pick-up, Manum had checked for scheduled DOE searches—*it better be accurate this time!*—and ensured their DOE contacts would be on the north wall so Tatem's people wouldn't see them in the desert.

They also scheduled an anti-Tatem driver to deliver their supplies to the source's house during their evening meal delivery. Samit had liaised with programmers so nearby security cameras would show video feed of a prior delivery while the driver brought the supplies into the house. Once the sun had set, the occupants would move them into the tunnel.

Of course, this meant always returning to the safe house in the dark. The alternative was staying overnight in Intercludae; however, not only had it been abandoned for several weeks, but they (and Tatem's people) had stripped it of supplies, and the DOE had searched it several times.

Samit looked around the room. His face was an impressive collection of purples, reds, and blues. "Who's getting supplies this evening?"

Everyone had done it but him as he needed to monitor and hack into the video feeds.

Breel raised her hand. "I'll go."

It was something different from the monotony of coding. While the risk of another search was possible, with the DOE focussed close to Lexum yet far from Intercludae's entrance, coming across officers was unlikely.

Breel nudged Cafrec. Taking the hint, he said he'd come.

"Been a while for me, so I'll go," said Vectus.

They always went in groups of four with Manum, Lexo, or Praxa as the fourth. Lexo and Praxa exchanged glances, expressions, and shrugs—a silent conversation.

Lexo nodded. "I'll go. After a good sleep, I'll be ready by then."

Thank goodness it's Lexo.

Praxa would only ignore Cafrec except to glare out of the corner of her eye whenever he joked.

Lexo and Praxa delivered breakfast to the DOE officers while everyone else started working. The day dragged until suppertime, which was a earlier than usual so Breel and the others could eat before leaving.

They each brought a backpack, flashlight, and dart gun. As they walked to get the supplies, Lexum's walls loomed closer. Ignoring them, Breel fell into step with Cafrec, lagging a few feet behind Vectus and Lexo.

Cafrec's hand found hers. "Nice to get out."

It was a bright day, though not hot enough to break a sweat which was a nice reprieve from the previous day. The moderate amount of cloud cover blocked the blinding sun. The breeze was light enough that it didn't churn up sand.

Cafrec said in a low voice, "I'm glad it's Lexo with us."

"Same."

"I don't get it."

Breel shrugged. "I suspect Praxa's not used to humour after living in Lexum. After all, Tatem doesn't give allow citizens to be funny."

Cafrec lifted an imaginary microphone to his mouth. "Automatic Mortae if I so much as hear a chuckle!"

Breel laughed even though it wasn't laugh out loud humorous.

"Silence!" said Cafrec in a voice that would've echoed inside the house.

Vectus and Lexo glanced back. The former raised an eyebrow then, noticing Cafrec's fist in front of his face, smiled. "Ah, pretending to be Tatem."

Cafrec pointed at Vectus. "Smiling is an automatic Mortae!"

"Well, the population will drop," said Lexo.

"I don't think so." Cafrec grinned as he ran a hand over his hair. "I've already made sure you have nothing to smile about."

"Isn't that the sad truth." Vectus turned back to his conversation with Lexo.

Ahead, the suburbs stretching from horizon to horizon came into focus.

Cafrec dropped his voice. "But Vectus and Lexo appreciated my humour even though they're not used it. Even Samit has laughed. Why not Praxa?"

Not knowing enough about Praxa to guess why she disliked Cafrec's jokes, Breel had no answer.

Unless she's the spy... It'd explain her lack of Tatem bashing participation.

"Hey."

It was Lexo, brow knitted with concern, who had slowed to walk in step with them. "Could you please lay off Praxa?"

Breel's face burned.

I wish the sand could swallow me whole.

"Why does she glare at me all the time, man?" Cafrec asked.

Lexo shook his head. "That's not for me to say."

Cafrec frowned. "She hates humour?"

"Again, not for me to say. Please don't give her a hard time."

"In all fairness, he hasn't," said Breel. "Cafrec's said nothing to her."

Lexo raised a hand. "I know. But please go easy on her."

Praxa's the one making it obvious she doesn't like Cafrec, and Lexo thinks Cafrec's the bad guy?

Here they were trying to overthrow Tatem to start a society in which people had the freedom to pursue the life they wanted to live. Yet Lexo was telling them to go easy on Praxa (*whatever that means*) because she didn't like Cafrec's jokes.

What a hypocrite!

It was tempting to ask Lexo to explain, but continuing the awkward conversation was unappealing, especially with several hours of walking ahead of them.

Cafrec nodded. "Okay. You're a good friend to her."

"And she is to me. We've been close for years."

It was in that moment Breel realized she knew nothing about Lexo and Praxa's relationship and how they came to be against Tatem. Curious, she asked, "You know each other from school?"

"Yeah, we do."

"What made you turn anti-Tatem?" Breel asked.

Assuming he's more willing to share about himself than about Praxa.

Lexo had no issue explaining. "My parents and I always had a decent relationship. We saw my grandparents a lot who, like my parents, worked in the Department of Sanitation. My father and his father are plumbers. While my father fixed residential plumbing issues, my grandfather worked in government buildings including the retirement home. When he and my grandmother turned sixty and, you know, Tatem forced them to retire, man, he got angry."

The group walked around a bush covered in so much sand that only a couple of skinny leaves poked out of the top.

"Ah," said Cafrec. "One of the lucky ones who love their job."

"No," said Lexo. "Well, maybe. I dunno. When the Department of Households came to move them, they hadn't packed a single thing. He refused to go to the retirement home, having been inside it countless times before. The driver called the DOE and...well..."

Mortae. What a way to reward good working citizens.

"That's awful," said Breel. "I'm sorry."

Such stories were a constant reminder of why their efforts in ridding Lexum of Tatem was the right thing to do.

Lexo shrugged. "I don't remember them well, but it was difficult, especially for my father. However, even though he'd been close to them, he said they deserved it and Tatem knew what he was doing." He grimaced.

Hearing stories about Hargamites thinking that death is the only punishment for breaking the law was enough to make any anti-Tatem's stomach churn.

They slogged through a deep area of sand. Afterward, they took a minute to dump sand out of their standard-issue shoes which had turned from black to gray with sand-caked soles. No matter how often they tried to clean their shoes, even tying them resulted in gritty hands.

Lexo wiped his hands on his pants. "That day I realized I hated Tatem. Unable to talk to my parents, I talked to Manum. Somehow, I knew he was safe."

As they continued, Lexo described how Manum had been there for him, talking to him about his parents and grandparents while Lexo pretended to need extra help with weightlifting. Throughout his childhood, whenever he needed a listening ear, Manum was there. However, his relationship with his parents was never the same again.

"You're lucky you had him," Breel said.

Lexo nodded. "Sounds like his son is similar. You both know him, right?"

They explained they did, but not well. Breel started to say he'd been a favourite teacher who treated his students with respect but stopped herself since Vectus was walking feet away ahead of them. Instead of describing Mr. Gaimster, she told Lexo how she understood his loyalty to Manum.

"Thanks," said Lexo. "I appreciate that."

He jogged ahead to walk with Vectus, churning up sand. Breel's thoughts drifted back to Lexo telling Cafrec off for commenting on Praxa's lack of humour.

If Praxa's a hypocrite for telling Cafrec not to be himself when we're trying to fight for such freedom, maybe she's the spy...

But Praxa was so meek, it was hard enough picturing her as a DOE officer let alone a double agent. Not finding Cafrec funny didn't seem to be a legitimate reason to suspect anything. The best thing to do was monitor her.

***

It took less than half an hour to walk to the warehouse from which they could enter Intercludae. By that time, the sun was on the horizon, casting an orange hue over the remnants of the suburban buildings.

Tatem had filled the warehouse with confiscated items after the civil war. Items from computers, clothing, art, musical instruments, stoves, and lawnmowers filled the ginormous building. Breel suppressed her grin while recalling first seeing the warehouse one month ago. Before then, she'd never seen stacks and stacks of artwork. It told of a time when people appreciated and valued art—a time in which Breel wanted to live.

They wound their way through the items to a yellowed refrigerator against a wall. Breel opened the door to reveal a trapdoor where its bottom had been. On it was a keypad and a brass handle. She punched in the word *Intercludae* then, a moment later, a whirring sounded as the trapdoor unlocked.

Opening it revealed a thirty-foot ladder followed by a dark passageway. One by one, they descended, entering a culvert with a fifteen-minute walk to Intercludae. When Breel and Cafrec had first ventured through the tunnel, a doorway spanning its width had blocked Intercludae's entrance. After the tunnel attack, the DOE had left it opened to aid in quicker searches, not realizing that it made supply retrieval easier for Breel's group.

Lexo led the way, gun out, along the tunnel. When they arrived at Intercludae, he investigated for signs of the DOE while the others waited near the entrance. It wasn't until Lexo motioned for them to follow that some tension released from Breel's shoulders.

They walked into the spacious musty main room which had been the ex-DOE training area. The DOE had removed all weapons and clothing, leaving the room even more empty than before.

They didn't linger which was just as well as Breel shuddered at the thought of staying in that room for too long. Instead, they turned into a claustrophobic side room which had housed computers and surveillance equipment. Now, plastic shards from sledgehammered monitors littered the ground. The DOE had taken the computers.

Off the room was an entrance to another tunnel six and a half feet in diameter. It ended five miles away underneath their contact's backyard. Tatem's people had cleaned the tunnel after the attack, so according to Manum it looked better than it had in years. Lightbulbs in the ceiling every few feet lit the way, reflecting off the culvert's corrugated metal sides. The clanking of four pairs of feet on metal was the only noise. For the first few miles, it was wide enough to walk two-by-two, so Breel and Cafrec followed Lexo and Vectus.

"I was thinking last night about how nice this has all been," said Cafrec.

"Oh?"

Does he mean being outside Lexum? Or being with me?

"Well," said Cafrec, "for one, I can be myself! And you, too, right?"

Her heart sank.

He means being out of Tatem's control, not me.

But Cafrec was right. He could crack jokes and make fun of Tatem all he wanted. If she had the time, Breel could draw. Even having the option to draw improved things.

She searched for his hand in the dim, yellow glow. "For sure. It's weird not living in fear of that."

Other fears had replaced the worry of revealing her true self to the wrong people. The DOE finding them. Not achieving their mission. Her father being pro-Tatem. Never having the chance to draw again. The always present fear of death.

Cafrec rubbed his thumb on her hand. "Having you throughout all this has made things so much easier, especially back in Lexum. Not to mention when Famut told us about our"—he lowered his voice—"genetics."

Breel glanced at Vectus and Lexo. Vectus's mouth moved but the clanking feet drowned out his voice.

Good, that means they can't hear us either.

Having Cafrec to go through everything with made it easier. However, part of her wished he struggled with it as much as she did. Since he wasn't close to his family, it was hard to say whether he understood how much Breel anguished over what Famut and Centia had done to their genetics.

Nonetheless, she was glad to have him with her and told him so. "I can talk to you about things I can't talk about with my mother or Trafis."

"You can?"

Light illuminated his smiling face.

"Well, yeah," said Breel. "You're easy to talk to. And I wanna share those things with you."

Except for Famut, Cafrec was the first person with whom Breel could be transparent. No doubt it was because, other than Famut, he'd been the first person who shared her views on Tatem. However, even now that her mother and Trafis were anti-Tatem, she didn't have those discussions with them. There was something comfortable and safe about sharing her private thoughts with Cafrec.

The tunnel narrowed, so they released each other's hands then Breel walked ahead of Cafrec.

"I know what you mean," Cafrec said. "It's been a while since I've had someone to talk to about anything and everything."

It took an hour and a half to reach the end of the tunnel which was a wide circular area with a ladder to a door in the ceiling.

There were no supplies.

Chapter Seventeen

Lexo put a finger to his lips, his gun already out.

No! Not again!

Breel's hand trembled as she removed her gun from its holster. Before her mind could zoom back to when Tatem killed Famut, she forced herself to concentrate on the present moment. The damp, musty smell of the tunnel. Cafrec's heavy breathing. The light reflecting Lexo's blonde hair as he looked up the ladder.

You can do it this time, Breel. Don't freeze.

Lexo climbed the thirty-foot ladder. A rasping noise drowned out Cafrec's breathing. Breel startled, heart in her throat.

Who's that!?

She spun around to look behind them, but nobody was there. The noise got louder. Cafrec and Vectus had stepped closer to Lexo but neither looked around for a noise.

Oh, it's my breathing!

If the situation wasn't so serious, Breel would've laughed.

But it was a critical moment. The supplies weren't there which meant something had gone wrong. It could've been anything.

A neighbour noticing a delivery of more than a small box of food.

Samit's video feeds failing.

The Department of Households moving the house's residents, or the DOE arresting them.

The residents telling the DOE about the delivery.

They had no way of knowing.

Lexo turned his head then put his ear against the door.

Breel's heart hammered against her ribs. At any moment, the DOE could open the trapdoor and, if so, there was no way they'd be as lucky as last time.

She stepped beside Cafrec then reached for his hand as Lexo descended the ladder. He led everyone a few dozen feet into the tunnel.

Everyone leaned in as Lexo said, whispering, "I put my ear to the trapdoor, and I heard nothing. What should we do?"

It wasn't an immediate concern because they always had essential supplies delivered before needing them in case of an issue. With a two days' supply of food for everyone, starvation wouldn't be immediate. But leaving without finding out what had happened made little sense. If the DOE were involved, delaying their inevitable capture was pointless. As it was, it'd be easy for officers to sandwich them in the tunnel. If the DOE had planned that, they'd already trapped Breel and the others.

"We're here now so should investigate," said Breel.

Lexo nodded toward the door in the ceiling. "The DOE could be up there, though."

"If they are, it's already too late."

As she explained her thoughts, she glanced back toward Intercludae. There were no shadows or sounds suggesting anyone was there; however, that didn't mean they weren't waiting to arrest them in Intercludae.

Cafrec patted her back. "Too late? Cheery thought."

Vectus tapped his gun on his arm. "She has a point. The tunnel's more than long enough for them to block our exit without us knowing."

Lexo looked from him to Breel. "You're saying that it doesn't matter what we do because if the DOE are in the backyard above us, they're likely waiting in Intercludae, too?"

Breel nodded. "More or less. Tatem's desperate to find us, so I doubt he'd risk losing us if he had a lead."

Cafrec nodded. "I see your point."

Vectus lowered his gun. "Let's wait an hour to see if our contact opens the trapdoor. If not, I'll peek through it to see what's going on. With luck, there aren't officers, and the cameras won't catch me because it'll be dark."

Lexo shook his head. "No, all cameras are infrared to see in the dark."

Of course, they can.

But then Breel realized something. "The camera shouldn't be a problem."

Lexo shot her a confused look. "Uh, it's a big problem."

"But the supplies aren't in the tunnel yet, right? That means Samit's still feeding the house and backyard cameras the fake videos. He won't flip to the real video feeds until our supplies are in the tunnel."

The dim light obscured Cafrec's grin. "She's right, guys."

"Good call," said Vectus.

"Of course," Breel added, "that's assuming Samit wasn't caught."

Cafrec laughed. "Mr. Lexum's Best Hacker? No way!"

Even Vectus smirked. "If it comes to it, I think we need to assume Samit has control of the camera. Shall we wait a while and if there's nothing, I'll look?"

Everyone agreed. Breel sat, attempting to lean against the wall but gave up as the curved culvert made it uncomfortable.

Moments later, a scrapping noise echoed throughout the tunnel. Breel gasped—the sound was coming from the trapdoor. Lexo was already standing, gun pointed toward it. The others scrambled to their feet as it opened. Breel aimed her weapon, repeating *I won't freeze, I won't freeze* to herself over and over.

"Hello?"

It was a soft whisper from a woman descending the ladder. Both her hands were on the rungs, so at least she wasn't holding a gun. Once she was closer to the ground, the poor lighting revealed her uniform and Career Group stripings.

Black pants.

Sunshine yellow sweater.

Neon yellow stripings around her biceps.

She was a DOE officer.

Chapter Eighteen

As the DOE officer stepped off the ladder, Vectus grabbed her muscular arms, holding her body against his, before she could retrieve her weapon. Breel, Cafrec, and Lexo pointed their guns.

The officer's eyes widened then she chuckled. "Whoa, nice welcome party."

Who is she?

"It's okay," the woman said. "I'm your delivery contact."

Everyone changed glances. Vectus didn't release her. The officer talked in detail about how the deliveries occurred and the prior deliveries she received.

Satisfied, Breel said, "We didn't know you're a DOE officer."

"Oh? Well, I am. Sorry for the delay. I had to wait for a neighbour to go inside." She rolled her eyes.

Breel's heart still thought it was sprinting so took a few moments to slow to its normal rhythm. Vectus released the officer and Lexo lowered his gun. The woman smoothed her uniform then pulled back her auburn shoulder-length hair.

Cafrec wiped sweat from his brow. "Thank goodness. We were worried."

The officer scratched her head. "Yeah, I figured. Sorry. I'll get the supplies, okay?"

Cafrec grinned as she ascended the ladder. "Nothing like some unnecessary excitement in an otherwise dull day."

Vectus clapped a hand on his shoulder. "I could've done without it."

A few minutes later, the supplies were in their backpacks. When they approached the end of the tunnel an hour and a half later, Breel's leg shook as she imagined the DOE waiting for them with their guns out. But no one was there.

***

Everyone attended the next day's post-breakfast meeting including Praxa fresh off her guard duty night shift. Thanks to two locks and two cameras someone had included in the delivery, they could now leave the furnace room unguarded during the day. Lexo and Vectus had followed the included instructions to install the cameras, aiming them at the furnace door. They could view the live feed which Samit kept opened on his laptop for monitoring.

Manum announced his son had emailed him good news.

Samit, his nose and much of his face still a colourful bruise, said, "Lemme guess. He's decided to come, so you want an exception to our rule?"

"No, I wish," Manum said. "The news is we have several new recruits. Three are new Leaders of Today who are eager to help. One said her parents and two sisters are onboard as well."

There was a buzz of excitement as everyone expressed their happiness, and gratefulness, that more people had joined the cause.

Manum continued. "Her father is head of one of the food storage facilities, so will help simplify the logistics of bringing us food. In other news, the head of the Department of Logistics pulled the mother of a past student from her regular job to help plan the anniversary."

Having an insider for such a big event was an enormous help. Planning how to take advantage of it with so little information had proven nearly impossible. Getting details from someone involved meant a better chance of discovering something valuable.

Samit frowned. "But how'd we know they're on our side?"

Manum sighed. "What, now you're not trusting anyone?"

"It seems too convenient."

The Samit vs. Manum show was more than old—especially their lack of trust for each other's people.

Tired of it, Breel stepped in. "What's the point of recruiting others if we don't trust them? My uncle and Centia did this all the time, and I don't think anyone doubted their judgment."

Cafrec patted her leg. "She has a point."

Samit drummed his fingers on his crossed arm. "What's her usual job, Manum?"

Breel flopped back against her chair, relieved the argument had ended.

"Something to do with scheduling," Manum said. "She'll need an email address."

Only Samit protested but outnumbered, he agreed to provide her one.

"This'll be great," Trafis said. "Mother, no more looking through anniversary emails. We'll hear everything from her!"

Cafrec snorted. "I wouldn't count on that."

"Why not?" Trafis asked.

"Because this is Lexum," Breel said. "Everyone's only told what they need to know, so she'll only know one small slice of information."

Samit nodded. "Hopefully, it's a good slice. Trafis and Criba, you'll still need to review anniversary information."

Trafis threw his head back and groaned.

***

Manum visited Breel and Cafrec later that morning. His face was back to normal, having healed much faster than Samit's.

"We need to talk. Go for a walk?"

They agreed, as they'd yet to have a walk that day. A few minutes later, they were outside with their guns in holsters and blinded by the sun high in the sky.

Manum walked with a solemn expression. "Listen, it's pretty clear that Tatem's anniversary announcement will be about replacing the Nito Test with genetic engineering."

A chill hit Breel's body despite the warm breeze. "Yeah, we figured that, too."

"I could tell based on your stunned expressions. I was hoping you'd tell everyone."

He paused as if waiting for them to apologize or explain why they had yet to mention it.

Breel took interest in a stubby bush. Years without wind protection had left it slanted with sand covered leaves.

"My mother can never know," Breel said.

Manum's expression softened. "I understand your hesitation."

"It's not hesitation. I'm not doing it."

Manum frowned. "You can tell everyone without mentioning your own genetics. They don't need to know that part."

"But what if they guess?" Cafrec asked. "Imagine them finding out who I am? They'll think *I'm* the spy. As it is Criba said my eyes look like his."

Manum cocked his head. "I assumed you didn't care much, Cafrec. You make fun of Tatem all the time."

Cafrec dropped his gaze. "Just for jokes. If I make fun of him, I can't be him, you know?"

"Well, okay," said Manum. "But why would they guess that? You only need to tell them about the genetic engineering Tatem ordered Famut and Centia to do and those they did for our own purposes. You don't need to mention yourselves. They'll never guess it."

He had a point. Especially for Breel, nobody would assume she was related to Xorem.

"Mentioning genetics at all hits too close to that topic," she said.

Manum put a hand on her shoulder, causing her to stumble over the loose sand. "I understand, but it's imperative that everyone knows what Tatem's been doing. We can't keep it a secret. If you don't tell them by tomorrow's evening meeting, I will."

Breel stumbled on an even bigger mound of loose gritty particles, getting some in her shoes. "You'd do that?"

"Absolutely. I didn't have students and people I care for die for nothing. I'm here to do everything I can to avenge their needless deaths." He glanced away, blinking back the tears. "Tell them or I will."

Breel's heart raced.

What if they figure it out? My poor, poor mother...

Though Xorem was Breel's biological mother, Breel didn't think of her in that way. She unknowingly donated an egg—that was all. It didn't change that Breel's true mother, the woman who had looked after, loved her, and supported her, was Criba. But there was a risk of Criba thinking otherwise and that wasn't something Breel wanted.

Ahead, a palm-sized green lizard scampered across the sand. Breel had learned about them in geography class. According to Famut, most "facts" about the desert, such as its vicious animals, had been lies to prevent citizens from attempting to escape. Though it was her first time seeing a lizard, she couldn't drudge up any excitement. Her stomach churned at the thought of her mother finding out the truth.

Cafrec put an arm around her, squeezing her. "He's right."

Breel sighed. "I know. I just don't like any of this genetic talk."

Not only was such knowledge uncomfortable, but it was a constant reminder of how Famut had gone behind her parents' backs. Though she forgave him, she had to find that forgiveness within herself every day. Some days, it was easy. Others, it was near impossible.

"I don't like it either," said Cafrec. "But let's get it over with so they don't think we're hiding anything and suspect *we're* spies."

"Smart decision," said Manum. "It'll be fine."

Try as she might, Breel couldn't muster the same confidence.

Chapter Nineteen

Samit called the post-lunch meeting to order. "If all goes to plan," he said, "Clonis will arrive tomorrow evening."

The room erupted in excited conversation. A few days ago, they didn't even know Tatem had a brother and now they were about to meet him.

Breel met Trafis's eye from across the table. Grinning, he said, "This could be the key to us winning against Tatem."

"I wouldn't get your hopes that high," said Samit.

Too late.

Anticipating meeting someone who could provide insight into Tatem was enough to raise anyone's hopes into the stratosphere.

"But..." Samit paused, waiting for Manum and Lexo to finish their conversation. "But I'm sure it'll give us a tremendous advantage. Lexo, I want you and Praxa to meet him at the end of the tunnel at nine in the evening. It'll be dark enough by then."

I sure hope Breh's right and Clonis can make the trip.

Seven miles was a long way for someone of his age who'd spent most of his life locked in a room.

Samit flipped his pen around his thumb. "You won't get here until late, but we can't have you meet him earlier. It needs to be dark when Clonis enters the tunnel in Lexum to prevent neighbours from seeing."

"I understand," said Lexo. "If what Breh said is true, I'm sure it'll be fine."

When Samit called for other updates a few minutes later, Breel's breath hitched.

Just do it. It'll be okay because you don't need to tell them anything about yourself...

Swallowing hard, she said, "Cafrec and I have one."

Cafrec squeezed her leg. She placed her hand on his, grateful for the support.

"Cafrec and I, well..."—*Just say it!*—"We think we know what the anniversary announcement will be."

Samit blinked. "You do?"

"How'd you find out?" asked Trafis. "Isn't that our job?" He motioned to himself and Criba.

Breel ignored him. "When we arrived in Intercludae, Uncle Famut told us about these experiments the government was conducting."

Vectus groaned. "Oh gee, why am I not surprised? What horrid thing did Tatem do this time?"

Breel tried to find the words, but her mouth was dry. She took a sip of her water as Cafrec took over. "They used everyone's DNA to determine which genes increase or decrease the risk of certain traits and skills."

Lexo cocked his head. "Huh?"

Everyone else stared at them as if trying to decipher gibberish code. Remembering that she and Cafrec only knew about genetics because of Famut and, in Cafrec's case, Centia, Breel explained. "Our genes are passed down from our parents. They help determine things like our personality and appearance. A gene is a section of DNA."

"They're unique instructions for our bodies," said Cafrec. "For example, they learned which gene gives someone a creative ability, which makes someone rebellious, and so on. Famut and Centia's jobs were to use genetic engineering to turn those genes off or on as required. So, if someone had the rebellious gene, they'd turn it off so the citizen would be less likely to rebel."

"Genes are a programming language, then," Vectus said.

"Exactly," said Breel.

So far, so good…but it's not over yet.

"It also fixed the Demna Exam issues," said Breel.

Samit cocked his head. "You mean they reduced the failure rate? How?"

Breel fidgeted in her seat.

Take a deep breath…here we go…

"They looked at what sorts of genes each unborn child has," she said, "and based on that, determined which Career Groups are most suitable, then engineered them to be a better match. Maybe they only had three of five genes Tatem wants in a bricklayer, so they turned on the other two to ensure the Nito Test result would be bricklayer. Having the natural skills and aptitude for bricklaying, they'd ace the Demna Exam."

Everyone was silent. It was a lot to take in, especially for a group who knew nothing about genetics.

When Criba spoke, Breel's muscles seized.

Please don't guess it, please don't guess it.

"You're saying they manipulated our personalities and abilities, so we'd act how they want us to act and be skilled in a pre-chosen Career Group?" Criba asked.

The tension in Breel's muscles dissipated. "Yeah."

Criba tsked. "Wow. That's awful."

Trafis frowned. "I don't get it. I remember Uncle Famut telling us about genes, but how'd they do all that?"

"He didn't tell us the how," said Breel. "Only that they did it."

"And here's the biggest part," said Cafrec, leaning in. "They were comparing the genetic and Nito Test results to tweak the genetic engineering process. We think Tatem will announce scrapping the Nito Test, so Career Groups will be genetically determined."

Everyone considered the gravity of the announcement. Criba started at her hands, shaking her head. It didn't look like she was in deep thought about her daughter's parentage.

Maybe, just maybe, I'm safe...

Manum smiled as he caught Breel's eye. She nodded in acknowledgment as he interrupted the silence. "We can't allow genetic engineering to continue post-Tatem."

"Of course not," Samit said. He turned to Breel to Cafrec. "You're saying that Tatem mucked around with every citizen's, what's it called, genes?"

Oh no...

Breel's body tensed as Cafrec said, "Not everyone. It's younger citizens, perhaps around thirty years and younger. Famut didn't say, but he was old enough to have been around when it started."

Criba clapped a hand to her mouth. She looked from Breel to Trafis and back again with wide green eyes. Lowering her hand, she stammered, "So, both of you?"

"And Praxa and I?" Lexo asked.

Breel's heart leapt to her throat as she gripped the edge of her seat.

This is the exact conversation I didn't want! If Mother learns that Uncle Famut engineered my genes for Tatem, will she think about the ways we're different? How I'm the only member of the family with curly hair? Will she suspect I'm not her daughter?

Breel's hand hurt from squeezing Cafrec's, so she released it. If Criba started thinking that way, the best Breel could hope for was that she never once doubted Breel was her biological daughter. It seemed probable. After all, Breel herself had never considered the possibility that she wasn't related to Criba.

That's because you had no reason not to.

But isn't that why your mother won't figure it out? She has no reason to doubt either.

Maybe I have nothing to worry about.

Before Breel could do her best to make Criba and Lexo feel better, Manum spoke. "Yes, Famut would have changed a gene here or there to enhance their abilities for the Career Group in which they already matched."

"Oh..." Criba's brow remained furrowed, but she didn't ask further questions.

Breel relaxed. The danger of Criba discovering the truth had passed—for now.

"Wait, wait, wait..." Samit crossed his arms. "Manum, you knew about this, too?"

Manum squared his shoulders. His chest rose as inhaled. "Famut told me because I was Intercludae's second-in-command. There wasn't a need to mention it until it was important."

"No need to..." Samit shut his eyes as he pursed his lips.

"Breel, Cafrec and I saw no need to burden everyone with this knowledge," said Manum.

A vein pulsed in Samit's forehead.

Breel tensed, ready for yet another argument. Or screaming match. Or assault. She dared not look at Manum. After all, it was her fault they hadn't revealed the genetic engineering sooner.

Samit groaned. "Fine. Perhaps you're right."

Whoa, Samit's agreeing with Manum?

Everyone did a doubletake at this rare occurrence. Samit rested his hands flat on the table then leaned forward. "But let's agree to tell each other if we have important information about Tatem from here on out."

"Of course," said Manum as the others nodded.

Satisfied, Samit turned to Breel. "More keywords for you to pull from emails. Genes, genetics...anything like that. Criba and Trafis can read through them."

As conversation turned to a more exciting and far less disturbing topic—Clonis's arrival—Breel let herself a moment to relax and release the tension in her muscles.

Criba hadn't suspected anything. All that worrying and refusal to mention the Nito Test had been for nothing.

She pulled herself back into the discussion. Everyone agreed to ask Clonis questions to learn more about Tatem, especially whether he had a weakness they could use to their advantage.

Cafrec grinned, his eyes sparkling. "Don't we know his weakness? He's far too into his hair." He mimicked Tatem.

Samit rolled his eyes. "We mean a real weakness."

"You're assuming Clonis wants to talk," said Manum.

Samit frowned. "Breh said he does."

"Oh, Breh said! Did it occur to you Clonis may have lied to escape isolation? To have some semblance of freedom?"

He's right! I didn't even think of that. If he's anything like Tatem, that's something he'd do.

Manum raised a hand before Samit could speak. "I'm just saying you shouldn't set your expectations too high. Once he's here, we're stuck with him. That's great if he's useful. But if he's not, we're guarding him for nothing."

"You're full of cheer, Manum," said Cafrec.

Lexo frowned at Manum. "It sounds like you don't want him here."

It was the first time he seemed against Manum's perspective.

Manum shook his head. "No, he needs to come. I just don't want us assuming he's the answer to everything."

Cafrec saluted him. "Noted, President of Cheer."

Trafis laughed and even Samit smirked.

Manum glared as he squared his shoulders. "The DOE didn't kill my students for us to get sloppy with Clonis."

Cafrec flinched. He opened his mouth then closed it again.

Cafrec doesn't know what to say? That's a first.

Vectus raised a hand. "I understand your point, Manum, and I agree. We'll take precautions, as Samit said."

They discussed what they'd do including constant supervision—"Calling it guarding will give him the wrong idea" said Manum—and not allowing Clonis access to their computers. Since those steps meant that it'd be impossible for Clonis to contact an enemy, they agreed they could talk freely around him.

Regardless of what Clonis would bring, like it or not, things were going to change.

Chapter Twenty

At half-past eleven, everyone except for Samit—at his desk—sat in the living room waiting for Lexo, Praxa, and Clonis. They expected the threesome between twelve and one in the morning, but it all depended upon Clonis's endurance.

Criba and Trafis drummed their fingers on their legs. Breel and Cafrec sat side-by-side in silence. Manum and Vectus stood in the corner, talking in low voices. Every few minutes, Manum peeked out the living room window's blinds.

One minute, they were discussing what Clonis could teach them about Tatem. The next, Breel woke at the sound of the front door opening. She removed her head from Cafrec's shoulder. Samit emerged from his desk. Trafis, slouched in a chair, blinked sleep from his eyes. The others looked around bleary-eyed.

Guess I'm not the only one who fell asleep.

Breel's watch said it was a quarter to one.

Lexo stepped through the doorway, followed by Praxa then Clonis. He wore a gray sweater without stripes on the biceps—*What department and Career Group are those for?*—and had waist-long, wavy, and scraggly salt-and-pepper hair. His unkempt beard was dark brown.

Like Tatem, Clonis was around six feet tall, putting him a good half a foot taller than Lexo and Praxa. He looked to be at least ten to fifteen years older than Tatem, putting him in his early to mid-eighties.

Praxa placed one hand on Clonis's shoulder while fixing her wind-blown hair with her other hand. "Everyone, meet Clonis."

Lexo motioned for Clonis to step into the living room, but he stayed in the doorway, taking everyone in. He stared at Cafrec the longest. Breel tensed, but a moment later, his eyes travelled to Trafis.

"Come in," said Vectus with a smile.

Clonis stared, unmoving.

"Uh...does he talk?" asked Samit.

"Does he talk," said Clonis. His gruff voice was surprising given Tatem's smooth tone. "He's got a name, you know, and he's standing right here."

"Oh," said Samit. "Of course. Welcome, Clonis."

Clonis's eyebrows shot up. "What happened to your face?"

Samit glared at Manum. "I was punched."

Clonis leaned forward, studying him. "Geesh, been decades since I saw a punched face. It was a nurse, see. Apparently, another resident thought she deserved it, but the nurse never could figure out why. One minute she was dealing with the man's IV pole then wham"—He punched Lexo in the shoulder—"he punched her."

Lexo grimaced as he rubbed his shoulder.

"Sorry," said Clonis. "It's also been decades since I was around so many people. Last time must've been at a party Hargam held in the estate, see. Invited all these fancy people. Wanted to get on their good side. Of course, he had them all killed, see. Been a long time. Decades, like I said."

Trafis's jaw fell. "Decades?"

"Decades, young man."

"Sorry to overwhelm you," said Criba.

Clonis scoffed. "Eh, I just wanna sleep. You'd be tired, too, after that long walk at my age."

Trafis's face fell. Breel shared his sentiment as she, too, had hoped to hear at least some tales from Clonis which involved Tatem. But that'd have to wait until the morning. Getting the hint, everyone said good night, leaving Lexo and Praxa with Clonis. As per the agreed upon sleeping arrangements, Clonis would bunk with Lexo and Manum in the bedroom beside the living room.

"I've never seen clothing like that," said Trafis as they headed to their bedrooms. "No stripes? I mean, we don't have stripes, but he wore that in Lexum."

"Must be what the retirement home residents wear," said Breel.

I guess once you retire, you no longer need stripes because no one cares what your Career Group had been.

She shuddered at the thought of wearing a plain gray sweater. At least the awful stripes provided a splash of colour.

I bet he'll look forward to our sweater selection.

Sleep couldn't come fast enough. In the morning, they'd learn more about Tatem.

***

When Breel woke, Praxa was still asleep. Samit complained when neither she, Lexo, or Clonis came to breakfast.

"Give them a break," Vectus. "They all walked a long way late at night and Clonis isn't young."

Despite Samit's protests, they agreed to take the morning off then, once everyone was awake, talk to Clonis as a group. Samit, as usual, continued working. Manum slept after a night of guard duty but had asked them to wake him for the chat with Clonis.

Breel and Cafrec spent some time alone in the living room, sitting on the couch and discussing the future.

"You can draw, and I can make people laugh," Cafrec said.

Breel hoped for nothing else. But so far, despite no longer living in Lexum, her dream didn't seem any closer. However, that was the case for the entire anti-Tatem resistance. Pursuing their dreams would have to wait until Tatem was gone but staying positive about the post-Tatem future was becoming more and more difficult.

"You look sad," said Cafrec. "What's wrong?"

Breel swallowed hard as Cafrec entwined his fingers with hers. "I'm finding it hard to be so optimistic. There've been so many attempts to overthrow Tatem that I wonder if it'll ever happen? Will any of us ever be free to do what we want with our lives?"

Cafrec frowned then kissed her. "Well, if that's not what'll happen then what's the point of doing all this? You'll be an illustrator, Breel."

"As a Career Group though?"

"I'm sure you can! If not, you can always draw for a hobby because they won't be illegal." He tucked a curl behind her ear then wrapped his arms around her. "You'll get to draw, don't worry."

Cafrec, ever a ray of positivity, was right. If people couldn't have the freedom to do what they wanted, continuing Famut and Centia's work was pointless. In the future, she could draw whenever and wherever she desired. She may have to take some courses to be in the Illustrator Career Group, but she was willing. Her and the others working toward freedom to achieve their dreams would encourage others to do the same.

Chapter Twenty-One

Two hours after breakfast, Praxa sauntered into the living room where Breel, Cafrec, and Criba sat.

"I'll get you a plate," Criba offered.

Praxa sat then adjusted her pyjamas. Everyone joined her as she ate her eggs, toast, and sausage. Even Samit turned away from his work.

Praxa yawned then frowned, noticing everyone staring at her. "What is it?"

"What's he like?" asked Breel.

Praxa glanced at Lexo's empty seat beside her. "I like Clonis. Says whatever's on his mind." Her voice sounded strained as if from lack of use. "Talks a lot though, turning everything into a story."

Yeah, that was obvious last night.

Praxa chewed then swallowed some sausage. "Nurses took him outside several times per week, but he hadn't been in the desert since he was a teenager, so it excited him. He walked fine, though a little slow. He said he can't wait to look around where he grew up. We told him that may not be possible."

Wow, Praxa can string more than a few sentences together.

"Did he understand why?" Criba asked.

Praxa shrugged. "Not sure. He hates Tatem and will help us though."

Cafrec clapped. "Excellent!" He laughed when Lexo and Manum entered the room. "That applause wasn't for you, by the way."

Lexo gasped. "Don't see why not." He chuckled.

Criba got them food as they took their usual places beside Praxa.

"Glad he had no problems getting here," said Samit.

"You talking about me?"

Breel jumped at the gruff voice. Clonis was standing between the kitchen and dining room with one hand on the wall as he surveyed the table. He wore a navy-blue sweater. His hair was unbrushed.

Criba stood. "Would you like some breakfast?"

He inched closer to the table. "Whatcha got?"

"Eggs, toast, and sausage."

"All right."

Criba retrieved a container from the fridge. "How much would you like?"

"How much you got?"

"Whatever you want."

His eyes widened. "Are you serious? No one's ever asked how much I wanna eat before."

Breel laughed to herself as she, and everyone else, could relate. The Department of Food only sent a certain amount for each meal, so the only times anyone could eat more were at departmental dinners. Breel had attended one, and it had more food and variety than she'd ever seen in her life.

"How about two of each and two spoonfuls of scrambled eggs?" Criba asked. Clonis grunted in agreement. "Take a seat."

He sat in the empty seat beside Vectus, adjacent to Manum.

"You people could learn a thing or two," he said.

That's a strange way to make friends.

"What'd you mean, Clonis?" Lexo asked.

Clonis raised an eyebrow as if it should be obvious. "Cleaning. Dust and sand everywhere! Dried toothpaste all over the sink. Hair in the shower." He shuddered. "My childhood home was cleaner! My parents were sticklers for cleanliness because it's so hard to keep clean in the desert, see. Sand got on everything! But every single person had a job to do each day which made it manageable. Mine was to shake out the beds every evening, so they'd be as sand-free as possible for bedtime."

He detailed the other jobs which included sweeping, washing the floors, and cleaning the toilet, shoes and countertops.

Nobody had considered cleaning except for doing the best they could when they first arrived. Sure, they'd noticed it getting dirtier. But wiping the dust and sand off the floors was the first time anyone had ever cleaned, so they didn't know how to remove toothpaste from the sink or food stains from the counter. After moving in, the only cleaning they did was washing the dishes.

"I guess it didn't occur to us," said Breel.

Clonis tsked. "Hargam's fault, I guess. I'm also used to housekeepers, see. But unlike you, I grew up not having one, so I know how to take care of myself. I'll teach you the ways."

They thanked him. When Clonis asked where their supplies were, his jaw dropped as Samit said they had some cloths and soap. Vectus offered to ask for cleaning supplies in their next supply delivery.

Criba passed Clonis his plate. One moment, he had a pile of eggs and two sausages and slices of toast. The next moment, he scooped the remaining scrambled eggs onto his last bit of toast.

"Would you like more?" Criba asked.

"No." He handed her the plate. "The toast's a little dry."

Cafrec laughed. "I've never seen wet toast!"

Clonis stroked his beard. "Hmm, no. I suppose not."

If too-dry toast is his only complaint, that's good.

Criba returned to a quiet table as everyone waited for Clonis to speak. He looked from person to person before saying, "I take it you want me to talk."

"Tell us about yourself," Breel said.

"Ha. You think there's stuff to say?"

"Start with your childhood," said Samit.

Clonis laughed. "Start? Start and end, you mean. There isn't much to talk about after childhood." He leaned back, stroking his beard. "Not sure how much you know, but we were poor, see. Lived out here in the slums. Parents worked in the factories, making little money. Only parents who worked as shift leaders or factory supervisors could afford to pay someone to look after their kids, so we were on our own most of the time, see."

"How many siblings do you have?" Criba asked.

"Eight. Hargam is the third. I'm a year older."

Breel did a double take. Clonis's weathered face made him look far more than one year older.

"No one cared whether we went to school, so we didn't go often. We ran around playing and stuff, see. Hargam was...different. Always doing something which drew in other kids. They thought he was the best until they knew him better. Our younger siblings hung around him because if they allowed him to treat them like servants, he was less likely to harass and abuse them. He saw himself like their parent, see. Sometimes he'd punish them by holding their heads underwater."

So, he was a monster then, too. Surprise, surprise...

Clonis drank coffee from a brown mug then grimaced. "Our parents never believed me because they thought Hargam was perfect. I wasn't perfect, see. They blamed me for most of his wrongdoings. One day, something happened. I didn't find out until years later, but Hargam talked someone into bringing him through the tunnels to look inside Lexum. The government didn't allow us lower class in the city, see."

Manum rested his arms on the table. "What's the purpose of the tunnels?"

Clonis shrugged. "As I recall, to smuggle supplies to and from Lexum. Anyway, Hargam changed after seeing Lexum, see. Stopped playing and started going to school. After a couple of years, he was second in his class."

So Tatem had wasted his life until he saw what he was missing.

Samit cocked his head. "But he told everyone he was first which is how he became a government official."

Clonis wagged a finger. "No interrupting. The girl in first disappeared, see. No one knew what happened, and no one found her. Very suspect."

Ah, there it is. I bet I know where this is going...

"Your brother?" Cafrec asked.

Clonis grimaced at another sip of coffee. "No evidence but yep, I believe that. Hargam became top of the class. Getting the university scholarship gave him the only lower-class government official seat. Didn't talk to him much during that time though as Hargam wanted to be one of them and the government forbade us from visiting, not that I wanted to. But he came back home sometimes to brag, see. Even started talking differently. All Lexum sounding. He changed his looks with fancy hair and suits. Hargam told us what we were missing, making us see we weren't getting everything we should. One day, he suggested attacking the upper class."

Whoa. That's bold.

Vectus raised a finger before Clonis continued. "You're telling us that the civil war was your brother's idea?"

"Yep. Didn't you learn that in history class?"

Breel shook her head. "No. We learned he 'saved' Lexum from the civil war. Not that he started it. Must've had a lot of influence."

Clonis shrugged. "Ah. Guess telling you that wouldn't make him the hero. And yep, he did have influence. Well, one day, Hargam was the last living government official. Years later, he told me he had visited each one on government business to murder them. Came unannounced so there'd be no record of his visit."

Breel shuddered. The civil war would've been a stressful time for the government officials. No doubt they'd have welcomed Tatem, open to discussing ways to stop the attacks.

Clonis examined his nails. "Hargam brought lots of changes. I thought he was different because for once it seemed he was putting the entire lower class first—not just himself. He was doing things for us, see."

"You mean you started respecting him?" Criba asked.

"Yeah, kinda."

The thought was frightening. However, if Clonis thought Tatem was doing a good job, many others would've thought the same. Somehow, he conned everyone into thinking the best thing to do was for him to remain as president.

Manum tsked as others shook their heads at the thought of Clonis respecting Tatem.

"But...but why?" Trafis asked.

"Because it didn't seem selfish, see. Everyone had a job that made sense for them. No education? Here, have it for free. We no longer lived in terrible conditions. Everyone had suitable homes, suitable jobs, and enough to eat. Money didn't matter. In time, he abolished money."

No wonder people worshipped Tatem. He set things up to save the lower class, so they'd hail him as their hero.

Clonis stroked his beard. "But, as you know, the upper class rebelled. During the rebellion, I saved Hargam's life when a man tried to stab him, getting me in the shoulder instead. I lost blood, but Hargam got me to the hospital in time." He pulled down his sweater's neck to reveal a two-inch-long white scar.

"Now," he continued, "because of these changes, us older siblings were happy to be his advisors. At least until he started doing things we didn't like. We, and Xorem, begged him not to execute people. But he wanted to, see. Worst, he seemed to like it. One day, we begged him to stop, so he killed our siblings in their sleep—even the younger ones who weren't part of it."

Breel gasped.

Who kills their own siblings?!

Wait, this is Tatem...why am I surprised?

He had to remove his siblings because having them around telling stories of the horrible things he did growing up would reflect badly on him.

"He killed them because they didn't agree with Mortae?" Trafis asked.

"Yes, and for disagreeing too many times to other things, too, because our jobs were more to agree with him than to advise, see. Guess we disagreed too many times."

"Why didn't he kill you, too?" Cafrec asked.

"Because I saved his life. He put me in jail then isolation in the retirement home. He visited me though, see. Made nurses visit me, too. Had time outside each day. It was something, I guess."

"You've been there all that time?" Criba asked.

"Yeah."

Criba clasped a hand to her mouth, eyes wide. "You poor thing."

Clonis shrugged then downed the rest of his drink. He grimaced. "Ugh, your coffee tastes horrible." He placed the mug on the table. "Yeah, but I had visitors, like I said. Got to know Xorem, too."

A jolt of electricity shot through Breel. For the first time, she was talking with somebody who could tell her about Xorem's personality and relationship with Tatem. But nobody could know about her excitement, so she hid it deep inside.

Concentrating on keeping her voice stable and tone even, Breel asked, "What's she like?"

"Yeah, what's her story?" Samit asked.

Breel could've melted with relief that someone else was curious about Xorem, too.

"Grew up super wealthy. Hargam wanted her parents' house because it's on an estate and the biggest in Lexum, see. I think she let him stay then married him because she felt bad for the lower class and thought he's a good person for helping. But she ignores the bad things Hargam does, see. Don't think she believes some of it because she never leaves the estate to learn the truth. I told her what he did in childhood, and she called me a liar."

Tragpraev had also said Xorem lived too isolated to know much.

Just how Tatem likes it, I'm sure.

"What about Mortae?" Breel asked. "If she disagrees with it, why's she with him?"

Clonis shrugged. "Either Hargam got her believing it's a good thing, or she stopped caring. She doesn't mention it anymore."

Not satisfied with his answers, Breel asked, "But what's she like? Her personality, I mean." Realizing it was a strange question, she rephrased. "Who marries someone like your brother?"

"She doesn't enjoy seeing people suffer, see. She liked him helping us."

Samit raised an eyebrow. "You're saying she sees him as a saviour despite his actions?"

"Yep. The whole lower class did, too."

Breel wanted to gag.

My biological mother still thinks Tatem's a hero? Disgusting.

Clonis leaned forward. "How're we gonna overthrow him?"

Silence. Everyone exchanged glances. Criba's cheeks reddened.

Samit cleared his throat. "Uh...we're working on that."

"But there's a fiftieth anniversary party of his presidency in two weeks," Vectus said. "We plan on making our move then."

Clonis stared at the group, waiting. But nobody said a word. Clonis tutted. "Hmm...thought you'd be more prepared."

His words stung, but Clonis wouldn't understand everything involved, especially coordinating with their people in Lexum.

Clonis leaned forward on his arms. "Is my job to kill him?"

"No," said Manum. "If there's any killing, I get that honour. I'm killing your brother."

That's a bold statement to make.

No one said a word as they held their breath, waiting for Clonis's reaction. They'd never said killing Tatem was the goal. However, keeping him alive would be foolish, especially when his followers would be desperate to free him. As much as they didn't want more death, Tatem needed to be Lexum's last execution.

But Clonis's brow didn't furrow in anger. Instead, he shrugged. "Okay."

"You don't care that someone wants to kill your brother?" Trafis asked.

Clonis chuckled. "You have a sibling?"

"Yeah." He pointed to Breel.

He glanced at Breel. "Ah, her."

"Her?" What's that mean?

Clonis leaned back. "I take it she's not like Hargam. If she did things like strangle you or lied about you to your parents, you'd understand." He yawned. "So, if I'm not killing him, what'd you want me for?"

"We were told you exist," Samit said, "and that you can tell us about Tatem. Does he have any weaknesses or faults? Anything useful for us to know?"

"Anything we don't already know," added Breel.

"We already know he's into his hair and is a raving psychopath," Cafrec said.

Clonis laughed. "Oh yes, his hair. Forgot about that." He had a far-away look.

Reminiscing about some childhood experience, I guess.

Given the unclean state of the suburbs, it would've been horrible—especially for someone like Tatem. No wonder Tatem was concerned about his appearance.

"Anything?" asked Samit.

Clonis raised his hands, palms out. "Whoa, whoa. You can't expect me to answer immediately. I need to think, and I'm not the thinker. Hargam was the thinker, see. He was always thinking about how to fix things. I'm sure he knew everything he wanted in life even before starting university."

Samit rolled his eyes. "Visionary and ambitious. Great. Thanks for the new info."

"You're welcome." Clonis had missed the sarcastic tone. "I've enough of people so will leave you to think about that."

They'd have to wait to learn whether he'd share anything useful. However, there were two positives. He didn't like Tatem, and he was open to telling them everything he knew.

Chapter Twenty-Two

Clonis left the room.

So far, they learned Tatem had always been a monster, especially to his siblings and other children.

Not a surprise. I sure am lucky that Trafis is a good brother.

While Breel and Trafis didn't always see eye-to-eye, they got along and had never tormented or harassed each other—unlike Tatem, who'd have been a nightmare sibling making his siblings pay for not doing as he asked. It seemed impossible that kids would've liked him which meant that Tatem had manipulated them.

Samit groaned. "I don't understand why Clonis can't tell us anything. This guy is useless."

Geesh. Clonis hasn't even been here a day and Samit already wants him to recall every single relevant experience with Tatem.

"Give him a break," said Praxa. "It's a miracle he's as normal as he is."

Breel did a double take. Praxa speaking was one thing. Her defending someone, to Samit of all people, was another. Both Manum and Lexo smiled. The former patted her arm.

"I'm sure he'll tell us something," said Breel.

Vectus nodded. "I doubt he's thought about Tatem in that way for a long time."

Samit groaned. "Well, he needs to start. Just like we all need to get to work."

Manum went to bed after a night of guard duty. Breel and Cafrec headed to the storage room, but before Breel could sit, Cafrec put an arm around her, causing her heart to skip a beat. She jumped when he spoke, his hot breath hitting her ear.

"Did you notice last night when Clonis looked at me longer than anyone else?" he whispered.

Breel rubbed his back. "Yeah. But he hasn't mentioned it yet, so I'm sure he'll keep quiet about it."

Cafrec shuddered in her arms. "I hope so."

It was the first time he showed being bothered about being Tatem's biological son. Breel had always suspected that he cared but did his best to hide it. Breel started for her desk, but Cafrec took her hand, stopping her.

"What is it?" she asked.

Cafrec silenced her with a kiss. Her fears about everyone discovering their identities melted away. But once they started working, her mind swirled as the words on her screen ran together.

For the first time, she'd heard something positive about her biological mother—she cared about others. It was something, at least. The question was why Xorem stayed with Tatem. He would've been alluring at first given all the positive changes he made for the lower class. But even once he implemented Mortae, Xorem stuck by his side.

Perhaps she's ignorant, indifferent or easily manipulated? Whatever it is, she's a small woman for letting Tatem control her. That will never be my fate. Ever.

Yet, that wasn't quite true. Tatem had controlled her and everyone else for half a century. But the difference was that Breel and others had rebelled against him. Xorem had never done that.

She glanced at Cafrec to find him staring into the abyss of his laptop screen with an unmoving hand overtop his mouse. It was tempting to discuss it with him, but she sensed he wanted to be alone with his thoughts.

Breel's mind drifted back to Xorem then Tatem. Clonis had said he changed in university, doing everything possible to fit in including talking and dressing differently. Suits replaced raggedy, sandy clothing. He exchanged unruly locks for slicked back hair. Moved into Xorem's house after a life in miniscule rowhouses. Began maintaining composure during the news and Mortae, regardless of what happened.

It was all to create, then sustain, his new image. The last thing Tatem wanted was everyone seeing him as a lower-class citizen. However, he ensured everyone knew he'd been one, so they'd see him as a hero.

Then it hit her.

His image! That's the answer! We need to destroy his image.

It was perfect. They'd show Lexum evidence of Tatem's wrongdoings, poking holes in his image of a benevolent leader. Some neutral citizens would realize the truth then become anti-Tatem. They could even push the views of some Hargamites closer to the neutral zone.

Cafrec was the only person with whom she felt comfortable discussing these ideas, but he had started working. Not wanting to interrupt, Breel filed her thoughts away then turned to her own tasks.

First, she checked that the automatic import and email categorizing were working. Next, she wrote code to view email details before even opening the message.

It was approaching lunchtime, two hours into their work, when Clonis popped in. His beard was gone, and his hair brushed. Despite the long hair and sweater, his resemblance to Tatem was even more pronounced.

Breel and Cafrec turned to face him, motioning to the empty chair, but he stayed standing.

Clonis pointed to the basement's main room on the other side of the wall. "Hear you have some prisoners."

"Yeah," said Breel. "Not causing trouble at least."

Clonis laughed as he leaned against the wall. "I wouldn't count on that lasting. Smart having your own DOE officers watching them."

He walked toward Breel then stared at her laptop behind her. "Hmm...I've never used a computer."

Sitting in the chair they'd offered, facing them, he leaned toward Cafrec, eyes squinting. "You're the one."

Cafrec gasped. "I'm the what now?"

"Spawn."

Breel's insides turned cold while Cafrec froze, his hand gripping his chair's arm. Tatem had called Breel Xorem's "spawn" and Cafrec his "spawn."

"How...how d'you know?" Cafrec's breathing laboured. "Please, please don't tell anyone!"

Clonis frowned. "Who's there to tell?"

"Uh...everyone in this house," said Cafrec.

"Pfft." Clonis waved a hand. "Yeah, yeah. I won't tell."

When he looked to Breel, her insides turned to ice. He studied her with his average, non-sparkling blue eyes—*I wonder who in the family had Tatem's eyes?*—then nodded. "Yep, you're the other one."

Oh no! Now two people know!

Manum had proved himself trustworthy; however, Clonis had to gain such trust.

"How...how d'you know?" Cafrec's voice was high as he repeated the question.

Clonis leaned back as if speaking about something mundane and ordinary. "I knew he and Xorem wanted a baby. Well, she wanted a baby, and he wanted a successor. He didn't want anyone knowing that someone else had used their eggs and sperm."

"He told you that?" Breel asked.

"Hargam told me about lots of stuff. Guess you could say he still kinda used me as an advisor."

He took interest in his right hand.

"What'd you advise?" she asked.

Clonis removed dirt from under one of his nails, flicking it onto the floor. Breel shuddered. "Remember, I said we didn't give advice. I don't recall what I said, anyway. All I know is he wanted a child, and he got one. So—"

"I'm not his child!" shouted Cafrec.

Breel's teeth clenched as anger boiled inside her.

How dare he call Cafrec that!

Clonis's attention had yet to move from his hand. He'd moved to the next fingernail. "I bet he doesn't much like his...you, Cafrec, um...being against him."

Cafrec crossed his arms. "That's his problem."

"Not saying it's not." He stopped examining his hand to glance at Breel. "You look like Xorem, especially the hair, though hers is white now." He returned to his fingers, flicking more bits onto the ground.

Disgusting.

Breel didn't care what Clonis had to say about their appearances and told him so.

He shrugged. "Fine. Just thought you'd wanna know."

"We don't," said Cafrec. "Go away."

Breel tensed.

Don't think that's a smart thing to say to someone who knows so much about us.

Clonis shrugged, rose, then walked upstairs without a word.

Cafrec moaned. "I hope we can trust him. I don't want the others thinking we're spies if they find out."

Breel gasped. The thought hadn't crossed her mind. But it wasn't likely to happen since Criba, Trafis, Manum, and even Samit and Vectus could back them up, but anything was possible. They just had to trust that Clonis wouldn't spill their secret. However, Famut and Centia had used Xorem's eggs and Tatem's sperm on purpose which meant they could've done it to anyone. If this was common knowledge, it'd be a huge black mark on the trust everyone had in Lexum's reproduction process and Tatem himself. Tatem wouldn't have told Clonis this if he couldn't trust him which meant Breel and Cafrec had no reason to distrust Clonis. Cafrec admitted Breel was right.

"Earlier, I thought about what Clonis said in the meeting," she said.

"Which part?" Cafrec asked.

"How Tatem changing himself to be like everyone else shows he cares about his image."

Cafrec ran his fingers through his hair, eyes sparkling. "Duh."

Breel laughed but only because it was what he wanted. "We can take advantage of that."

Cafrec's brow furrowed. "What d'you mean?"

"By destroying his image."

"O...kay."

He stared. Waiting. Breel explained that they'd yet to figure out how to apprehend Tatem during the anniversary celebration. It was their only plan, yet all attempts at capturing Tatem during Mortae failed—including one month ago. Capturing him during the anniversary was no different.

Cafrec leaned forward then brushed back a lock of errant hair. "That's a good point. It'd also be at the Quaddro with Tatem standing on the platform in front of Lexum."

Encouraged, Breel continued. "Who's to say the elite force won't shoot us during the anniversary? Like last time, citizens could attack us on the platform while the DOE shoots darts into the crowd. Uncle Famut believed many citizens are on our side, and I don't disagree. However, many citizens stormed the platform during our Mortae, so he underestimated how many worship Tatem."

Years ago, there'd been a rare evening in which Tatem had been too sick to deliver his daily speech. The next day in school, a teacher cried on and off during a lesson with hands so shaky her writing on the whiteboard had been illegible. Students in one class had been so worried that their teacher postponed a test—a decision unheard of in Lexum.

"We need to do something different," Breel said.

Cafrec grinned. "That's something I love about you, Breel! You're always thinking."

Breel's face burned.

Cafrec patted her leg. "You're onto something because you're right, we keep doing the same things that don't work. What're your thoughts?"

"We nip away at his image, making our voices heard and encouraging others to be vocal, too. Once his status is at its lowest point, when there are fewer Hargamites, we apprehend him."

Cafrec smiled. "Yes! Destroying his image before taking him down is perfect! It's not something he'd expect which means we'll have a better chance of overthrowing him. I'm sure you have ideas?"

"I haven't gotten that far."

Cafrec leapt to his feet then grabbed a pen and sheet of paper from the stack on his desk. "Let's start!"

Breel grinned, her crossed leg swinging back and forth, as they huddled over the paper.

"Everyone sees the news," said Breel. "We can hack into it to air our views."

Cafrec wrote it down. "That's good."

Famut had always encouraged not just drawing but daydreaming about what could be. He often said her drawings may one day help others.

"I could draw!"

The words tumbled out but as soon as she said it, she saw her drawings exposing the truth about Tatem in the Governmental Offices atrium, school hallways, and other key places around town.

They spent much of the evening growing their list of ideas. Some were ridiculous (destroy the entire supply of hair gel) but most (anonymous letters of opposition to Tatem) were serious. They shared so many ideas and laughter that Lexo and Praxa peeked into the room, finding them sitting on the floor, limbs entangled, as they cuddled and brainstormed tactics.

Breel's drawings had only ever been an escape from the realities of life. But, if the group approved, it'd have a wider purpose. Everyone would see her art, encouraging many to rebel.

This plan would make her dreams a reality even before a post-Tatem world.

Chapter Twenty-Three

The post-breakfast meeting couldn't come fast enough for Breel, but she resisted the temptation to blurt out her idea while everyone ate cereal. As usual, Samit's laptop on the table showed the video feed of the furnace room door. There'd yet to be issues with the DOE—not even when Manum, Lexo, or Praxa brought them food. But as each day passed, it was hard not to wonder when they'd attempt something.

Cafrec fidgeted, tapping his heel on the floor. It stopped when he finished his breakfast, held his fork to his mouth, then said, "It is I, your one and only hero, President Tatem!"

"What're you doing?" asked Clonis, from his usual seat beside Vectus.

"Cafrec sees himself as an entertainer," Manum said.

Clonis clapped his hands together. "Ooh! How exciting!" He leaned forward, elbows on the table and hands clasped under his chin, as he awaited Cafrec to continue.

Cafrec cleared his throat. "Citizens, before your morning exercises, you must all state your loyalty to me." He raised a hand. "'I, insert your name, solemnly swear to be loyal to our dear President Tatem in every word and action. If I fail to uphold my devotion, I accept Mortae as my one and only punishment. May my death remind others about the importance of never wavering in loyalty to the best and greatest person to have ever lived.'"

For once, there was little laughter.

Vectus placed his spoon in his empty bowl. "Shocking he didn't implement that years ago."

Yeah, it's the sort of thing Tatem would require everyone to do.

As they finished eating, they discussed whether Tatem would word it as "our most esteemed dear President Tatem" or "our dearest and most benevolent President Tatem." But the moment everyone finished their food, Samit stood.

"Meeting is to order," he said.

He never lets us have our fun.

But then she remembered what she and Cafrec planned to suggest. The temporary forgetfulness showed how much Lexum missed by not having entertainment as an escape. Those brief few minutes bonding over how Tatem would word such an oath had melted away any thoughts of what they had to do.

Samit surveyed the table. "Anniversary ideas?"

Breel raised her hand. "Cafrec and I don't think we should get involved with the anniversary."

Manum forced a laugh while Samit cleared his throat. He rotated his wrist, inviting her to continue.

Breel reminded them of how Uncle Famut and Centia had failed in all their attempts to apprehend Tatem during Mortae and that doing so during his anniversary speech was no different.

Samit shifted his weight as the others murmured their agreement. "What're you proposing?"

"Image is vital to Tatem, right?" Breel asked.

Clonis nodded so hard his head blurred. "Oh yeah, more than anything."

Breel said, "We use that against him. We destroy his image to show citizens the real Tatem. If all goes to plan, more and more citizens will see our view and it'll be easier to capture him."

As discussion broke out in groups of two or three, Breel and Cafrec listened. Vectus suggested targeting Leaders of Tomorrow since they're more likely to change their views. Criba and Samit agreed that Breel's idea was an obvious solution. No one looked at her and Cafrec as if they were deciphering someone else's spaghetti code.

Not worrying about stepping on Samit's toes, Breel rapped on the table twice. "Sounds like you're all on board. We have with some ideas."

She recited their list including ideas such as airing interviews with angry citizens, distributing pamphlets discussing their viewpoint, destroying ammunition supplies, requesting citizens call in sick to work, and asking everyone to do the bare minimum at work.

By the time she finished, only Samit wasn't nodding.

"Creative thinking," he said. "However, no one will do it because it'll mean Mortae."

Breel and Cafrec had discussed that at length. While Samit was right, they could lessen the risk by starting with distributing pamphlets to introduce people to their thinking. They, instead of an inside contact, could air information during the news. Once there were more anti-Tatem citizens, they'd encourage more individual tactics. By that point, it'd be difficult for Tatem to find and murder everyone.

"As well," Breel added, "most citizens don't know how to help so we have to suggest what they can do."

Samit scratched his bald head. "I see your point."

"Any other ideas?" asked Cafrec.

Everyone stared into the abyss, deep in thought.

Good! They're thinking about it.

Cafrec leaned forward then looked down the table. "Clonis, what about things which Tatem made illegal? Anything we could encourage people to do?"

Clonis nodded. "Oh yes. He banned funerals which are ceremonies to say goodbye to the recently deceased. Hargam made them illegal because they celebrate the deceased person and not Hargam, see. Holding a funeral for every Vucapi would work. I remember before he banned them, there was a funeral Tatem didn't want to attend but—"

"Is this necessary?" Samit interrupted.

Clonis blinked in surprise. "Well, no."

"Okay. Funerals aren't a good idea because Tatem would make all attendees the next day's Vucapi."

Criba stepped in. "Manum, do we have enough DOE contacts to block submitted reports from Hargamites?"

Manum shrugged. "I'm not sure, but in theory, yes."

Criba drummed her fingers on her arm then thought aloud. "Well, let's say the pamphlets work. More and more people see the cracks so come to our side. We encourage them to rebel. There's a funeral and a protest or two. But by ensuring reports go to our people, Tatem would be slower to learn of the funerals and protests."

Samit sighed as he ran his hands over his face. His eyes were as droopy as ever. "And when they take a day or two to realize there've been no reports?"

Breel stepped in. "By that time, wouldn't the protests have spread? If more of them are anti-Tatem, there'd be fewer citizens reporting anyway and Tatem will be used to fewer reports."

Samit placed an elbow on the table then rested his head in his hand. "Again, you're assuming people will want to protest."

"And you're assuming they won't," Breel shot back.

Samit pursed his lips, his shoulders squaring.

He doesn't see how starting with posters and news reports can change the minds of enough citizens to make a difference.

"Give people more credit, Samit," said Vectus.

"What d'you mean?" Samit asked.

Vectus sipped his water. "When they realize the injustice, many people will fight back. If there's enough of them, Tatem can't arrest everyone. Not if he wants society to function."

"And the anniversary?" Samit asked.

Breel and Cafrec had discussed that, too. "We let Tatem make his announcement," said Cafrec. "We talk about it in our pamphlets and newscasts, giving the facts about the horrible things Tatem has done with genetic engineering."

"Good idea," said Vectus. "We let him make the announcement then use it against him."

Samit grimaced as Clonis picked his fingernails. "Clonis, do you think this will work? And stop that."

Clonis raised his head. "Stop what?"

Samit pointed to his own fingernails.

"Oh." Clonis laughed then placed his hands on his lap. "My mother always asked me to stop, too. Hmm wait...no, she didn't. She yelled, not asked. Hargam thought it was a disgusting habit and always told her when I did it, see."

"He's right for once," said Samit. "Can you answer the question?"

Clonis waved a hand. "Yeah, yeah. Hargam doesn't like anyone saying bad things about him, see. So yeah, he'll get mad all right. And the more people stop loving him, the madder he'll get."

Cafrec nudged Breel. "You didn't tell everyone the best part."

Oh!

Breel couldn't hide her grin. "I can do the pamphlet and poster drawings."

Criba squealed, clapping her hands to her mouth. "Oh, Breel! What a great idea. Your dream will come true!"

Breel smiled so much her cheeks hurt. "And Mother, you can write the text."

Criba's eyes shone in a way Breel had never seen. It was as if seventeen years of worrying about her family disappeared with the click of a mouse. "Yes, I could!"

Everyone agreed that Breel's idea was worth trying. They'd use global tactics and let citizens know they didn't have to break the law if it made them uncomfortable. But, for those who wanted to do something, they'd have a list of ideas.

When Vectus said he'd contact the Department of Households about adding drawing supplies to their next delivery, Breel resisted leaping out of her chair in excitement. "That'd be amazing! Thank you!"

As the group returned to work, Breel and Cafrec grinned at each other, thrilled that everyone had agreed to the idea. Being used to assassination attempts, Tatem wouldn't expect non-violent assaults, which gave Breel and the others the upper hand.

Chapter Twenty-Four

The morning flew by. Breel and Cafrec worked on their usual tasks but also discussed the new plan, including other ways to tarnish Tatem's image.

When Samit brought everyone to order during the post-lunch meeting, Clonis interrupted. "I gotta go to my old home."

Silence followed. Based on what the suburbs looked like, his old home was falling apart. If the roof had caved in, he wouldn't even be able to go upstairs.

Why would he want to return?

Samit groaned. "I was speaking. Wait your turn. Does anyone have ideas to harm Tatem's image?"

When Clonis spoke, Samit protested but stopped when Clonis answered the question. "During the civil war, we'd find these posters hung places. They'd make fun of Hargam, see. I remember one showed him in tattered clothes walking on people wearing fancy clothing and lying in the streets."

Showing lower-class Tatem walking on the upper class? Clever.

Clonis turned to Breel. "Got me thinking about you drawing posters and pamphlets to tell the truth. Can you also draw pictures making fun of Hargam? Make him look evil, for example."

"Eviler, you mean," said Cafrec.

"How'd I do that?" Breel asked.

Clonis sighed. "I thought you're creative? And he loves his hair, right? Have him running his hand on his head."

He's suggesting that I draw Cafrec's ridiculous ideas!

She hadn't considered it. However, it had merit since appearance was so important to Tatem.

"I see where you're going," Breel said. "But Tatem will remove them."

Clonis already had a solution. "That's why we hang as many as possible then replace them as soon as they're torn down. They made him real mad last time, see. One poster became two and two became four then there were so many he ordered some loyal people to hunt for and destroy posters. Of course, he said nothing about them in public, and I figure he won't want anybody knowing this time either."

Breel's hands tingled at the thought of drawing. Keeping her excitement in check, she asked, "Do I have permission to work on this?"

Vectus raised both his hands. "Whoa, slow down. I believe posters tarnishing his image is a good idea if done in moderation, but what do the others think?"

Even Samit agreed because, like the more text-based posters Breel and Cafrec had suggested, they'd draw attention and, best of all, get the fence sitters thinking then jumping over to the anti-Tatem side.

Samit tapped his pen on the table. "Breel, before you start, we need to determine what you'll draw, which we can discuss once you have those supplies. Other updates?"

There were none, so Samit turned to Clonis.

"I can say what I wanted to say?" Clonis asked.

Samit nodded. "Why d'you need to return to your home?"

"I remembered Hargam kept a diary, see."

Kept a what?

Everyone exchanged confused glances.

"Oh yeah," said Clonis. "You're all too young to know about diaries. It's a book in which people wrote about their day and their thoughts and feelings."

Whoa.

The diary would be perfect for learning about who Tatem had been, where he wanted to go, and how he planned to get there. Knowing his thoughts and feelings, not to mention how his mind worked, could make a huge difference to their cause.

But the concept of sharing one's thoughts and feelings, even to a book, was strange. After all, Tatem forced citizens to live in such a way that the average person didn't have time to experience enough thoughts and feelings strong enough to need to write them.

Except for me...Maybe growing up with a diary would've helped. But no, it's a good thing I didn't have one.

If a housekeeper had found a diary alongside her drawings, Tatem may have made an exception to the law and punished Breel with Mortae regardless of how many warnings she had.

Manum crossed his arms. "What makes you think this diary will still be there?"

"I found it hidden under a loose floorboard, see."

Noticing everyone's confused looks, Clonis said, "Like this house?" He pointed out the wooden floor and how some boards lifted near the edge. "Over time some boards loosened, see, making it easy to hide things under them."

"Wouldn't he have taken it when he left?" Criba asked.

Breel agreed. Leaving it for anyone to read was careless. After all, it likely had incriminating evidence if not of his doings in childhood, but about what he hoped to achieve.

"I'm sure it's there," said Clonis. "He didn't want reminders of our childhood, so I'm sure he didn't take it, see. He may have forgotten about it."

If Tatem had planned as much as Clonis claimed, destroying the diary before moving seemed the obvious solution. But when Breel asked, Clonis insisted that wouldn't have happened in case Tatem needed it later.

Samit asked, "I assume you read it?"

"Of course."

Samit motioned for Clonis to continue. "Then what's it say?"

Clonis shook his head. "Oh, you younglings. That was decades ago when I was around their age, see." He motioned to Breel and Cafrec. "I can't remember what it said, only that he said bad things."

Samit groaned; however, it was just as well. Seeing the diary and reading it themselves was preferable to relying on Clonis's memory.

Samit said, "You want to return to your childhood home, but we stay here because it's far away from Lexum's wall, giving us more time to prepare for DOE searches. However, we've learned our people can't always influence searches which is why we keep close to here when out for a walk." He glared at Breel then Criba and Trafis.

Yeah, we know, we messed up.

Samit continued. "Even if we take all precautions, it's risky going that far. Clonis, you're sure it's there?"

"I already said I was."

Samit asked for opinions. Cafrec agreed it was worth the risk. It wasn't clear whether his eagerness was to appease Clonis or to learn about his biological father. Regardless, Breel understood.

In the end, the group agreed the risk was worth learning about Tatem's innermost thoughts.

Clonis grinned. "Glad you wanna find it. Can't wait to see my home."

Hundreds of tiny townhomes squishing hundreds of people together isn't much of a home to me.

But Breel kept her opinion to herself. She, too, would give anything to see her childhood house again.

"And this diary thing exists, right?" asked Samit. "This isn't some ploy to go there?"

Clonis's jaw dropped. "Wow, calling me a liar?" He pointed a thumb at Samit then whispered to Vectus, "Is this guy always such a jerk?"

Vectus cleared his throat. "Samit has a point. If it's there, you've earned our trust. But if not..."

If not, we can't do anything because we can't return Clonis to Lexum.

Clonis shrugged. "Well, I'm not lying, so you"—he pointed to Samit—"can apologize when we get the diary."

"Fine," said Samit. "Manum, work with the DOE to arrange the best time to go."

"Of course," said Manum. "The good thing about being far from Lexum is that we can go during the day as the DOE on Lexum's walls won't see us."

While that was true, the suburbs were huge with no way to tell each house apart. Finding it would take hours, if not days, so coordinating the ideal time seemed impossible without knowing how long it'd take. But when Breel voiced these concerns, Clonis shook his head, claiming that he'd never forget which house was his. He said it with such conviction not even Samit questioned him.

"Could Breel and I come?" Cafrec asked.

Samit frowned. "I was going to ask Manum and Lexo or Praxa."

"They can, too. But Breel and I saw these houses, so we can help orient."

Breel saw right through Cafrec as they had no reason to go. He was just curious about seeing Tatem's childhood home. Breel tensed at the thought of another DOE encounter; however, she wanted to support him.

"Cafrec and me could be helpful," she said. "Also, I'd like a longer walk."

"I don't see why not, Samit," Manum said.

"But it could be dangerous," Criba said. "What if more DOE..." She trailed off.

Manum waved a hand. "No, don't worry about that. There've been more searches than normal, but they're near where Luap and others planted evidence. I'll work with him to find an optimal time."

But Samit and Criba didn't change their minds. The former was being unreasonable and Criba wanted to keep her daughter safe. However, the others saw no harm in Breel and Cafrec coming, outvoting Samit and Criba.

Clonis returned to his fingernail picking. "I don't see why so many of you need to go. I can get there myself, see."

"Praxa and I will protect you if there are DOE officers," said Manum.

Clonis waved a hand. "Pfft. I don't need protection because you said no officers will be there. Plus, nobody would shoot someone who looks like Hargam."

"Best to be safe," Manum said.

"And these two?" Clonis pointed to Breel and Cafrec.

Putting an arm around Breel, Cafrec grinned then said, "We're ready for adventure!"

I'm glad that living in cramped quarters hadn't affected his spirits.

Breel laughed and smiled. Cafrec made her days brighter and his attitude was the main reason her outlook had yet to turn bleak. Someday, though not as soon as she'd like, this would all be over and together they'd enjoy a world in which every day was bright.

Chapter Twenty-Five

That afternoon, Breel tweaked her email categories, adding new keywords to capture more emails such as "aptitude" to the Nito Test category, "gene" to the genetics category, and "event" to the anniversary category. After testing and making a few minor changes, most emails categorized as expected. Sometimes categories tagged irrelevant messages; however, that was preferable to missing emails, so she kept the sensitivity high.

What Breel wanted to do was draw, but there was little point until they finalized the posters. Plus, she'd yet to receive the drawing supplies. Besides, the more database work she did now, the more drawing time she'd have later. At least going through emails allowed for reading those which caught her eye and that kept things interesting.

The genetic engineering-related emails had been the most alluring given that many mentioned both Famut and Centia.

An email between two geneticists at the fertility clinic said, "Glad we're on the same page. Given that Centia had the opposite opinion, I know we're doing right by Lexum."

The email didn't mention what they were doing.

An email from a Career Group head to a Nito Test developer said, "I looked over your suggested test changes for the Farmer Career Group. Total garbage. We don't care whether someone *wants* to work outside.

We only need to know whether they're capable of physical labour. I'll give you another chance to get this right."

Breel searched for the next email to see whether the developer had achieved expectations or became a Vucapi. Their head's email said, "Much better, but I've made some revisions. I don't expect perfection this early in your career, but I expect you to try harder."

Yikes. I bet Samit was just like this hardnose.

Since Cafrec had worked under Samit for a year, Breel read him the emails then asked how Samit compared.

"Shall we talk about it outside?" Cafrec asked.

Breel agreed. They were out of the house a few minutes later, after checking in with Manum on the DOE situation. They walked out the door, crossing their fingers that Manum had received correct information this time.

The bright sun was setting as the wind blew sand everywhere. Breel held her hair back to keep the wind from whipping it around. Cafrec took her hand then led her to the side of the house. The difference was immediate. Sand no longer clawed at her eyes and her hair stopped attempting to escape her grip.

Cafrec grinned. His eyes sparkled like Tatem's but also, not like Tatem's. Cafrec's were full of life and love whereas Tatem's were the soulless pits of a sadist.

He pulled her closer. "Better?"

Her heart skipped a beat. "Much."

The wind was but a distant memory as they kissed, Cafrec's hands making a bigger mess of her hair than the wind ever could. All her troubles melted away, much like drawing had done for her in Lexum.

At some point, Cafrec pulled away. "Samit could be mean like that, too."

"Samit?" Breel frowned then remembered the emails. "Oh, wait, right."

Cafrec smiled as she fixed the knotted hair on her head. "Samit once said"—he spoke in a deep voice for his best Samit impression—"'If this is your best, Cafrec, why aren't you wearing a salmon-pink sweater with coffee-brown pants?'"

Breel grimaced. Insinuating Cafrec's work was so bad that he belonged in the Department of Sanitation, Lexum's least prestigious department, wasn't only offensive to Cafrec but to those in the department.

Cafrec tucked a lock of hair behind her shoulder. "Another time, he said if he wanted a 'nonsensical mess,' he would've asked a six-year-old to do it."

"Wow. Was it that bad?"

"No, I don't think so. His expectations were too high as he wanted me at the level of the man I replaced, but he'd retired so was super experienced."

While that made sense, Breel wondered if there was another explanation. Vectus had admitted to pushing her and Cafrec on Famut's request, so it was possible that Famut had asked Samit to do the same.

But Cafrec forced a laugh at her suggestion. "Even if Famut asked him, I doubt it would've made a difference. He's just...Samit, you know?"

"He needs to learn how to chill like you."

But the day Samit became easygoing would be the day Tatem stopped getting pleasure out of killing innocent people.

***

Later that day, Clonis walked into Breel and Cafrec's room without knocking, already talking. When Breel raised a finger while typing an email, Clonis sighed.

After finishing her message, she turned around to find him sitting, chair against the wall, with his legs stretched out.

"You ready to talk to me?" he asked.

"I was finishing something."

"Yeah." He groaned. "Can't wait for those cleaning supplies to come tomorrow!"

The last thing Breel wanted to do was clean especially since she'd receive the drawing supplies at the same time.

Clonis frowned. "You made a face, Breel."

"I've never cleaned in my life. Nobody has."

Clonis threw his head back and laughed. "No, people have but they're in the retirement home, see. Even Hargam cleaned."

"Everyone did?" Cafrec asked.

Another laugh. "Of course. Parents worked long days in a factory or warehouse, so kids did most of the chores. Hargam got out of doing chores as often as he could though. One day when he was supposed to sweep and dust the kitchen, our parents were furious when they came home to find it worse than before. Somehow, Hargam convinced them it'd been *my* job, so I got in trouble for it not being done, see."

It was a wake-up call when Clonis explained what sorts of chores they did such as buying household items and food, cooking, washing dishes, cleaning, and a host of other things.

Geesh, how'd the kids have time to study?

"But things were different for the upper class, right?" said Breel. "They had housekeepers? People cooked for them?"

Another laugh. "No, only the super wealthy like Xorem did, see. Everyone spent hours per week doing these things before Hargam came. He made everyone specialize to increase productivity."

Becoming an expert in one thing meant maximizing your utility to society which was why Tatem made doing things not related to one's Career Group illegal. But it was news that pre-Tatem people could do many things.

Making everyone dependent upon each other was a smart move for Tatem to keep citizens in line. His system worked if there were enough citizens in each Career Group. Intercludae had functioned because of representation from many Career Groups. But at first, they would've had issues with the lack of certain Career Groups just like Breel and the others without housekeepers or cooks. Yet, everyone had done these things fifty years ago.

"We can't keep it this way," said Breel.

Cafrec stared into the abyss. "Yeah, you're right."

"But...when did you do these things?" Breel asked. "Between working and studying..."

Clonis pursed his lips as the corners of his mouth upturned into a smile.

Geesh, he's hiding yet another laugh.

"People worked a certain number of hours," he said, "but outside work, their time was their own, see. Want to work on hobbies? That's fine. Feel like sitting outside doing nothing? Go ahead. They didn't force anyone to take classes."

A world in which people had the freedom to live their lives how they wanted had been Famut's goal. Now it was Breel's goal. But it wasn't enough. It was clear from living with different Career Groups that people needed to know how to cook, clean, and more. The post-Tatem world

be a change but being self-reliant and capable of doing many tasks would
be worth it.

Chapter Twenty-Six

The following day, in between their work, Breel and Cafrec discussed what Breel could draw. Even better, unable to wait for the proper supplies, she sketched to practice drawing Tatem.

When she first put a pencil's tip to paper, a charge of exhilaration coursed throughout her.

Yes, this is one of the reasons I came to Intercludae...

The freedom to draw when she wanted. What she wanted. Where she wanted.

Knowing that drawing didn't mean risking a Mortae sentence was magical. Surreal. Two months ago, she'd never have believed it. But there was no longer a housekeeper from whom to hide her drawings nor her parents to see and worry about her actions. Only herself, the pencil, and paper.

Unfortunately, it meant drawing a lot of Tatem but one day, she'd draw other things. For now, drawing anything, even Tatem, was enough.

***

Manum, Vectus, Cafrec, and Lexo left in the afternoon to get supplies. There'd been talk about whether both Manum and Lexo should go in case the imprisoned DOE attempted something; however, there'd be more to carry than usual with the cleaning supplies and extra food, so everyone agreed the two strongest people should go.

Before everyone ate supper, Breel helped Praxa bring the DOE's meals downstairs. They placed the five plates of chicken breasts, rice, and vegetables and mugs of decaf coffee on Praxa and Lexo's desks outside the furnace room door. The sound machines on either side of the door whirred. At first, it'd been annoying but now it was an ignorable background noise.

Praxa grabbed her gun from her desk then motioned to the door. "I'll unlock it then stand at the entrance. After they move to the far wall, you'll place their food on the floor inside the room."

A wave of uncertainty swept through Breel as she pictured the officers attacking her while she bent over to place a plate on the floor. "And they haven't tried anything yet? Even their leader?"

"Nothing."

Breel took a deep breath then told Praxa she was ready.

After unlocking the door, Praxa opened it, blocking the way between the officers and Breel. A shuffling noise sounded as Praxa motioned for Breel to get the plates.

Breel took two plates then stepped beside Praxa. Blankets and pillows covered one corner of the room. As ordered by Manum, they'd stacked empty plates and mugs from their lunch near the door. The five officers sat along the far wall wearing the uniforms they'd refused to replace with non-Lexum clothing.

The leader frowned from the corner. "Why's a programmer here?"

Praxa and Breel said nothing, not daring to say both Manum and Lexo were away.

Breel set the plates on the floor then left the room for the others. Praxa stayed in the doorway, observing the officers with her gun pointed.

"You're both lucky to be alive," said the leader as Breel returned. "Escaped Vucapi can't live forever, you know. Soon, you'll have your Mortae."

Ignore her.

Those words became a mantra not because the officer upset Breel, but because biting her tongue wasn't easy. Saying anything risked revealing information or getting them angry.

Breel picked up the last two mugs. As she set them on the floor, movement caught her eye. She dropped the mugs, shattering them and spilling the coffee. Before she could chide herself, one of the young women leapt to her feet.

"Stay back!" Praxa shouted.

The officer ran at them. Praxa shot her without hesitation, but it didn't matter. The other four had already surged toward Praxa and Breel.

Praxa shot the middle-aged man who fell as Breel scrambled to her feet. The others were close enough to touch Breel and Praxa, but the fallen man blocked their way. They stepped around him while Praxa's next dart missed her target.

Breel recalled Manum telling her in Intercludae that dart gun chambers held five darts.

She won't have enough ammunition...

"Breel, move!" said Praxa.

Quiet Praxa had barked an order. Breel obeyed as Praxa shot a third officer. Next, she aimed for a young woman when the leader tackled her. They fell beside Breel in a mass of tangled limbs, the leader atop of Praxa, pounding her with a fist. Praxa caught the first two blows with a protective arm but wasn't any competition for the woman.

She's going to kill her!

Breel grabbed the leader's arm before she could land another punch, but the officer wrenched free of Breel's grip like it was nothing then pummelled Praxa more.

"Oh no!"

Breel spun around at Trafis's voice. He stood near the desks, jaw dropped as he stared at Praxa and the officer. Then, noticing Praxa's gun on the ground near her foot, he grabbed it, pointed, then fired. The leader fell unconscious on Praxa, causing the air to leave Praxa's lungs in a *whoomph*.

Breel and Trafis rolled the woman off Praxa who nodded her thanks as Trafis helped her sit. A bruise was forming on the back of her hand, but her face had been saved from damage. Praxa pulled back her hair with a shaky hand.

"Thanks, Trafis. Quick think—Where is she!?"

The other officer!

Breel and Praxa leapt to their feet, looking around, but the officer wasn't in sight. Praxa was halfway to the stairs when a small voice said, "I'm here."

It was the young woman, no older than Breel, standing in the furnace room's doorway with tears in her eyes. "Please...please don't shoot me. I'll stay in here."

She backed into the room, tripping over her fallen comrades, until she stood against a wall.

Praxa marched into the room. "Never try that again."

"It wasn't my idea. Please don't tell the others I could've escaped."

"We won't," said Praxa.

They dragged the leader into the room with the others then locked the door. Praxa returned to her desk. Breel sat in Lexo's chair, arms shaking, while Trafis sat on Lexo's desk.

Praxa pushed her sleeves up to her elbows, revealing purplish bruises. "We got lucky."

"Are you okay?" Breel asked.

"Yeah. At least it's not my face."

"You were amazing!" said Breel.

There was more to Praxa than met the eye. Not only did she take out three officers within seconds, but she only had bruises after taking on someone far bigger than her. Yet, Praxa had only smiled her thanks. She hadn't bragged about what she'd done. Instead, she suggested they eat and tell the others what happened.

After the evening news, they discussed whether it was a coincidence that the officers had tried something when Manum and Lexo were away. In the end, they decided it was impossible for them to have known and, instead, had acted when they saw Breel, rather than an ex-DOE officer or muscular Manum, assisting Praxa.

After the meeting, Breel spent time with Criba and Trafis in Trafis's room in the basement. The moment Breel and Criba entered, Trafis pushed back from the desk. The chair wheels slid a few feet across the concrete floor.

"Are you both okay?" Criba asked, looking from Breel to Trafis as she and Breel sat on Trafis's bed.

They said they were, but Breel didn't tell Criba how scared she'd been. Instead, she shrugged, pretending it hadn't been a big deal. Deflecting the question, she asked Criba how she was holding up.

Criba shrugged. "Okay. At least until what happened with those officers in the desert and now once again. Good thing for Praxa and you, Trafis."

Breel voiced her agreement. That was twice in which she owed Trafis her life if not lack of injury.

Criba sighed. "Does spying on your father feel wrong to you? I'm glad we can see what he's doing, but it doesn't feel right."

Breel understood but having the updates made her rest easier. However, it was still impossible to know whether Duknum was furious at them or himself, or whether he had moved on and forgotten about his family. Emails and reports suggested the latter but there was only so much he could say without the DOE considering him a traitor.

"Do you think he wishes he came with us?" Trafis asked.

Breel considered the question. Despite considering Tatem "a good man," Duknum had never gushed about him. While he was never one to get emotional, dealing with his family departing and turning against Tatem would've been difficult. However, it didn't mean Duknum had or would agree with their views.

"I'm not sure," Criba said. "He's always so adamant about following the law."

"Yeah, to the nth degree," said Breel. "Mother, why is that?"

Criba leaned back as her gaze rose to the ceiling. "It's because of his childhood. Famut was a great older brother. He never bullied your father or made him feel less than himself. However, everyone commented on Famut being a future doctor, his intelligence, and his likeability. Then there was your father. Smart, but not in the same league. Quieter so harder to get to know. Fewer social skills. Everyone would speak to Famut but ignore your father, so he felt like no one ever cared about getting to know him. The only people who didn't put Famut on a pedestal were their parents."

Breel had heard bits and pieces of this, but never that Famut had overshadowed him to such a degree.

My poor father.

Criba placed her palms flat on the bed. "Your father said the worst of it was Famut doing questionable things that weren't *quite* illegal. A few times, Famut even smooth-talked DOE officers out of giving an official warning. Meanwhile, your father got a warning for something he didn't even do. The officer didn't listen no matter how hard your father and his parents tried telling the DOE he didn't do it.

"So, he grew up resenting Famut and fearing him jeopardizing the family. He went on high alert for anything that'd trigger a DOE investigation on family members. He was as careful as possible and wanted his children to be careful, too."

This was new to Breel, and if she'd known it years ago, it would've helped her to understand Duknum's reasoning. If he'd explained his fears and why he had them, she'd have been far more likely to stop drawing.

But no, he insisted I obey without listening to my perspective. He figured I'm enough of an Uncle Famut fan he didn't want me learning the things Uncle Famut did as a kid. Why'd he allow Trafis and me to see Uncle Famut if he hated him?

But when she asked this, Criba shook her head. "No, he never hated Famut. He was jealous, that's all. Believe me, I tried convincing him to tell you all this, so you'd see his viewpoint, but he didn't want you knowing."

Trafis put his feet on the bed then crossed his ankles. "It's like we're learning about him for the first time."

Yeah, which is ridiculous. There was no good reason not to tell us. He could've left out the parts about his jealousy and Famut sweet-talking the DOE.

Criba smiled as she patted Breel's hand. "That's why he was so delighted when you got the Department of Education, Breel. Our daughter in the most prestigious department! And you, Trafis, in the Department of Teaching. Every parent hopes their children will get into better departments than them. Breel, I hope you didn't stress over which department you'd get."

Breel hesitated. She'd never told her parents how much it had bothered her.

Deciding to be honest, she said, "I did stress. I"—her cheeks burned—"didn't want the DOE or occupation. Even sanitation would've been better!"

Criba smiled. "Understandable not wanting to work at the DOE or with your parents. Well, I hope your father can forgive us."

Breel disagreed. "Mother, we're the ones who need to forgive him. He put Tatem and society before us."

"That's not his fault," said Trafis.

It was true. Tatem forced everyone to put society first.

"Do you think he's rethinking everything?" Trafis asked.

"I'm sure he is," said Criba.

And, I hope, it's opening his mind to what Tatem's like.

But, of course, there was no way of knowing Duknum's innermost thoughts. They could only hope he had seen Tatem's true colours.

Chapter Twenty-Seven

The next morning, after the post-breakfast meeting, Clonis raised a broom into the air. "Time to clean! My parents were right about one thing—if everyone helps, it'll get done quicker."

Breel sighed. She'd have to wait longer to test the drawing supplies. She had five pencils of varying hardness, a pack of forty-eight coloured pencils, three sketchbooks, an eraser, a pencil sharpener, and a ruler. She had little time to use them as after Cafrec and the others had returned from the supply run the previous night, they debriefed about the attempted escape. Breel only had half an hour to draw before getting to bed. Having only used graphite pencils, blending various blues to draw the sky was a thrill like no other.

But drawing would have to wait again. Clonis organized the cleaning supplies on the dining room table, explaining what each was and how to use them. There was a vacuum, two brooms, dusting cloths, a toilet brush, and cloths and chemicals to clean the kitchen and bathroom.

Clonis instructed Breel and Cafrec to dust the basement. When Clonis gave Samit that job, Cafrec laughed so hard he cried.

"I bet he did that on purpose," said Cafrec a few minutes later as he and Breel dusted their desks.

As Breel found a dusting rhythm, it didn't seem too bad of a task, but she couldn't imagine doing it every day. Clonis said they had to dust daily because of the sand, so it was a relief to know they wouldn't have to do it as often once they returned to Lexum.

They finished cleaning in no time and, for once, the house sparkled. Standing in the kitchen, everyone grinned while admiring their work, though Trafis kept sneezing due to the displaced dust triggering his allergies. The sinks glistened. The counters shone. The floor was clear of sand and dirt. Tatem made it seem like people could only be and do one thing, but they had all cleaned. It wasn't as good of a job as a housekeeper—the counter still had stubborn stains—but it was far cleaner than expected.

Clonis clapped Praxa on the back. "See? You can all do this! Cleaning the kitchen and bathroom every day or two and the rest of the house every few days will have it looking this good all the time."

When Breel sat at her desk a few minutes later, she even felt different. Just knowing the room was room made her feel more relaxed.

Breel had just started her database duties before drawing when Clonis entered. He leaned back in the spare chair, hands behind his head. "What were your Career Groups?"

No hello or may I join you?

"Computer programmer," Cafrec said.

Clonis's eyebrows raised. "Huh. Wow. Computers everywhere, I guess. I never used one, see. I bet that's easy to believe, since we were poor. But even in Lexum I didn't use them. I gave Hargam advice, not that I knew much, but I guess he thought his siblings were the best advisors since we weren't upper class spies sent to kill him. But once he murdered our siblings, I wanted to murder him, too."

His looked to the floor as he said this last part.

He misses his siblings.

While Breel still had her sibling, she, too, had lost someone dear to her. In fact, she had lost Famut twice—five years ago when he disappeared then one month ago when Tatem shot him. Breel would think about Famut even at Clonis's age, just like he continued grieving his siblings.

"Was he ever a decent brother?" Cafrec asked. "When you were kids, I mean."

"Ha! Didn't you listen to a word I said, boy? He could talk a mouse into approaching a cat. However, no adult ever thought anything bad about him, see. When us kids said he was bad, well, it wasn't Hargam who got in trouble. One time, Hargam called a girl names in front of her brother, so he pushed Hargam."

Clonis punched the air with his fist. "POW! Just like that. They were standing on top of a short hill near the cliff, so Hargam lost his balance then fell down the hill backwards. You should've seen him rolling!"

He laughed, smacking a hand on his leg then rotating his hands to mimic Tatem's flying limbs.

"Oh, Hargam was mad. He burned a small box of treasures the boy had. When the boy told his parents and my parents, Hargam said I did it. They even found matches by my bed, but they weren't my matches, see. All the adults believed Hargam, of course."

"He framed you," said Cafrec.

"Yeah, and not for the first time. He wasn't a good brother, see. Around adults, he pretended to be, but whenever the rest of us told them Hargam did something, they never believed us. They didn't know he was bullying and torturing kids and animals. Of course, like I said, once he saw inside Lexum, he changed. Wanted to become one of them, see. He had things he wanted to do, so stopped wasting time playing around."

"Did that make things easier for you?" Breel asked.

Clonis nodded. "Oh yes. Once he cared about school, he didn't have time for bullying. It was great. Yeah, those were better days. Hargam went to school and studied like his life depended on it. For him, it did. He wanted to learn and show everyone he could do something great, see."

Tatem's a horrible person, but I can't blame him for wanting that. If I were him, seeing the grandeur of Lexum, I'm sure I'd have would've worked hard to get that scholarship, too.

Tatem had wanted to have a better life and needed to prove himself. If he'd been born inside Lexum with access to excellent schools including postsecondary education and many Career Group options as an adult, there was a chance he never would've become president. He ascended to president the way he had by being a hero to the lower class. Without manipulating them to garner their support, it would've been difficult.

Cafrec had more questions. "What were your parents like?"

Clonis shrugged. "Okay, I guess. Had to work all the time, like all the adults, to make as much money as they could. Since I was the closest in age to Hargam and often the one telling on him, they liked me the least. Thought I was trying to ruin Hargam's life, see. Accused me of making up stories to wreck his scholarship chances because they thought I was jealous. I wasn't. He had no friends so what was there to be jealous about? Once Hargam started working hard at school, they suggested we should, too. But they didn't go on about it too much since they knew we'd work in the factories, anyway."

It was impossible to imagine a world in which the government didn't force children to attend school. Kids unsupervised while they played all day...but playing what? Famut had introduced Breel and Trafis to some games, but they'd get old after days and months and years on end.

I bet Tatem was cruel for his own entertainment.

The way he failed to conceal his grin while talking about Mortae proved his craving for enacting such punishments. Before Mortae, he'd satisfy that need using his siblings and other children. Now he could use everybody.

"What happened to your parents?" Cafrec asked.

Clonis wrapped a lock of hair around a finger. "They died during the war. In their last moments, they learned what Hargam was like. Some upper-class people kidnapped them then broke into the estate, bringing them to Hargam's office. The kidnappers said they had people surrounding the house, ready to burn it. They gave Hargam the choice of saving our parents or the house."

"Gee, I wonder what he chose..." Breel shuddered.

Clonis nodded. "Right in front of them, too. Said they're old, so it didn't matter. I didn't hear about it till later. Worst of all, nobody was there to burn the house. They only did it to confirm the type of person Hargam is, see."

His poor parents...

After years of being under his manipulative spell, they watched as Tatem ordered their deaths to save a house. At eighteen years old, he put a building ahead of his parents' lives.

What a horrific way to discover your child doesn't care about or love you. Is he even capable of love?

If Tatem shooting Famut in cold blood was any sign, choosing the house wouldn't have been a hard decision to make. His list of people and things warranting saving would be small with the house topping the list. It sounded like Xorem made the cut, too, since after killing Famut, he showed her tenderness and love when she felt faint.

What's she got that no one else has?

"The more I hear about Tatem, the eviller I realize he is," Cafrec said.

"Yeah," said Clonis. "My brother isn't the best guy."

"That's an understatement," Cafrec muttered.

"Is it just him?" Breel asked. "What were your other siblings like?"

Clonis's gaze fell onto the wall behind Breel and Cafrec, zoning out as he reflected on his long-dead family.

"Fine. No meanness there." Clonis laughed. "I remember one time we talked about ways to kill Hargam even though we'd never do it, see. But Hargam heard then told our parents. It was one of the few truths he ever told them. They were super mad. We all got the strap good that day. Hargam rarely got the strap, of course, and I got it far more than the others."

Gee, I've never appreciated Trafis for being a good brother!

"I'm sorry you had such an awful childhood," Cafrec said.

Clonis waved him off. "Not for you to say sorry. Anyway, that's some of the bad stuff from my childhood, but there was a lot of good. We were a close sibling group, see. Played all day long, rarely went to school, and most of the time had no adults telling us what to do. We had fun."

That's why Tatem mandates everyone works and studies all day long—he doesn't want a society like that.

While on the surface, ensuring everyone work and improve themselves sounded like a great idea, Tatem had taken it—and everything else—to the extreme.

Clonis tsked. "Too bad Hargam ensured you don't have time for fun. A real shame. I can't imagine studying all day and night. How boooor-ing."

It was true. It was hard not to be envious about parts of Clonis's childhood. However, Breel was under no delusions about how unlucky his family and the rest of the lower class had been.

At least now no one in Lexum is poor. I guess that's one good thing Tatem did.

"What I wanted to talk to you about was those drawings," Clonis said.

"These?"

Breel held up her drawing of Tatem in his suit standing in front of his desk. She'd yet to colour his tie cherry-red and her fingers itched to do so.

Clonis's jaw dropped. "Whoa! How'd you get so good when my brother doesn't allow you to draw?"

Breel's face burned. "I did it in secret over many years."

His grin could've competed with Cafrec's. "Good for you! But gee, you're lucky he didn't have you killed."

Breel shuddered at the recollection of her failed Mortae alongside most of the people living with her.

Tatem amping up the crowd.

The chanting citizens awaiting their deaths.

Tatem's psychotic smile.

Feeling every single eye of Lexum on her as Tatem announced the Deliverer who'd give the injection.

She shuddered again.

No, don't think about it. That's in the past. You won't have another Mortae.

But I could if we fail.

No, stop.

"That's what you want to show people?" Clonis asked, pulling her out of those dark thoughts as he examined her drawing.

"No," she said. "I'm practicing."

She explained that she and Cafrec wanted to get across Tatem's evil ways but had few ideas.

Clonis nodded. "That's because Tatem didn't let you be imaginative. When we were kids, we drew little vees above eyes to show someone's evil. You can also make his eyes red."

Breel studied her drawing for a moment. The red eyes made sense but not the vees. "Can you show me?"

Clonis leaned over her desk while Cafrec stood to watch, a hand on Breel's shoulder. His hair smelled like vanilla courtesy of the communal shampoo bottle. Taking a pencil, Clonis drew two vee-shaped lines above each eye.

The vees did something to the drawing—but evil wasn't her first guess.

"He looks angry," said Cafrec.

Clonis shrugged. "Well, I'm not a drawer. You need to practice. Draw the eyes different, too."

It was worth a shot. The moment Clonis left, Breel coloured the tie by blending a few reds, then she spent most of the morning practicing drawing Tatem to look evil. She experimented with drawing narrower eyes and arching the eyebrows. Exaggerating Tatem's grin added to the look. Right before lunch, she picked up her masterpiece—there was no mistaking her intention of portraying Tatem as an evil man. No vees needed—just artistic talent.

Chapter Twenty-Eight

During the post-lunch meeting, Breel offered to show an example drawing.

Samit stepped to the side. "Why don't you stand up here?"

Breel's body vibrated as she stood beside Samit. She held up her drawing of Tatem in front of his desk with his narrowed eyes and smile—always wide and deceivingly friendly. His mouth was larger than usual, the corners near the edge of his face. She'd added a hint of red to his eyes.

"That's great!" Trafis said.

Criba touched Breel's arm and beamed. "You're so talented! All your years of drawing has paid off."

Breel basked in everyone's compliments. Only Praxa—staring at the table—said nothing.

When Breel sat, she felt like she was soaring high in the sky. After many years, others seeing and enjoying her work was her dream come true. But the elation plummeted to nothingness when Samit confronted Praxa about her lack of participation. When Praxa didn't answer, Manum defended her.

Samit glared. "I wasn't talking to you."

Vectus stood, extending a raised hand to each of them. "Don't you two start this again. If you want to fight, do it on your own time." He looked across the table to Praxa. Speaking softer, he said, "I've also noticed you looking away when we, especially Cafrec, degrade Tatem."

Praxa stared at the table. "I'm uncomfortable with it."

Breel strained to hear her.

"Hmm..." said Samit. "If you can accuse someone of being a spy for putting in more work than anyone else and not liking people reading their screens, then I can accuse her of being a spy for not wanting to speak what should be her true feelings for Tatem. Stop defending her. Praxa, tell us the truth. Now!"

Pandemonium erupted. Manum stood so fast his chair toppled to the floor. He marched to the other side of the table, walking behind Clonis, Cafrec, Breel, and Vectus, yelling at Samit. The worries and tension which had disappeared when Breel showed her drawings flooded back to the forefront as her heart raced. She leaned forward as if that'd get her out of harm's way.

Oh, please don't fight right behind me.

Praxa sat stunned as Lexo put an arm around her then said something unheard over Manum. Breel's heart ached for Praxa as her lower lip trembled.

Vectus yelled over Samit and Manum. No one else said or did anything—there were already too many people involved with emotions running high. Trafis glanced back and forth between Samit and Manum, bewildered at something which, for Lexum, was an abnormal situation.

"You take that back!" said Manum. He grabbed for Samit as Vectus held him back.

"You didn't care when Vectus mentioned Praxa not joining in," said Samit, "but when I do—"

"*Enough!*" Vectus's voice rang. "The fact is, we have reason to be suspicious."

Manum stared daggers at Samit, but when Vectus let him go, he returned to his seat.

Sitting, Vectus turned to Praxa, eyes softening and head tilted. "I'm not saying you're a spy. What I *am* saying is we need reasonable proof that you aren't one."

"Lexo and I are proof," said Manum.

"Yeah," said Lexo. "We can vouch for her."

Praxa shook in his arms. Her eyes brimmed with tears.

Samit scoffed. "Lexo, that means nothing. When you thought I was a spy, it didn't matter that Cafrec has known me for a year."

Manum placed a hand on Praxa's shoulder. "We've known Praxa for much longer than that."

"I've known her for more than half my life," said Lexo.

But Samit demanded that Praxa prove she's anti-Tatem.

Lexo gritted his teeth but spoke with a level tone. "Your situation was different, Samit. Praxa works no more than everyone else and takes part in other things."

"That means nothing coming from you," said Samit. "Everyone knows Praxa's your best friend."

The arguing continued and Vectus attempted to mediate. When Samit suggested Vectus intimidate her to get out the truth, like with his students, the colour drained from Praxa's face. Manum opposed it.

It was a standstill.

No one spoke.

This is awful. If we can't trust each other, who can we trust?

Breel racked her brain for a solution—for anything. If Manum and Praxa refused having Vectus force her to talk, all she could do was explain.

"Praxa?" Breel hesitated. Joining in was like jumping into a room of DOE officers with her drawing notebook. Praxa, Lexo's arms still around her, looked up. "First, I don't think you're a spy. The way you handled the officers when they attacked us..."

If Praxa was the spy, not only would she have let them attack Breel, but the search leader wouldn't have pummelled Praxa. But no one else had been there to witness how she reacted to their initial attack.

Breel continued. "I'm curious why you don't join in degrading Tatem. If you explain why you're uncomfortable, we may understand."

Praxa stared at her lap. It took a moment for her to speak. "Okay, I guess I need to, don't I? My parents are staunch Tatem supporters and raised my brother and me to be the same. He was eight years older than me. Cafrec, you remind me of him."

But she hates Cafrec!

Cafrec blinked with confusion. "I do? Oh, wow. Cool."

Praxa shook her head. "No, not cool at all. He was a great big brother, and we were close despite the age difference. He joked and did illegal things like talking to people in other Career Groups to learn from them. His Mortae was six months before his Demna."

She brushed away a tear while Lexo gripped her tighter. Breel knew from Criba that watching the Mortae of one's sibling, especially at such a young age, was traumatic. Praxa's pro-Tatem parents would've thought he had it coming.

Praxa cleared her throat. "My parents weren't maternal and after he died, they were worse. I retreated into a shell but instead of helping me, my parents became stricter. They didn't allow me to have opinions. If I hinted at disliking someone or something, they punished me. I could never do right in their eyes even though I never had a warning. I don't take part in saying bad things about Tatem because of it."

Breel's parents had been strict, too, but they never punished her for expressing her own views, and they'd only been strict out of love. Praxa's story had been genuine, no doubt about that. Her behaviour seemed understandable.

But one thing was unclear. "How were you convinced to come to Intercludae?" Breel asked.

Manum stepped in. "I introduced her to Lexo, one year ahead of her in school, thinking they'd hit it off. I told her there's more to life after getting out of her parents' home and she could have a far better life in Intercludae."

Samit shook his head. "You're a walking contradiction."

Manum groaned. "What is it now?"

"You convinced Praxa to ignore parental approval and go to Intercludae. Yet you talked on and on about your son not coming here because he wasn't doing what *you* wanted."

"That's different," said Manum.

"Praxa," said Vectus, ignoring the tension, "you're saying it's ingrained in you to not express your opinion or say anything that someone could interpret as making fun of Tatem, right?"

"Yes."

Vectus nodded. "I understand. Some of us have been at this a long time. Whether or not we lived in Intercludae, we could express ourselves to other each through email. But you've had little opportunity for that, so it's natural to fear it after society and your parents forbade it. I was lucky as my parents had lukewarm views of Tatem which cooled as the years went by. They were young teens during the war, so remembered the good he did because, horrible as most of the things he's done are, he did a lot of good at first. My parents never expressed their lack of support for fear of influencing me to have illegal views which could risk my life. However, as I got older, I knew."

If only my computer programming classmates could hear him. I can't believe I used to hate him.

They could always count on Vectus to settle arguments and be the voice of reason. The more Breel got to know him, the more she liked him. He'd gone from one of her least favourite people to one of her favourites.

As Praxa smiled at Vectus, some of the tension in her face disappeared.

"All that to say," he continued, "I can't imagine how difficult it was growing up in a household like yours."

"Thank you, Vectus."

"You're saying you're convinced she's not a spy?" Samit asked.

Vectus folded his hands on the table. "Yes, I am. I'm sure we've all experienced this to a degree. I taught Breel and Cafrec, and I knew Famut and Centia had influenced them, so I figured they're anti-Tatem. However, they had to hide their views. As you know, I hid my views by making myself seem like a huge Tatem supporter while shoving programming down my students' throats."

"Yeah, seeing you in Intercludae shocked me," said Breel.

"I thought you were a Hargamite for sure," said Cafrec.

Vectus cringed. "That was my goal."

Samit sighed as if he *wanted* Praxa to be a spy. "I see. What do others think?"

One by one, as the group said they didn't think Praxa's a spy, the colour returned to her face.

"Fine," said Samit. "However, I'm watching her. Understood?" He looked at Praxa.

"As do I with you," said Manum.

Samit looked ready to throttle him but then the corners of his mouth upturned into a smile. "That's fair." He glanced at his watch. "Almost time for the news."

Chapter Twenty-Nine

The next day, Manum said the DOE had set everything up for them to retrieve the diary. Between drawing without repercussions and Samit demanding Praxa prove she's not a spy, Breel had forgotten all about it.

She didn't tell anyone about fearing the trip, concentrating instead on helping Cafrec fill backpacks with food, water, and flashlights in case they were out after sunset. Running into the DOE officers had shaken her confidence in their DOE sources. Manum assured everyone that coming across more officers was unlikely, especially with new searches being miles away; however, the risk wasn't zero.

Breel, Cafrec, Manum, and Praxa armed themselves then left with Clonis after lunchtime. The warm air hit them the moment they stepped outside. An azure-blue sky stretched from horizon to horizon without a wisp of cloud while the sun beamed like a giant oven in a Department of Households video.

This is going to get hot...

"Nice day, at least," Manum said.

Having an afternoon of seeing sky and sand rather than walls and breathing in the warm, fresh breeze instead of stuffy old air was more than enjoyable despite how warm they'd get.

Clonis gazed upward, arms wide. "Wow! Look at this! Couldn't see this when I came in the dark, see." He turned in a circle, admiring the scenery—not that there was anything to see other than rocks, piles of sand, and the occasional small bush. "This sure feels like home. Yep, got the desert. The scorching sun. The walls far away."

Praxa patted Clonis's arm. "You've missed it."

"Hargam locked me in that retirement home for decades. I miss everything."

"We should get moving if we want to be back by nightfall," Manum said.

The Lexum suburb was a sprawling assortment of rundown buildings. Clonis didn't take them toward the rowhouses closest to Lexum. Instead, he walked toward the nearest section one mile west.

"Clonis, walk ahead of us to set the pace," Manum said.

"Don't want the old guy to fall behind?" Clonis asked, stepping in front of the others.

"We don't want to go too fast for you," said Praxa.

"Yeah, that's what I said."

Clonis swung his arms, whistling as his head turned in all directions, soaking it in. Breel and Cafrec—hand in hand—followed with Manum and Praxa beside them.

"Did you ever see Lexum while growing up?" Manum asked.

"Nah," said Clonis. "Lexum was for the upper class. They didn't want us there, see. Only person I know who saw it was Hargam but that's only because he snuck in for a few minutes."

Everyone stepped closer to Clonis who grinned so much his mouth would hurt. His head spun as if on a swivel as he gazed at the landscape. Despite his age, as he walked on the sand, he counterbalanced his weight when the sand shifted whereas the sand often caused Breel and the others to slip

"Did you wish you could?" Cafrec asked.

"Of course!" said Clonis. "Everyone imagined what it looked like. I asked Hargam so many questions after he bragged about seeing it."

"I would've been jealous," said Manum, walking in stride with him.

Both Clonis and Manum's feet shifted with their next steps. Clonis kept walking as if it hadn't happened while Manum slid, a hand stopping his momentum before he fell headfirst into the sand.

Clonis laughed. "Close one! I wasn't jealous because I knew I'd work in the factories and never thought things could be different. But Hargam changed things, and we all liked him for that, see."

"We learned about the riots and civil war," said Praxa.

The sand moved underneath Breel's foot, so she did what Clonis did and waited for the shifting to end before taking a step then putting her weight on it.

"Yeah," said Clonis, craning his head skyward, "the upper class didn't like us getting everything they had. But we had more people, and they couldn't evict us from Lexum. Things seemed great at first because Hargam followed his plan to improve our lives."

"And," said Manum, "along the way he got the lower class believing that his laws, most of which only benefitted them, were for the best. That got most citizens on his side."

"Yep, most people thought he was great." Clonis raised his arms then lowered them and his head, mimicking people worshipping Tatem.

"They still do," said Breel. "It's sickening."

"He always loved attention and thought he was better than everyone else," Clonis said.

Tatem never hid his love for the crowd's adoration. He riled up citizens during every Mortae, getting them chanting with their arms in the air, excited to witness someone's death.

"Speaking of your brother," said Manum, "Thoughts on his other weaknesses, beside his image being important?"

Clonis pointed ahead. "His diary will tell us."

"And if it's not there?" Manum asked. "Let's say by some miracle no one took it. After fifty years, who knows what condition it's in. What about water damage?"

Clonis's brow furrowed. "Uh..." He motioned to their surroundings. "We're in a desert."

"Okay," Manum conceded. "What if an animal ate it?"

"Few animals in the desert."

"Yes, but if it's there, it's likely in poor condition."

Clonis bent over to touch a knee-high bush with brown leaves. "Don't see why it wouldn't as it's hidden under a floorboard. No animals can get it and only me and Hargam know it's there."

"Does he know you know about it?" Cafrec asked.

Clonis's laugh made him sound decades younger. "No! If Hargam knew I read it, I sure wouldn't be talking to you today."

"He would've killed you for reading his diary?" Cafrec asked.

Clonis frowned. "Being against anything he believes or thinks is dangerous, no matter how minor. Didn't you hear me when I said he killed our siblings for disagreeing with his laws?"

Cafrec looked at Breel in horror.

Not sure why he's surprised...it's not different from other things Tatem's done.

But she needed to make concessions for Cafrec since he shared DNA with Tatem. Breel wanted be there for him but knew enough not to talk about it unless Cafrec did first. Sure, she, too, had a biological parent different from the one she thought; however, Xorem wasn't Tatem. As far as they knew, Xorem was naive, sickly, and easily manipulated. She wasn't a psychopathic killer with such an ego that she demanded society worship her.

Conversation dwindled. The wind was a moderate breeze with gusts that whipped Breel's hair across her face. She kept pushing it back; however, it became as fruitless as keeping her shoes and pant cuffs clean of sand.

Clonis whistled when the suburbs were close enough to see details. Time and neglect had caused the wooden buildings to become as dilapidated as the other set of rowhouses. Refuse, bricks, wood, and pieces of roof cluttered the ground. Metal groaned in the wind.

"Wow, I never thought home could look worse than when I lived here," said Clonis.

"Where'd we go?" Manum asked.

"This way."

He led them to the area farthest from Lexum and closest to the trees.

"We lived a quarter mile from here," Clonis said.

The first rowhouses—each only eight feet wide—were indistinguishable from the others with broken glass, crumbling bricks, and holey roofs.

"Everything looks the same," said Manum. "You sure you know where to go?"

"Trust me," Clonis said.

He stopped twenty feet in front of the first house in the row, turned to his left where a factory lay some two hundred feet away, then counted the streets they passed. Breel tensed at every intersection, her muscles relaxing when no DOE officers appeared.

"It's up next," he said once they passed the sixth street and set of rowhouses.

At the intersection was a three-foot high, round structure made of bricks with a wooden arm and crank. "We got our water from this well by turning the crank to lower and raise a bucket on a rope." The rope and bucket were long gone.

Dozens of rowhouses extended the entire length of both sides of the street. They walked down it, winding their way through the shingles, wood, glass, and leaves. In one area, over twenty houses were a pile of rubble with only crumbling brick towers left standing.

Clonis pointed to the ruins. "From a fire. With this many wooden houses connected they spread fast. Luckily, this one only burned a few homes, but I remember a fire that destroyed one hundred."

One hundred!? That's horrifying...

Citizens of Lexum didn't deal with fire so, except for a brief informational video at school, Breel had never seen one.

"Were fires common?" Praxa asked.

"Oh yes, they were in the winter when we used woodstoves because unsupervised children stayed at home. Our parents only allowed the older kids to use the woodstove. Hargam thought he was too good for it and never used it. He didn't wanna get his hands dirty."

"What's a woodstove?" Breel asked.

Clonis laughed. "We put wood in a stove to heat our homes, see."

"Like the ones at the Department of Food?" Cafrec asked.

"Yeah, I guess. Except those are for cooking and these were for heating homes. It was a lot of dirty work because we had to chop wood, pile it outside the house, fill the stove, stoke the fire to keep it lit, and remove ashes. Be grateful for furnaces. These bricks"—he pointed to the brick stacks at the back of each house which matched the crumbling brick towers in the ruins—"were chimneys to remove smoke from houses."

In Lexum, heat was always there, so it wasn't something anyone thought about.

Having to go through so much work to have heat sounds awful. I've sure taken a lot for granted.

But that thought caused an unpleasant taste in her mouth. After all, it was Tatem who had given everyone such luxuries.

Clonis pointed to the trees in the distance. "We got our wood from the treeline near the cliffs. Back then there were more trees, see. Sometimes us kids played games in them, but parts of the forest were close to the cliff, so we had to be careful not to fall over it. Falling down a hill, like Hargam once, was one thing. But I don't think anyone who fell off the cliff lived."

"It's that steep?" Manum asked.

Clonis nodded. "Oh yes. Our parents told us not to go near it but of course we didn't listen. We played there a lot."

They continued down the street. Some houses were in ruins while others had a missing roof or windowpanes. After a few minutes of meandering through piles of garbage and materials on the road, Clonis stopped, pointing to a house on their left.

"Here it is."

Chapter Thirty

Clonis pointed to a rowhouse as indistinguishable as the rest except for the number *328* above the doorframe with an upside-down *3*. The roof was intact, but the door and windowpanes were gone. A small stack of wood lay against the house alongside a few dozen bricks covered in sand.

"That's my house," said Clonis.

"You sure?" Breel asked. "How'd you know it's not house 328 in another row?"

"I know how many streets away we were from the factory, see."

Everyone waited as Clonis looked upon the skinny two-storey with a smile, perhaps recalling an incident with his siblings. Something creaked in the wind, and a ball of dust, dirt, and shredded material blew across the road until getting stuck in a pile of shingles. Breel and Cafrec passed out the flashlights from their backpacks.

A few minutes later, Clonis stepped toward the house. Cafrec passed him a flashlight from his backpack.

Clonis examined it with an upturned nose. "What's this?"

Cafrec turned it on then swept his arm toward the doorframe, casting light into the doorway. "Flashlight. It'll be dark inside."

"Ooh!" Clonis's face lit up as he took it then moved it around, the light bouncing between his childhood home and those on either side, while walking through the threshold. The others followed, squeezing into the foyer which was a few feet wide and six feet long. A layer of dust and sand covered the floor and the five-foot-long bench against the wall.

Clonis pointed to the bench. "We put our shoes under there. They weren't good shoes, though. Lexum got those, so we made them from leftover scraps. Had to glue the soles on and they didn't stay glued long, see. We always got sand in them, so it was easier for us kids to run around with bare feet. Our parents didn't like it though because it made our feet and the floors even dirtier, see."

The house opened into a single room. Age had warped the wooden kitchen counter. It had a chipped white ceramic basin on one end along with an iron stove with two elements. It looked like a miniature version of the stoves in the Department of Food videos.

Clonis patted the basin, sending dust and sand into the air. "That was for washing."

Along the wall across from the counter and stove was a sand-covered table with two chairs on either end and a bench along each side. One bench hugged a wall so that only the person sitting on the end could get out. To the left was the woodstove—twice the size of the kitchen's stove—and the chimney.

The staircase and a door were in the back corner. Clonis opened the door which led to the backyard which contained a wooden building, three feet by three feet. Eight feet from the door was the next house.

"An outhouse—our bathroom," Clonis said.

Cafrec's jaw dropped. "You had to go outside?"

The inside of the house was bad enough. But going outside to do one's business in the dark and cold of night was cruel.

No wonder the lower class worshipped Tatem. Indoor bathrooms? Plumbing? Heat? It was life changing!

As they ascended the narrow, rickety staircase, everyone took great care of the occasional missing or broken steps. There were three bedrooms—one had a double bed, another three twin beds, and the last five twin beds. The bedframes were wooden slats with the remnants of thin mattresses on top covered in stains, dust, and sand. Each room had one to three wooden wardrobes.

"Boys in one room, girls in the other," Clonis said. "This was the boys' room."

To say it was the biggest room was a generous statement. At eight by eighteen feet with all five beds against one wall, there was little space to walk between them. Wardrobes on the opposite wall took up the remaining space.

Breel shuddered at the lack of privacy.

No wonder Tatem wanted out...

Clonis opened a wardrobe, sending more dust and sand into the air. He knelt, head disappearing as he bent into the wardrobe.

"These don't have bottoms," he said. "Made it easy for Hargam to hide his diary."

Moments later, he reappeared, a small book in hand.

In that moment, Breel realized she had her doubts about the diary's existence. But Clonis had been right, giving them an incredible find. Reading Tatem's innermost thoughts and feelings would provide a wealth of insight and information.

Clonis wiped dirt off the black cover as everyone crowded around him. He opened the book, revealing yellowed pages filled with small and tidy cursive writing.

Cafrec had already leaned in to read the first page. Breel and the others stepped closer to do the same.

"I'm sixteen today," Tatem wrote. "It's about time. Means there's one year until my scholarship. My parents and siblings don't seem to care about being poor and not having the same rights as those inside Lexum—but I do. I'm done with it."

Nothing of consequence in that. But what's the appeal of writing private thoughts which anyone could find and read?

"Is that what people do in a diary, talk about whatever they want?" Breel asked.

"Yep, that's about it," said Clonis.

He turned the page which had an entry written a few days later. "I hate Clonis more than usual. He tried getting me to deal with the woodstove, and I said no. He didn't listen. Well, I sure showed him. No one messes with me."

"Gee," said Cafrec, "what'd he do?"

Clonis shrugged. "Probably burned my arm. He was always burning us on the stove, see."

"And your parents didn't put a stop to it?" Manum asked.

"Didn't you listen? No, they didn't, because either they were working or Hargam said it was our fault, so they blamed the rest of us." He pushed back his right sleeve to show a two-inch-long scar between his elbow and wrist. "From him pushing me into the stove." Next, he lifted his shirt, revealing an even longer scar from below his ribcage to his waist. "He tripped me, then I fell into the stove."

He shared other scars including one on his other arm and another on his lower back. Tatem had also scarred the front of Clonis's right leg by whacking him with wood then trying to pierce him with it. Imagining Tatem threatening Clonis like so wasn't difficult.

Breel asked, "How much did he write in this?"

Clonis turned to the last entry which was a few pages before the end of the book. "Looks like wrote right until he left for school in Lexum."

Everyone leaned over him to read it. "I'm out of here!" Tatem had written. "All my plans have gotten me where I wanted. No one can say Hargam Tatem isn't ambitious. Just they wait and see…I'll leave this diary behind to avoid people in Lexum seeing it. But in case I need it later, I'll hide it where it's safe and hidden. After a few years, I'll return to destroy it."

Cafrec whistled. "Wow, he planned on becoming president for a long time."

Clonis snapped the diary shut. "Yep. All the time he'd say things like 'when I'm president…' as if that was supposed to scare us. But he did many of the things he said he'd do, see."

Manum's brow furrowed. "Are you saying he planned a civil war to become president?"

Clonis nodded.

If he was right, Tatem had ensured he got the scholarship to become a government official. Next, he got Lexum warring to destroy society, warranting new laws and making himself seem like the lower class's saviour.

The most worrying part was Tatem's track record for achieving his goals. If his vision to become Lexum's dictator happened as he wanted, it was a good precedent for him to replace the Nito Test with genetic engineering. If the diary had shown anything so far, it was that Tatem would stop at nothing to achieve his goals.

Everyone wanted to read more; however, returning home was important to avoid any potential last-minute searches. Cafrec placed it in a bag before putting it in his backpack then everyone followed Praxa downstairs, being careful to avoid the broken and missing steps. She peeked out of the doorway, looking both ways before jumping back into the house.

"There's something out there!" Her voice was shrill.

Breel's heart constricted. "DOE?"

Praxa raised her weapon, glanced outside for half a second, then moved back inside. "I dunno but I hear scratching from a few houses down. I don't think it's the wind moving something."

Breel's heart pounded like when she had walked into the first day of the Demna Exam.

If it's one of our own people, they would've told us...it must be the DOE. Thank goodness Praxa and Manum are here.

"Stay here," said Manum.

He nodded at Praxa. They raised their weapons then Praxa followed him outside.

Chapter Thirty-One

Breel's heart raced. Cafrec's and Clonis's laboured breathing was audible in the narrow entryway.

If it was the DOE making the scratching sound Praxa had heard, she and Manum would have to take them out. Then they'd have to wait for the officers to wake from the tranquilizers before escorting them back to the house. Once more, their DOE sources would need to plant evidence suggesting they captured the officers in a different area. It had worked once—so far—but twice was a stretch.

Dread filled Breel. Part of her wanted to flee out the backdoor but she couldn't abandon Cafrec and the others. She listened for a sign of what was happening but heard nothing over the wind rustling garbage on the street. Then out of nowhere came laughter.

No! The DOE's laughing while shooting them!

Cafrec shot Breel a quizzical look as Clonis stepped toward the doorway.

Breel's heart lurched. "No, wait!"

Too late. Clonis walked outside as if they weren't in a precarious situation. Then he, too, laughed.

"What the...?" said Cafrec, looking at Breel.

Standing on the road, Clonis waved them over. "Come out, it's okay."

Breel didn't move. But then Manum and Praxa also called them. Taking a deep breath, she took Cafrec's proffered hand.

Manum and Praxa stood two houses away, guns holstered, pointing to something a few feet ahead. A brown tail bobbed in the distance as its red four-legged owner trotted away, manoeuvring around the refuse.

"Just a fox," said Manum. "Harmless."

They'd learned in school that foxes then kill people—but it was more lies so no one would leave Lexum.

What a scare over nothing.

Clonis grinned. "I miss fox!"

"What'd you mean?" Breel asked.

He licked his lips. "Yum!"

Breel gagged. "That cute little animal?"

"Yep. Plenty of foxes, at least until I got older. Free meat, see."

It was hard to judge someone for doing what they needed to survive.

If I lived like that, I'm sure I'd try fox, too.

There was a lightness to Breel's steps as they meandered through the street. The DOE hadn't found them, and they got Tatem's diary. If anything held his secrets, it'd be this book.

Cafrec, in front of Breel, navigated around broken glass. "Clonis, how'd you find his diary?"

Clonis navigated a pile of bricks sticking out of the sand. "I saw him writing on his bed once, and he closed it the moment he saw me. I knew it wasn't schoolwork because he always did that at the table, and I'd never seen the diary, see. One day, when he was at school and our siblings were running around, I spent all day searching for it. I read it every week until he left. The few times he visited I checked if he had taken it, but he never did. I think he forgot it was there."

Probably far too busy studying and learning how to live in Lexum while contemplating overtaking the city.

"Did everyone have a diary?" Cafrec asked.

Clonis's weight shifted as they avoided broken shingles. "Nah. Some did but most couldn't afford to waste the paper, see. Hargam was supposed to use that book for school."

Breel shielded her eyes as the sun peeked at them from between the buildings. "I don't understand why he had a diary when others could find it."

"He may have found it easier to keep track of his thoughts or work things out," said Cafrec. "It seems he had a lot swirling around his head—hatred for his life, working hard in school, planning the future."

Cafrec's been thinking about this a lot.

It could be plain curiosity that kept Cafrec asking questions and thinking about Tatem's reasons, or it was wanting to know more to convince himself he wasn't Tatem. Yes, Cafrec had a deep-seated desire to learn as much about Tatem so much so that he walked with and talked to Clonis on the way back. The others followed within earshot.

"Thanks for not getting annoyed at my questions," Cafrec said after Clonis described how Tatem once threw out food to punish his siblings.

Clonis clapped Cafrec's back, causing Cafrec to stumble over the sand. Breel steadied him.

"Of course!" said Clonis. "It's nice talking to people anytime I want again. I was wary at first, but you all seem okay. You hate my brother, at least, and that makes you fine by me."

Manum, walking with Praxa, joined the conversation as the suburbs disappeared behind them. "We're all grateful. No sense in wasting an opportunity to learn more about our enemy. I, too, have questions, though Cafrec's covered many of them, and I hope the diary can answer the others."

Clonis gestured to the open desert. "We got the time. Ask away."

Breel squeezed Cafrec's hand when her foot slipped on some loose sand.

Manum said, "After the civil war, when did you and your siblings start questioning his motives?"

Clonis stepped over a fern. "We always knew, but we ignored it because he was doing good things, see. We couldn't ignore it once he started executing citizens though."

Manum frowned. "You're saying you were okay with him forcing people to change jobs, staying president after promising to reinstate a council, and barring freedom of speech?"

"No, we did. But he made it seem like they were the only options."

He manipulated them well. Choose me to get everything you need...or choose someone from the upper class and continue being mistreated. But if his siblings stopped him early, how many lives would they have saved? How different would Lexum be now?

If Clonis and his siblings had stopped Tatem, everyone could be living with choice and freedom of speech without Mortae and draconian laws. Because they didn't, Breel and the others had to do everything they could to make it their future.

Chapter Thirty-Two

It was a good thing that they only had one mile to walk, as Clonis's pace slowed. He even slipped on sand a few times, prompting Manum to walk by his side. On any other day, Breel would welcome the walk instead of staring at a screen, but today the quicker the walk, the faster they'd read the diary.

Cafrec's questions slowed Clonis further; however, nobody told him to stop since they, too, wanted to know the answers.

"How'd you handle being in that room for all those years?" Manum asked when there was a lull with Cafrec's questions.

Clonis shrugged. "Hard at first, but like I said, Hargam visited me a lot. And Xorem and a few others. Hargam and I played checkers. I watched a lot of television."

Breel searched her memory for the word "checkers," but nothing came to mind.

"It's a game," Clonis said when she asked. "You play on this board with pieces and—oh, never mind."

Breel had only ever played games in secret with Famut and Trafis. Her heart fell knowing that Clonis had played games with boards and pieces...whatever that meant.

"So Tatem and you could play games but not us," Cafrec said.

"He just played with me," Clonis said, as if that made it better. "He was good at it. Always beat me, but that was okay. He was always the thinker, like I said. But yeah, it got lonely. And I was sad about my parents and other siblings."

Cafrec scoffed. "Why'd you keep seeing Tatem after what he did to them?"

Clonis laughed, tossing his head back. "Like I had a choice!"

Whispers of darkness sat on the horizon when they arrived back at the safe house. The smell of spices from Criba and Lexo heating supper was a pleasant welcome.

Criba removed a plate from the microwave. "Oh, thank goodness you're all safe!"

Samit spun his desk chair around as Vectus and Trafis walked into the kitchen. "Well?" Samit asked.

"We got the diary," said Cafrec.

There were cheers, and everyone also expressed their relief. The group sat at the table then they recounted their journey, including the scare with the fox.

Trafis leaned forward, staring at the diary on the table in front of Cafrec. "Anything good in it?"

"We only read a few entries," said Clonis.

Cafrec looked from Clonis to Samit. "I could read more right now."

Samit nodded. "Fine. But be careful as that's an old book."

Cafrec grinned at Breel then invited her to join him in the living room. They sat on the couch, her arm around him, as he turned to the third entry.

Tatem wrote, "Clonis complained to our parents about his arm hurting from the burn. They told him to not be such a wimp—ha. We had a math test today. When I studied last night, Clonis asked what letters are doing in math. He's such an idiot."

Wow, he was egotistical even back then.

"Doesn't sound as if he likes his brother," Cafrec said.

Breel nodded. "I get the sense he didn't like much of anyone."

Subsequent entries were similar with stories about how he wronged his siblings, calling everyone names including parents, siblings, neighbours, and teachers. He also made frequent comments about how much better he is than everyone else.

The diary suggested Tatem had conflicting feelings about his parents, often in the same entry, such as, "Father came home after midnight. Not sure why the man works so hard for next to nothing, but I commend him for working harder than most. He scolded me for being awake, saying sleep is more important than studying. I told him he knows nothing about studying. Got the strap for that comment. I told Mother about it before she left for work, and she railed on him. Good! But she said all my studying's a waste of time since only one student gets a scholarship. She doesn't understand how important it is to me, nor how I'm guaranteed to get it."

Guaranteed to get it...

"This diary gets scarier and scarier," Cafrec said as Breel shuddered.

They agreed that Tatem saying he was "guaranteed" to get the scholarship was proof that he planned on killing the top student months before doing it. Adult Tatem gave her the creeps and based on what they'd read so far, he gave off the same bad vibes back then, too.

Tatem continued. "It's ridiculous that only one student gets a scholarship to continue school. Education should be free, giving everyone the same opportunities no matter where they come from. No one should grow up wondering whether they'll have enough to eat. But the world isn't that way which is why I need this scholarship."

Cafrec's jaw dropped as he read it. "This is what he ended up doing!"

The hardest part about reading his vision was agreeing with it. At age sixteen or seventeen, Tatem had described his ideal world. Within a few years, he changed Lexum to be how he'd envisioned.

Cafrec flipped the page.

"After our math test," Tatem wrote, "Prima still has the highest mark in the class and most other classes. The teachers talk as if she'll be getting the scholarship. No, she won't. Her average is only two percent higher than mine. I won't be stuck working in a factory because of two percent. Part of me hoped I wouldn't have to do this, but picturing myself doing it makes my fingers prickle with excitement. I'm thrilled that—"

Cafrec shut the diary before Breel could finish reading.

"Oh man," he groaned, tossing the diary onto a couch cushion. "I can't believe he looked forward to"—Cafrec swallowed hard—"killing somebody."

If the first few pages were that bad, the rest leading up to the murder would be worse.

Chapter Thirty-Three

Breel and Cafrec sat in silence digesting that teenage Tatem hadn't only planned to commit murder but had looked forward to it.

Cafrec leaned forward, head in his hands. "He's a sick, sick person."

Breel put an arm around him, drawing him closer. "Yeah. Do you want me to read it and let you know about anything important?"

Cafrec sat back against the couch then turned to Breel. His face had turned a light shade of green. "Yeah, it's best if I don't read it."

Breel kissed him then whispered, "You're not Tatem. You're you."

"I know."

Criba announced that supper was ready, so they made their way into the dining room as Lexo placed a platter of mixed vegetables on the table. His eyes brightened when he saw them walk in. "Anything interesting?"

Cafrec slumped into his chair. "He talked about wishing Lexum had the things he eventually changed such as free schooling and food for everyone. But he's sick in the head."

As all eyes landed on Breel, she nodded in agreement. "The entries we've read are disturbing."

That surprised nobody but Samit declared the details would have to wait until their meeting.

***

They congregated in front of the television after supper. Beside Breel, Cafrec tapped his foot and squeezed her hand. Clonis stood in the corner, finger to his lip, as they listened to the reporter drone on.

"Today's biggest event was when five rebellious Leaders of Tomorrow stormed the Governmental Offices to attack President Tatem leaving the building. You'll be relieved to hear our dear president is alive and well."

Cafrec rolled his eyes. "What a relief!"

Tatem came on the screen a few minutes later. A grave expression with downcast eyes replaced his usual smile.

"Citizens, it is a sorrowful day. Someone brainwashed five Leaders of Tomorrow into thinking attacking me is okay. They are no longer with us, thanks to my security. What has Lexum come to?" He shook his head, tsking. "This doesn't just affect them but also their parents who grieve for their corrupted children. But, to these parents, you deserve this because the fault lies with you. It is your duty to keep your children in line which means when they do not embrace the collective, you fail society. These Leaders of Tomorrow were to become fruitful Leaders of Today who pay back Lexum tenfold for all the education and support given to them. But because you could not parent them, it was all for nothing."

He paused. Before the failed Mortae of Breel and others, Tatem had never broadcasted such incidents. But after their escape, making an example of anyone following in their rebellious footsteps was commonplace.

Tatem sighed. "I have thought long and hard about the best course of action. If citizens think attacking their well-protected leader is okay, what stops them from attacking anyone else? We do not want to live in fear that rebellious people could maul us when we walk out our front door. That is not the Lexum I want, and I know it is not the Lexum you want.

These attacks must end, but it seems our current laws are not enough to prevent them."

Here we go again.

Breel's nails dug into her leg. No one made a sound as they awaited the grand reveal of what inane law Tatem would mandate next.

Tatem sipped his water then ran his hand over his hair. "As of today, I have enacted a new law." His eyes lit up; the fake sombreness gone. "If a Leader of Tomorrow engages in illegal acts, both they and their parents will be punished with Mortae."

Clonis's jaw dropped. "Whoa."

Nobody else reacted. Not only had Tatem already threatened this, but it was a miracle he had waited this long to do it.

Tatem continued. "Right now, the parents of these rebellious Leaders of Tomorrow have two DOE officers knocking at their door, demanding entry. All ten will have their Mortae tomorrow afternoon in punishment for their children's deeds."

He paused, the corner of his mouth twitching while attempting to maintain a sad expression.

Tatem touched his hair. "Make no mistake, citizens. If a child living in your house disregards any law, we will punish them and you regardless of Career Group. It is irrelevant if they are otherwise a perfect child in your eyes. You are biased. Someone breaking a law is not thinking about society or embracing the collective. We do not tolerate such selfishness."

Breel gulped as she ignored the sidelong glance from Trafis.

This was me mere weeks ago.

Her drawing would've sentenced herself and her parents to Mortae. They'd have died after years of warning her about drawing's dangers and urging her to follow the law. Her acts would've sent Trafis to live among other orphans until he passed the Demna Exam. Breel tried not to think about it.

Tatem said, "Some of you will think this law is too harsh, that Leaders of Tomorrow should still have warnings, and their actions should not affect their parents. But your children reflect you, and if you are not raising them to embrace the collective, then you, too, deserve punishment."

The new law would cause hundreds of citizens to be killed by Mortae. Innocent Leaders of Tomorrow disobeying their parents or talking to Leaders of Tomorrow in a different Career Group and class would make them and their parents become Vucapi.

Tatem pointed at the camera. "I will meet any disagreement on this or any other law with Mortae. If any citizen speaks out against our ways, against the collective, we will recognize them as a rebel. You either agree with us or are one of them. If you are on their side, we will find you.

"Citizens, we live in a critical period. Speak to your children to ensure they understand our ways are the only ways. You know the consequences if they do not fall in line. Until tomorrow, good night."

Samit turned off the television.

"Yikes," said Manum. "This is terrifying."

As Breel stared into the abyss of the blank screen, her thoughts drifted to her father.

Is he glad I'm gone so he and Mother aren't in danger because of my drawing?

It wasn't an answer she cared to think about.

"It's a sad day for Lexum," Criba said.

The number of deaths would increase. Tatem had said Career Group didn't matter despite there being a delicate balance of Career Group supply and demand. As Tatem killed more people, it would create a desperate need for certain Career Groups.

Databases without a computer programmer to maintain them.

Classes without a qualified teacher to teach.

Farms without farmers to plant, tend to, and harvest food.

Doesn't Tatem realize he's creating a huge spaghetti code mess that even the best of programmers would have difficulty figuring out?

Samit stood, placed the remote on the television stand, then returned to his seat with a groan. "I'm not surprised."

"I don't think any of us are," said Criba. "But you don't have to be surprised to be sad."

Samit nodded. "True. More reason to overthrow the sleazeball."

Breel forced a laugh. "Sleazeball? That's tame for Tatem."

Cafrec nodded. "You mean psychopathic monster."

"Bang on," said Criba.

Clonis bit his lower lip. "My television didn't have the news. I don't think he wanted me to watch this stuff."

Breel frowned. "But what did you watch, then?"

"Old shows."

Old what now?

Clonis laughed. "Right, right. A show, like...people pretended to live different lives, and videoed it for people to watch, see."

"Yes, I remember my grandparents talking about television shows," said Vectus. "People watched them for entertainment."

Then, fifty years ago, Tatem outlawed television shows, games, hobbies, and anything else that didn't "contribute" to society. All out of his desperation to have the "perfect" society.

Clonis nodded. "Yep. At least, the upper class did. Not us, see. But he let me watch them."

It was yet another advantage Clonis had had over everyone else. A wave of jealousy washed over Breel. Watching people pretend stuff for entertainment sounded weird, but it would've been a welcomed break from studying all day long.

Chapter Thirty-Four

The group returned to the dining room to discuss Tatem's speech around the table.

Samit tapped the table. "We must impress upon our sources the importance of being careful. For some, it may be better that they pause doing things for us so they can stay safe."

"I disagree," said Manum.

Oh, here we go.

Samit would argue back as if his opinion was the only one that mattered. Instead of a civil conversation, Manum would quip back. At some point, Vectus would break them up.

But that's not what happened. Instead, Samit invited Manum to explain. If something had happened for them to be civil to each other, they hadn't told the others.

Manum said, "They all agreed to be on our side. We pass along tips and wisdom for being careful but advising they stop assisting us is counterintuitive."

Samit sighed. "And having our people die isn't counterintuitive? They can lie low until the anniversary party. I thought you of all people would agree with me, Manum. We don't need more deaths."

Criba cocked her head, confused. For once, Samit wasn't being insensitive but both he and Manum had valid points.

"Obviously, you're right," said Manum. "But my people didn't die just for us to tell everyone, 'Oh, it's a little more dangerous now, so stop what you're doing.' No, we need everyone to do their part."

And your son...?

But Breel didn't dare mention Mr. Gaimster. Desperate to prevent an escalation, she said, "Samit, I agree to an extent. But isn't it for our people to decide? If they feel it's too risky, they stop; otherwise, they keep going. Because I also agree with Manum that it's always been dangerous and there'll be more dangers to come. We can't tell everyone to back out now because things got riskier."

Samit agreed as did Manum after a moment of reflection. Besides, it was up to everyone to decide what they felt comfortable doing.

"Onto the topic of the evening," said Samit. "Tatem's diary."

Breel and Cafrec outlined his childhood exploits bullying the other kids, and his general thoughts on their way of life and what he wished it was like. Samit asked Trafis to finish reading it and mark any important passages to report them during meetings.

Trafis smiled and straightened his posture. "Me?"

"You were in the English Teacher Career Group, so it seems most suitable for you." He handed Trafis the diary, who took it as if it'd break from the lightest touch.

Bet this is the first time he's happy about his Career Group.

"Onto our second topic," said Samit. "Destroying his image. We brainstormed ideas while you retrieved the diary. In fact, some of us have been doing that for a few days."

Samit said Vectus had wondered if they could distribute pamphlets to everyone through meal deliveries, but they didn't have a food packer on their side. However, Lexo had an anti-Tatem childhood friend in the Department of Expansion who said they had another source whose job involved preparing curriculum materials for continuing education courses then sending them to package preparers. This put them in a prime position to add the pamphlets.

The source said they'd put the pamphlets behind the front cover of the books so only the recipient would see them. It'd take a while to determine whether the book printer, package preparer, or warehouse stocker had added the pamphlets.

Including pamphlets in Department of Expansion deliveries wouldn't cover every Leader of Today; however, enough would receive them over time to spread the word about the strange, anti-Tatem materials. It didn't include Leaders of Tomorrow, but it was a start.

Best of all, sending the pamphlets with educational materials meant people would assume they're official documents. Recipients would retrieve the box of Department of Expansion course materials from their doorstep then open it, their eyes popping at the sheer amount of coursework. Seeing Duknum's thick computer programmer coursebooks had made Breel cringe. Years ago, she'd flipped through one. The text was smaller and denser than her schoolbooks yet still over one thousand pages.

After seeing the amount of work ahead of them, citizens would notice the pamphlet with Breel's drawing of Tatem on the front.

A thrill raced through her. They'd be sending her work for citizens to see. Her lifelong dream was about to happen even before overthrowing Tatem.

"You look excited."

It took a moment to realize Samit was talking to her. "Yeah," she said. "We're sending my drawings to hundreds, perhaps thousands, of people!"

Criba reached across the table to pat her hand. "Both our dreams will come true."

Samit said once Breel and Criba finished the pamphlets, they'd email them to a contact with printer access. A DOE officer would hand deliver them to their Department of Expansion contact who'd slip one inside each textbook before sending them to the package preparers.

"So? Thoughts on the plan?" Samit asked.

Breel loved it. Not only did it lessen the risk for any one person it meant that people would see her work. Her drawings were for a noble cause, helping others see their perspective and, perhaps, become anti-Tatem.

"It's a great start," said Manum.

Samit blinked in surprise.

Cafrec raised his arms. "It's a miracle!" Then, serious, he said, "I can't wait to see what the pamphlets look like."

Samit tapped the table. "This is top priority. Criba will write the content then Breel will draw something that matches. Breel, we also want to proceed with your poster idea. The picture you've already drawn will be great for one, but we want more."

"Such as?" Breel asked.

Lexo answered. "Some can poke fun at Tatem, and others can show our views. We're thinking at least half a dozen variations distributed at different times to keep them fresh."

"Ah," said Breel. "Unlike the posters in school?"

They only changed at the start of each school year.

"Exactly," said Criba. "Variety means people will pay more attention."

The moment Samit adjourned the meeting, Breel was on her feet. But remembering the diary, she thought she better speak with Trafis before drawing. She followed him and Criba into the living room. Trafis sat on the couch with his knees bent and feet on the cushion beside him, then placed the diary on his legs.

Noticing Breel, his smile widened. "This is my first task that makes me feel as useful as everyone else!"

"You're reading the emails to get important information."

Trafis scoffed. "Yeah, but anyone can do that. You, Cafrec, Vectus, and Samit have your programming skills, Lexo and Praxa are ex-DOE, Manum has lots of connections. It's about time that Mother and I are the best people to do a job."

"He gave you and Mother the emails because you both took advanced language classes."

Trafis didn't look convinced. "Well, whatever, but I'm glad for a break. Can't wait to read this, so go away."

Breel laughed to herself. Before she could get to the basement stairs, Cafrec called her name from the front door. His shoes were on. "Walk, Breel? I've already checked with Manum, and it's safe."

At night? Something's up.

She'd rather draw than walk, but Cafrec had done a lot for her, so she wanted to be there for him, too. So, she put on her shoes, took the gun Cafrec offered, then walked outside.

The moon and the stars provided decent lighting. Since Manum had asked Cafrec to stay close to the house, they headed a few hundred feet away. Breel admired the twinkling stars.

Cafrec wrapped his arms around her, hugging her from behind. "Isn't this romantic?"

She nodded, expecting him to kiss her, but he rested his head on her shoulder.

"Can't believe we got that diary," he said. "Breel?"

His tone suggested a serious question coming. When Breel first met him, Cafrec had rarely been serious. But their situation had changed that.

"When you look at me, do you see Tatem?"

"Oh." It wasn't an unexpected question.

Breel hesitated because when she looked at him, she *did* see Tatem.

"Personality, I mean," said Cafrec. "I know about my stupid eyes and hair."

Phew.

Breel faced him. His eyebrows knit together in concern. "Cafrec, no. I don't. You're different—even your eyes."

His expression relaxed. "What d'you mean?"

It took a moment to find the right words. "His eyes are soulless. Yours are full of heart."

Cafrec's breathing changed, slowing. "You think so?"

"Oh yeah. I know so. Trust me. You're not him. And if you were? I wouldn't be with you. I love you. You're not Tatem. I'm glad you're with me because it's made everything from starting as a Leader of Today to now more bearable. Though I miss the more jokey Cafrec. You told jokes *all* the time."

"Well, I still joke sometimes. But yeah…I guess because I'm worried about being like Tatem, I'm back to my old self. Except when I make fun of him, I suppose."

Breel released him, keeping her hands on his arms. Cafrec avoided her eye.

"Old self?" she asked.

He took interest in the wind blowing grains of sand across a rock. "My parents didn't appreciate humour, so I kept it inside. I started showing my true self after moving out." His eyes met hers, causing her stomach to flip then flop. "It wasn't until I met a certain person that I had someone I could be myself around."

"Who was that?"

He raised an eyebrow.

Oh! Me. I'm the person he can be himself with.

Breel grinned. "I feel the same about you."

Chapter Thirty-Five

Breel was in her element. When drawing, every hour that passed felt like a minute instead of the two or three hours it often felt like when coding. It was the way she'd always wanted drawing to be—peaceful without worrying about someone catching her.

Cafrec moved his chair beside hers then kissed her cheek. "This is the happiest I've seen you yet!"

He was in a playful mood, but all Breel wanted to do was draw.

Cafrec looked at what she was doing. "This looks amazing, Breel!"

He's too kind.

She'd drawn a rough sketch of a closeup of the Quaddro's platform. There'd be heads in the foreground chanting during Mortae. Tatem would stand on the platform, running his hand over his hair with the text "Nothing can come between me and my hair!" underneath.

When Breel admitted she didn't have the talent for generating ideas, Cafrec told her to use her imagination. But she didn't have one. After all, there was a reason she only ever drew what she saw. So, the drawing had been Cafrec's idea, of course. He took to devising ideas for comical drawings like Samit bragged he took to hacking.

I hope that changes after Tatem.

***

The next morning, Breel hopped out of bed. After getting ready for the day, she sat on the couch, angled toward the hallway to watch when Trafis emerged from the basement as, having gone to bed before her, she'd yet to speak to him since he began reading the diary.

I don't understand why he went to bed early with Tatem's diary to read. If I had the diary, I'd have stayed up reading! Who wouldn't want to intrude on the privacy of a man who's caused so much death, grief, trauma, and oppression?

"Hey, Trafis," she called when he appeared in his pyjamas five minutes later.

He turned, blinked to focus his blurry eyes, then yawned. "Breel, what is it?"

"You finished the diary?"

He sauntered into the room then sat beside Breel. "Not all of it." Another yawn.

"Well then...?"

"Well then what? I'm not allowed to sleep? I went to bed late reading some of it as it is."

He left without another word.

How could he have only read some of it? Why's it not important to him?

Then it hit her. It *was* important to Trafis—just not *as* important. He didn't have the ulterior motive of learning more about Cafrec's biological father. For him, it was only learning about Tatem the psychopathic monster. Breel and Cafrec would have to be patient.

***

Once everyone finished their pancakes, Samit stood. "Trafis, what'd you find?"

Trafis had the diary on the table beside him with strips of paper, words scrawled on them, marking pages.

He patted the book. "I'm three-quarters through and found some interesting things. He talked a lot about a girl named Prima. The one you mentioned, Clonis."

"Oh yes, she was top of his class," Clonis said. "Mysteriously disappeared days before the scholarship winner announcement. But I wasn't fooled. I knew it wasn't a mystery."

Trafis picked up the diary. "Tatem said a lot about her. He was obsessed."

"How'd you mean?" Samit asked.

Trafis thumbed through a few page markers before finding the one he wanted then read, "'My competition stayed inside the classroom to work when the other students went outside, so I did the same. I asked her stupid questions about school and her family which I've heard others ask, but she ignored me. No problem. I can get around that.'"

Prima was yet another person Tatem wanted to manipulate to achieve his goals.

"He talks about gaining her trust," Trafis said, "then his plans for getting her interested in seeing inside Lexum. One day, he says he'll show her Lexum tomorrow, then never mentions Prima again. A few weeks later, he got the scholarship."

He killed her. He led her somewhere to kill her.

"That's not all," Trafis said.

Samit nodded while examining his pen. "Good."

Samit's bored? Doesn't he realize this is proof that Tatem killed the top student?

Trafis turned to another page. "Here's something from a few months earlier: 'My parents are suddenly interested in all my siblings attending school. None want to go. Father said it's either school or quitting school to work in the factory, so they all pretended to attend school. I told our parents, since if my siblings worked, we'd have more money. I stifled my laughter with a pillow as Father punished them. But Mother stepped in, convincing Father not to let them work since the factory is dangerous and schooling is pointless since they'll work in the factory if they go to school or not. When Father tried to get them to work harder for the scholarship, none of them cared. What a bunch of slackers, not caring to better themselves or their situation. Mother and Father seem to think I'll support the whole family once I'm working in Lexum. Nope! Not even if I didn't have big plans.'"

Tatem's parents had seen him, and later their other children, as the ticket out of poverty. But only Tatem had cared about rising to the top. If he hadn't stirred up a civil war, life would've continued as it always had. Instead, not long after, he was president, Clonis isolated, and the rest of the family dead.

Samit frowned. "That doesn't tell us anything new. Any weakness or something we can use against him?"

Trafis nodded. "Oh, yes." He looked through the slips of paper, turned to a page near the beginning, then read, "'There were embers in the woodstove when I returned from school. Of course, my siblings were playing in the forest. I hauled Clonis back to rekindle the fire. I've seen what fire can do, so I'm not touching that thing. Bad enough that we need a constant fire in the house.'"

"He's afraid of fire?" Breel asked.

"Sounds like it," said Cafrec.

Whether they could use this weakness against Tatem remained to be seen; however, everyone agreed that knowing Tatem feared something was helpful.

Samit thought for a moment. "That's good, Trafis. Anything else about fire?"

He turned to another marked page. "A couple of months later, before murdering Prima, he wrote, 'One section of houses two streets over burned in the night because a kid played with the woodstove. Three families burned to death (good riddance) and four more will be lucky to survive.' He talks about it more the next day. 'I couldn't sleep because of dreams about the fire burning my family while I stood by and laughed. Then it burned *me* as *they* laughed. Because of the dreams, Prima did better on today's test. Other fires better not ruin my chances at the scholarship.'"

Trafis closed the diary with a snap and satisfied smile.

"It's natural to be afraid of fire," Manum said. "He could be talking about a normal fear that's a little heightened because of a few childhood incidents."

Having a natural fear of fire was news to Breel but that's because she only knew about it from a video. Manum knew about fire from his parents who'd been around before Tatem came into power. But most citizens had never seen fire, so had no reason to fear it. However, given how it destroyed homes and killed people, Tatem's fear didn't sound unreasonable.

Clonis stroked his beard. "Uh, no, I'd say Hargam fears fire more than others. He was the only person I knew who refused to use the woodstove, always having some excuse, see. 'I'm wearing clean clothes' or 'I threw out my back so can't carry wood inside' or 'I'm busy with schoolwork.' Hearing about burning houses or factories always made him real quiet."

Tatem had refused to touch the woodstove and had such terrible nightmares about being burned that Prima did better than him on a test.

Based on that, everyone agreed that this was a weakness. The next step was determining how to exploit it.

While hearing from the diary had been fascinating, even more thrilling for Breel was sharing her drawings. Though some—Samit—thought showing Tatem loving his hair to be too much, the others agreed to using it. Breel showed her other drawing which, again, had been Cafrec's idea. In it, Tatem stood with his hand resting on a large, waist-high bottle labelled "Hair Gel."

Trafis laughed. "I bet that's the size of bottle he'd need each week! I wonder why hair gel isn't available to everyone?"

"Isn't it obvious?" Cafrec asked. "He uses so much we'd never produce enough for everyone!" He ran a hand over his hair then covered his mouth in mock fear. "Citizens! It's a terrible day...we've run out of hair gel! The horror is real!"

Samit rolled his eyes. "Yes, it'd be a real travesty."

Breel turned to Clonis. "Why does he use it, anyway?"

Clonis tapped his lip as he thought. "I bet it's because when we were kids, we only had one brush. The bristles were hard as rocks, so we didn't brush our hair, see. When he got that scholarship, he was desperate to look different."

It was more evidence that Tatem wanted to maintain a certain image.

Samit clapped Breel's shoulder. "Great job, you two. But we can stop with the hair jokes."

Cafrec shrugged. "Yeah, okay. We'll get more serious."

"And how are the pamphlets coming along?" Samit asked Criba.

Criba said she'd email everyone some drafts before lunch. Breel couldn't wait to read her writing—and seeing Tatem's reaction to the resulting posters and pamphlets. She and Criba were achieving their dreams while fighting against Tatem which was more than Breel could've ever asked for.

Chapter Thirty-Six

The anniversary was one week away. Their prisoners hadn't caused further issues even when escorted to the bathroom, and their DOE searches remained far away. The days blurred together, broken up by target practice and getting supplies. In that regard, it wasn't much different from living in Lexum as a student sitting in class or studying every day.

Not eating? Time to study.

Not watching the news? You must study.

Morning exercises done? Study time.

Sick? If you can walk, you're well enough to study.

Working—which Breel had only done for a couple of weeks—had been no different.

However, there was one key difference outside Tatem's grasp which made all the difference—everyone was doing this because they wanted to, not because the government mandated it. There was no surveillance spying on their every action and word, so, by Lexum's standards, they were free to do pretty much anything.

Best of all was drawing for their cause. Cafrec loved it, too, as it meant taking on many of Breel's database duties and decreasing his computer security involvement. However, he still did some of that work which meant that Samit often popped by to give him more tasks.

"How'd you get into hacking?" Cafrec asked after Samit gave him yet another task list.

Samit leaned against the far wall before answering. "I got permission to take hacking courses through the Department of Expansion."

Weird. Why would Tatem want *citizens with hacking skills?*

She voiced her thoughts.

Samit shrugged. "Yeah, it's a risk. Apparently, there were some citizens who figured out how to do it, and Tatem wanted people trained to catch them. I needed special permission from my head and director. They did a huge background search on me, taking longer than normal because of my relationship with Famut. When he left for Intercludae, either Tatem trusted me enough or forgot I knew him as the DOE didn't question me. A few times, Tatem himself ordered me to investigate hackers he was concerned about—to hack the hackers so to speak. Sanctus wanted part of it but Tatem denied him. He was jealous because he wanted something different from coding software for the Department of Health, but he's the only programmer able to do a specific task. I don't know details, of course."

It sounded like what Criba said about Duknum's relationship with Famut. Like Samit, Famut had gotten all the fame and glory, leaving Duknum jealous.

"There had been talk of waiting a few years to send you both to Intercludae after you learned how to hack," said Samit. "But taking Department of Expansion courses requiring high-level permission needs a perfect record."

Breel and Cafrec grinned at each other. They'd both had two warnings.

Samit tsked. "It's a serious thing, guys."

He was right. However, having no warnings was rare. Breel tried not to think about the current Leaders of Tomorrow who no longer had a warning cushion.

Samit removed himself from the wall then was halfway out the door when Cafrec asked how he managed to receive no warnings.

Samit sighed then returned to the wall, scratching his bald head. "I was never a troublemaker. I wanted to work on my computer all day so found it easy to walk away when Famut and Sanctus suggested doing things I didn't want to do. Famut was always living on the border between legal and illegal. I remember one evening he was up to his shenanigans instead of schoolwork. The next day, he talked our teacher into letting him finish his work over lunch. No warning."

Cafrec's eyes widened. "Wow, that's some skill."

Was it ever.

Not doing one's work or doing it poorly were common reasons for teachers to report a student to the DOE. The rare time in which Breel had witnessed someone trying to convince a teacher not to got them into deeper trouble. If it was bad enough, they'd receive a rare double warning.

"I remember your father a bit, Breel," said Samit. "Younger than me. Even though he adored Famut, there was animosity. He'd always follow Famut, Sanctus, and me on our walk home from school. Famut didn't want him tagging along, but he never said no. Your father liked Sanctus, but Sanctus ignored him as he was an annoying kid. Always chattering away."

Breel laughed. It was impossible to picture her father, Mr. Serious, as an "annoying kid" and "chattering away." Other than Clonis, the only person Breel had known who'd talked a lot was Ragula—her Intercludae roommate for the few nights Breel had been there. Ragula had talked and talked as if she didn't need to breathe, but had made Breel feel comfortable and at home. Unlike Clonis and Ragula, her father must've grown out of the habit.

When Samit left, Breel returned to her newest drawing in which Tatem stood on the Quaddro's platform, grinning at a small body lying at an unnatural angle on the ground. In the Platinum section, a man and woman cried in each other's arms. Below them were the words "Is this a man who cares about Lexum's citizens?"

The poster would resonate with many as most citizens had witnessed the Mortae of at least one family member. Only the most cold-hearted would say they were happy that Tatem had them killed for disobeying the law. Even the biggest Hargamites would have to feel at least a twinge of anger.

Or am I naive?

Tatem had indoctrinated everyone to believe Mortae solved disobedience. Some families tried rescuing the Vucapi during their Mortae, but they never succeeded as the DOE always guarded family members. But both Lexo's and Praxa's stories had showed some citizens were so pro-Tatem even the death of a loved one didn't faze them. During the Mortae, they stood like inanimate objects—unmoving, unemotional, and unaffected. The worse were those who chanted and shouted more than anyone else, relishing the death of their family member for breaking the law.

No, there were Hargamites for whom the poster wouldn't resonate, and they'd scoff at the crying parents on the poster. But they weren't the poster's target group. They wanted to show them to the majority—those citizens who weren't anti-Tatem yet didn't agree with all his laws and decisions. The posters and pamphlets may convince them to choose their side.

Chapter Thirty-Seven

The next morning at breakfast, a loud knock on the door reverberated throughout the house. Breel's heart rate skyrocketed, pounding as if she'd ran for hours. Her fork fell onto her plate with a clatter. Everyone exchanged wide-eyed glances as they sat frozen. It was only when Cafrec squeezed Breel's leg that she could move. She raised a shaky hand to place it on his own.

Whoever was at the door was right there, on the other side of the wall. If the mystery person or persons barged in then started shooting, Breel and the others had nowhere to go and no way to protect themselves.

Criba, a hand clutched to her chest, was the first to find her voice. "Should...should we see who's at the door?"

Manum was already on his feet. Breel didn't dare make a noise as he walked behind her to peek through the blinds.

"Oh!" he said.

It was an "Oh!" of surprise followed by a second "Oh!" of delight. Smiling, he hurried to the door.

"Get back here!" Samit hissed.

But Manum ignored him. Breel's breath hitched as Manum reached for the doorknob. Even Lexo leapt to his feet, but Manum opened the door before Lexo could stop him.

Samit smacked his hand on the table. "You fool!"

"Come in," said Manum, a grin plastered on his face.

Breel gasped when Ragula entered wearing the short-sleeved desert-coloured Intercludae uniform Breel had last seen her in.

Manum hugged her, getting sand on himself. "Isn't this great?! She's ex-DOE from Intercludae, everyone! I mentored her!"

I don't like this...I'm glad she didn't die in the tunnel attack, but how'd she survive? How'd she find us? Why now?

Breel was happy to see Ragula alive, but it made no sense. The others seemed to be thinking the same thing. Lexo sat back in his seat, brow knitted with worry as he stared at Manum and Ragula. Samit frowned as Criba and Trafis exchanged confused looks.

Manum's face fell. "You're not happy? How could you not be?"

He drew Ragula close, an arm around her.

Ragula took in the room. Seeing Breel, her eyes lit up. "Breel! I'm so happy you're okay."

"Me, too! We thought you died."

Samit cleared his throat. "It's been a month."

Manum waved a dismissive hand, insisting Ragula would have a good explanation.

"I sure hope so," said Samit, crossing his arms.

Manum retrieved a chair from the closet near the door then placed it between him and Praxa.

"Have a seat, Ragula. Tell us what happened."

Ragula ran her hands through her short, brown hair before sitting. "I think that's all the sand out of there. Thanks, Mr. Gaimster. Boy, do I have a lot to tell."

"Take your time." Manum grinned, unable to take his eyes off her.

Ragula smiled her thanks then shifted her weight in the chair. A ripped vest pocket flapped as she moved. "It started when Tatem attacked us in the tunnel. Being one of the last in the procession, I managed to flee to Intercludae. Knowing the DOE would raid it, I hid in that warehouse with all those old items."

It would've been easy to hide there as the gigantic building had more than enough random items somebody could conceal themselves behind or inside.

She wasn't the only one who had escaped the tunnel attack—Vectus had, too. Figuring that the DOE would be swarming Intercludae, he had filled a backpack with food and water then hid in the warehouse to see if another Intercludae resident escaped. When none did, he returned to Lexum via the pipe in the wall, staying hidden in the treeline, waiting for someone to leave. Lucky for him, it was the route Lexo and Praxa took a few days later when exploring the desert for a safe house.

But how'd they not see each other?

Ragula and Vectus had been in different tunnels during the DOE attack, but it was strange that Ragula hadn't come across Vectus while he grabbed supplies. The only plausible explanations were that the DOE had attacked their tunnels at different times, Vectus had arrived in Intercludae first, or for some unknown other reason they didn't cross paths in Intercludae. But Breel wanted to give Ragula the benefit of a doubt, so said nothing.

Ragula said, "I hid for a whole day before returning to Intercludae. I had left the door to Intercludae opened as I didn't want to attract the DOE to the sound of closing it, and when I returned, it was still opened. I assume the DOE wanted a second way inside rather than just the tunnel from Lexum. Anyway, Intercludae was pitch black, but I heard voices so sneaked into the kitchen for food then hid in an industrial oven. Over the next few days, DOE officers came and went. Eventually, they stopped searching."

"We've been there," Samit said. "How come you kept quiet?"

Ragula frowned. "I left after a week, I think."

If that was true, it explained why they never saw Ragula in Intercludae as she would've left around the same time they moved to the desert. Breel and the others didn't start journeying through Intercludae for supplies until a couple of days later.

"I considered staying with my old head or someone else on our side," said Ragula.

Manum placed a hand on hers, "I'm sorry to tell you, your head died. Mortae."

Ragula's jaw dropped and her eyes teared. "No! What happened?"

"The DOE questioned her and determined she was a spy."

Ragula's lip trembled as she stared at the table. "That's awful. She was a great person. Gave me the confidence to leave Lexum."

Manum hugged her. "I'm glad you didn't stay with her as they'd have sentenced you to Mortae, too."

Ragula wiped her eyes. "True. Good thing I realized the odds of getting into her house undetected would be low. I knew my best bet was staying in the desert."

Samit snorted then crossed his arms. "And you only just found us?"

They had every right to be suspicious. Somehow, Ragula had stayed alone without detection. Food, water, and proper shelter were at a premium but, despite having no ability to contact anyone to get them, she stayed alive.

Ragula explained further. "I found some water and nonperishables in Intercludae. After that, I explored the old suburbs a bit, finding a few supplies. When DOE officers came around, it wasn't too hard finding a hiding place in the warehouses. Meanwhile, I tried finding you even though I didn't know if anyone survived the attack."

"Only me," said Vectus.

Ragula's jaw dropped as her eyes widened. "Just the two of us? Wow…"

Samit had yet to uncross his arms. "Ragula, why didn't you look for others? That's what Vectus did. Why didn't you see him?"

Vectus spoke first. "I only spent a few minutes throwing things into a bag, so that'd be why we didn't see each other in Intercludae."

Ragula nodded. "Yeah, that must be it because nobody else was there once I returned to Intercludae. I stayed in the desert as I figured if anyone survived, they wouldn't return to Lexum."

"Why'd it take so long to find us?" Samit asked.

He sure is grilling her. But I guess that's good. This is too weird.

"I thought for sure you'd be in the suburbs," Ragula said. "After searching many of the buildings, I realized they're too close to Lexum and not habitable. After a while, I looked farther out, first making small trips then bigger ones."

Manum beamed. "And you found us. See, everyone? She's one of us."

But Breel wasn't sure. True, she had met Ragula; however, they didn't know each other. Putting Vectus's and Ragula's stories together, their missing each other in Intercludae no longer sounded suspect. However, Ragula lasting five weeks in the desert with only a dwindling supply of nonperishables was difficult to believe.

Samit shook his head as he tsked. "Listen, Ragula. I don't know you and some of your story makes little sense, which means I can't trust you."

Manum rolled his eyes, but Ragula shrugged, unfazed.

"I trust her," said Manum, patting her hand.

"That's great, Manum," Samit said. "But Ragula needs to do a lot more to convince me."

"And me," Vectus said.

A pained expression crossed Manum's, especially when everyone—even Lexo and Praxa—agreed.

Ragula frowned. "But why don't you trust me?"

Lexo, on behalf of him and Praxa, explained that while they'd worked together in Intercludae, they didn't know her well. As for Breel, they'd been roommates briefly. Manum threw his arms into the air, comparing it to when he vouched for Praxa after others expressed suspicion.

Samit spoke, but Vectus interrupted, talking to Ragula. "We have no guarantee you haven't been a spy for the past month. How'd we know that you aren't going to run to Tatem in the night? Or that you didn't find us days ago, told Tatem, then returned here now to pretend to be one of us while reporting to Tatem?"

Wow, he's right!

Ragula could've gone into Lexum, lived with Tatem or some other Hargamite while avoiding detection from the anti-Tatem group, then left to spy for Tatem. Being on Tatem's side meant she wouldn't have to avoid detection in Lexum.

Ragula placed her elbow on the table then rested on chin on her palm. "Well, I can't blame you for being careful. That's fine as I know it isn't about me personally."

Manum motioned to Ragula. "Isn't this proof? She understands our position! That can only mean she's on our side."

Samit groaned. "Manum, she could just be saying that."

"I assure you, I'm not," said Ragula. "But again, I understand if you think I am. What're you going to do?"

Everyone except for Manum agreed to not let Ragula use the computers or go outside without an escort. Samit demanded they also ban her from meetings and require Praxa or Lexo to always guard her.

Manum slumped back into his chair in defeat. "Don't put her with the DOE officers." He put an arm around Ragula. "I'm so, so sorry."

"I understand, Mr. Gaimster. It's okay." She turned to Samit. "What'll it take for you to trust me?"

"Calling Tatem a monster is a start," Cafrec said with a laugh.

Ragula frowned. "I don't enjoy calling people names but yes, you're right. He's a monster."

Samit's arms flew into the air. "Oh, it's a miracle! She's trustworthy! Let's allow her to email whomever she wants."

"There's no need for sarcasm," said Manum.

It was a relief when Samit didn't respond. Instead, he ordered Manum and Lexo to move one lock and camera from the furnace room to the room in which they'd hold Ragula. At night, they'd continue guarding the DOE as normal while watching the video feed of Ragula's room.

After going through these instructions, Samit raised an eyebrow. "Wait a minute..."

"What is it?" Breel asked.

"No, this won't do at all," Samit said.

"Let me guess," said Manum. "You don't trust the ex-DOE to guard one of their own?" Samit took interest in the table. "I see. Well, I guess the rest of you will guard in shifts instead."

"Perhaps not Breel either," said Ragula. "We were roommates."

Samit blinked. "Why're *you* suggesting that?"

"I need to prove my trustworthiness somehow, don't I?"

Lexo spoke. "Praxa and I don't know Ragula well. You sure we can't guard her, too? Having two guards at a time is a waste."

It took a few minutes to convince Samit who only agreed if Manum no longer did guard duty, leaving it all to Lexo and Praxa.

They put Ragula in the basement bedroom Cafrec and Trafis shared. It meant Lexo and Praxa could work at their desks while monitoring both the bedroom and furnace room. They'd move Trafis's desk to the living room with Criba. He and Cafrec would sleep in Vectus and Samit's room.

It didn't take long to move everything around. When they finished, Breel and Cafrec hurried to the storage room, eager to discuss the situation.

Chapter Thirty-Eight

Cafrec leaned forward, facing Breel at her desk. "So, d'you think Ragula's a spy?"

Manum said they should trust his judgment because he knew her well. But if Ragula was an expert at pretending to be anti-Tatem, it wouldn't matter how long Manum had known her for. It made it difficult to know whether Ragula was a spy. She sounded genuine and, like with Praxa, Manum didn't doubt her innocence. But parts of Ragula's story—not seeing anyone else and somehow surviving alone in the desert—made her suspicious.

Cafrec nodded as Breel shared her thoughts. "We've met many people great at pretending," he said.

Like Vectus. Who'd have thought that intimidating Mr. Progrio who sang Tatem's praises more than anyone I've ever known is anti-Tatem?

"If people are skilled at pretending to be Hargamites, I'm sure there are people pretending to be on our side," said Breel. "We need to be careful."

The truth would come out soon enough. All they could do was take precautions, and they were doing that.

***

The first order of business during their post-lunch meeting was the diary. As Samit called them to order, Trafis sat straighter then placed the diary on the table, his hand atop of it. When Samit asked him for updates, he grinned.

"Not much," said Trafis. "I mean, nothing that helps. Just interesting tidbits."

Everyone, especially Cafrec, leaned forward, motioning him to continue.

Trafis turned to a page near the end then read, "'On my walk home from school, I came across a burning house. Kids screamed my name from the top floor, begging for help. I wanted to watch them burn but didn't.'"

Manum whistled. "That's some phobia."

Breel agreed. There was no doubt now that Tatem was fearful of fire.

Trafis turned the page. "The next entry says, 'The kids died in the fire. Good riddance. Their parents had far too many children to feed, anyway. Apparently, the fire started because the youngest kid stuffed something in the woodstove without closing the door, so a spark landed on a sock. I heard Lexum doesn't have woodstoves. Thank goodness as I never want to be around them again. Untrained people shouldn't have access to woodstoves, ovens, and other things that can cause fire.'"

It was a precursor to some of the changes Tatem had made as president.

Is that why only people in the cook Career Group know how to cook?

Clonis stepped in. "Sounds like Hargam. He once watched a rat in pain, flipping and flopping and squeaking in a box. The other kids told him to put it out of his misery, but they didn't know he was the one who injured it, see. When he refused, the neighbourhood kids tried helping the rat, but Hargam stopped them. He watched for hours until it died."

Given that Tatem tortured anti-Tatem citizens, it wasn't hard to picture him torturing rats. He'd gone from watching rats die and wanting to watch children burn to viewing citizens' executions in a matter of years.

Trafis shared the second last entry. "'Tomorrow morning, I leave for university! I cannot wait. This is the best thing that's ever happened, and it's all because I'm better than anyone else. Well, I guess there was one worthy competitor, but she's nothing now.'"

Geesh, his ego was always the size of Lexum. And I bet winning the scholarship made it worse.

If Clonis had ever showed the diary to his parents, reading it would've shown them what their son was like. Tatem would've been arrested for murder and never become president. However, being the favourite, Tatem may have convinced his parents that the diary was a joke.

Trafis had finished, so it was Breel's turn to provide an update. She'd been drawing to go alongside the pamphlet text Criba had written. Each pamphlet would have the same message and drawings on the inside and back with several variations of the front text and picture. So far, the group had approved Criba's message and the graphic for one cover. Breel had sketched a rough draft then received approval to work on it.

She showed the draft pamphlet to the group, folded in half like a book. In the background, she'd drawn a man and woman hugging and crying on a couch. The text read "Grieving your loved one's death by Mortae? Their murder was cruel and needless. You know that and we know that. There is another way..."

The left inner panel read: "Fifty years ago, Hargam Tatem became president of Lexum. It was an extraordinary feat. He came from the lower class with a dream of bettering their lives. After winning a scholarship for achieving the highest grades in his class, he attended postsecondary school in Lexum. It was there that he saw how the other half lived. President Tatem envisioned ridding Lexum of poverty and ensuring equal opportunities for all citizens." In the background, a young Tatem sat at a desk working hard on his studies with piles of textbooks surrounding him.

By design, the panel didn't barrage Tatem. Everyone would read it because it'd come in a governmental package as presumed mandatory reading material. The facts would draw in the Hargamites, encouraging them to read on.

The right inner panel said: "But Tatem took things to the extreme. He enticed and encouraged the lower class to enter Lexum, starting a civil war. Tatem was the only government official not killed. His presidency was to be temporary until a new council was formed. However, Tatem abolished the council. When he moved the lower class into Lexum, the upper class protested them having the same rights and privileges, causing more civil unrest. To maintain control, Tatem started Mortae. Later came curfews, the Nito Test, and the Demna Exam. He forbade anyone from engaging in activities which do not benefit society." In the background Tatem stood behind a table at which five government officials sat slumped over—dead.

Their call to action was on the back. "President Tatem tells us what to study, what job we will have, whether we can have children, where to live, to whom we can talk. Disobedience means death. Life never used to be this way, and life doesn't have to continue this way. Many citizens are working hard toward a better Lexum. But we need more people helping to overthrow Tatem so we can make our city a place in which everyone can live and fulfill their dreams without fear of death. If you'd like to help, you may want to consider:

- Protesting in the streets

- Protesting during Mortae

- Calling in sick to work

- Publicly mourning for the dead

- Destroying posters favourable of President Tatem

- Completing barely passable schoolwork and Department of Expansion coursework

- Writing anonymous letters of opposition."

Behind the text was a drawing of Tatem with his head down and shoulders slumped while leaving Lexum through an opened gate. Around him, citizens grinned and clapped.

"Well?" Breel asked after passing it around.

Criba beamed. "Looks great. My daughter's so talented!"

"Goes to show how much drawing you sneaked in over the years," Cafrec said with his patented grin.

Taking it as the compliment Cafrec had intended it to be, Breel's face burned.

"My drawings are fine?" she asked

Vectus reached across Cafrec to pat her arm. "I'd say it's ready. Great job. You're drawing our freedom from Tatem and one day, people will recognize that."

Breel felt a great sense of pride at his words and the agreement that the pamphlet was ready. Samit gave Cafrec the go-ahead to send a copy to their Department of Expansion contact for printing and distribution. They'd distribute the pamphlet to thousands of people—the first step in Breel's idea for overthrowing Tatem.

I am *drawing freedom.*

Chapter Thirty-Nine

Breel left for a walk later that morning with Cafrec, Vectus, Criba, and Trafis.

It was another calm, sunny day; however, the blazing ball of heat would keep the walk short. The sand that found its way into Breel's shoes burned for a moment as it stuck to her sweaty feet.

Trafis patted Breel's back. "Those were great drawings."

"You're so talented," said Criba, walking behind her with Cafrec.

"So are you, Mother. We could make posters and pamphlets together after Tatem, too."

"Ooh, yes," said Cafrec, leaping right onto the idea. "I can see it now! Pamphlets telling citizens how to play games, how to find hobbies, and most of all how to feel guilt-free for doing those things."

He wasn't wrong. Citizens would need something to teach them how to live in a post-Tatem world. Criba agreed, saying she'd love to make such things with Breel.

All they had to do was overthrow Tatem. But while his diary was illuminating and interesting, it'd only shown his fear of fire and how he'd had an early vision of Lexum which he later fulfilled. It'd yet to reveal anything more.

Cafrec thought differently. He suggested that citizens should know the bad things Tatem did in childhood such as his murder of Prima to get the scholarship, abusing other children, and torturing and killing animals for fun. While not all citizens would believe the stories, the diary, Clonis, and citizens living in the retirement home who had known pre-president Tatem could vouch for the stories.

Maybe the diary will be more useful than I thought.

"It could get more people to our side," Breel agreed.

For the rest of their walk, they discussed how and when to use the diary's information. They agreed it'd be a waste to use it this early as the information in it weren't known facts unlike the information in their pamphlets. The staunchest Tatem supporters would claim they created stories to discredit him.

It was best to wait until other efforts had revealed more anti-Tatem citizens. Then, after leaking his childhood doings, Tatem would get more desperate. Taking drastic measures, he'd be likely to make mistakes which they could use to their advantage.

"We should get back," said Vectus. "I'm not sure leaving Samit alone with the others was wise."

"Oh gee," said Breel.

How sad that he's right.

They turned back about a quarter mile from the birch trees near the cliff. With nothing but desert between them and the house, they could see a lone figure walking toward them. Breel's heart leapt into her throat. When Vectus stopped without warning, she stepped on his heel.

"Sorry." She whispered as if that'd prevent the person from seeing them.

She squinted, but the person was too far away—and it was too sunny—to determine if they wore a DOE uniform. One person wasn't likely to be a DOE officer, but they couldn't be too careful. Breel retrieved her gun from its holster and the others followed suit.

Within a minute, the mystery person was close enough to see their sweater didn't have yellow stripes.

Thank goodness they're not a DOE officer. But who are they?

After another minute, the distance between them had decreased enough to see it was Samit. A wave of relief washed over Breel.

"What's he doing here?" muttered Vectus.

Samit moved with purpose, arms swinging and fists clenched. Many of his steps kicked sand into the air. His face was red, and flecks of blood stained his shirt. Breel sighed.

"Oh, not again," muttered Vectus.

Cafrec stepped closer to Breel. "I sorta wish I witnessed this one."

Not me! He looks even worse than last time!

Vectus hurried ahead to reach Samit. The others did the same, stopping a few feet away. A bruise covered half of Samit's right cheek—which had been a day or two away from healing after the last fight—and his eye was bloodshot.

Vectus sighed. "I guess we don't need to ask what happened."

Samit gestured to the house half a mile behind him. "All I did was nicely express my concerns about Ragula."

Nicely? I bet he egged Manum on.

Samit looked from person to person, as if waiting for permission to leave. When Vectus suggested he interact with Manum as little as possible, Samit nodded then continued walking toward the trees.

"You'll be back soon, right?" Criba asked.

Samit didn't answer.

***

"He had it coming." Manum shrugged as if he was in the right to punch Samit again.

Manum poured glasses of water for himself and the others from the kitchen sink as Breel, Cafrec, Criba, Trafis, and Vectus shook their heads. Unlike last time, Manum didn't have a mark on him.

Breel took the glass Manum handed her. "What'd he say?"

Manum leaned against the counter. "He said Ragula's a spy and even went on about Praxa again. I reminded him that everyone agreed Praxa's in the clear, and that I vouch for Ragula. Then he said we shouldn't waste our supplies and time guarding Ragula and the DOE. He even suggested we kill the DOE and I..." Manum lowered his gaze. "I may have compared him to Tatem. He threw a punch, so I defended myself."

He shrugged as if the result had been nothing. But the state of Samit's face said it wasn't "nothing."

"How much did you have to defend yourself?" Breel asked.

Manum pursed his lips. "Well...Praxa may have pried me off him."

Vectus sighed. Samit and Manum made it difficult to get things done. It was unlike anything Breel had ever seen before—but that may have been why. Samit and Manum had hid anger deep down for so many years and now they could let it out without fear of Mortae. If so, it was troubling because it meant such fights may be commonplace post-Tatem.

I guess we need some laws.

It wasn't anything Breel had thought of before. She'd only known Tatem's extreme laws, but the Samit and Manum show made it clear they needed laws to prevent pandemonium and violence.

Vectus cleared his throat. "Manum, I agree with Samit that guarding the officers is time-consuming and tedious. However, there's no way around it. You're right that murdering them makes us as bad as Tatem."

The others nodded. It was hypocritical to express their horror for all the murders Tatem had committed—or had others commit on his behalf—then kill people for being an inconvenience. Lexo and Praxa would continue guarding the DOE—and now Ragula—at night.

Over an hour after everyone returned to work, Samit joined Breel and Cafrec in the storage room. For the first time, he sat in their spare chair rather than stand against the wall. He'd changed into a crimson shirt—*to hide blood?*—and held an icepack to his cheek while he stared at the floor, avoiding their gaze. "I'm here to talk to Breel."

"Oh." Cafrec turned back to his laptop.

"Breel, I have a favour to ask." He paused, waiting for a response.

"O...kay. A new database?"

Please no, I only want to draw.

"No, nothing to do with databases. I'd like you to befriend Ragula. I know you don't know each other well, but you've at least met. Manum is too close and seems to have parental feelings toward her, so I don't trust his judgment. But, before you agree, I want the truth. Do you think she's a spy?"

Breel crossed her legs. "I don't *think* she is, but maybe it's more I don't want her to be. Parts of her story make little sense to me, too, so we must be cautious. If Tragpraev could fool Tatem into thinking he was his loyal double agent, Ragula can fool us."

What she didn't say was that Manum's potential reaction to her buddying up with Ragula worried her.

The last thing I want is for Manum to think I've joined Team Samit, but I guess there's nothing I can do about that.

Samit nodded. "Good. That's the logical thinking we need, especially with Clonis, Ragula, and Manum around."

Breel cocked her head. "You don't trust Manum, do you?"

Samit raised his hands in defence. "It has nothing to do with our past. Spend an hour or two each afternoon with Ragula but make her think you're doing it for her."

"Like I'm keeping her company, you mean."

"Right. See if she reveals secrets. If you're not in the middle of anything, I'd like you to start now. I'm sure I don't have to tell you not to tell Manum, Praxa, and Lexo that I asked you to do this."

"I understand."

One week ago, visiting Ragula would've been a pleasant break between the monotony of building and maintaining databases and sending emails. But, while visits would take time away from drawing, Samit's request made sense.

She kissed Cafrec goodbye then walked down the hall.

Chapter Forty

Lexo—whose desk had the keys to Ragula's and the officers' rooms—unlocked Ragula's door. Ragula had showered and wore a navy-blue sweater and black pants. She sat on a chair in the back corner, carving a hunk of birchwood.

"How goes the hobby?" Breel asked, sitting on the foot of the bed.

Ragula placed the wood—*a fox?*—on the nightstand. "I'm out of practice since I haven't carved since Intercludae and since there's no one teaching me, I have to figure it out myself. Oh well, what can you do? It was nice of Manum to remember and get me some wood and this knife. Not the best, but it's something."

She held up a small knife from the kitchen.

I bet Samit doesn't know she has it.

"Yeah," said Breel. "Manum seems to care about his people."

Ragula nodded. "He was like that when he taught, too. His size intimidated me at first, but he's such a warm, kind guy."

Wanting to change the subject to something useful, Breel said, "I bet you've been lonely this past month."

Ragula groaned then leaned back in her chair. "You have no idea! And the food..." She grimaced. "Not much to eat, especially in the last week. I was super relieved when I found you. So, why're you talking to me? I know you have a lot of work."

Breel's brain scrambled to come up with a probable lie. "There's a lull in making databases, so I begged Samit to let me visit you. Even Tatem's brother got visitors, so you should, too."

Ragula's brow furrowed. "His brother?"

"Yeah, that older man with us is his brother, Clonis."

Recognition dawned on her face. "Oh! Yeah, he does kinda look like him. Wow, his brother!" She lowered her voice. "I didn't know he had siblings."

Talking about Tatem's family was the perfect invitation to discuss their opinions of him.

"Tatem had seven siblings," said Breel. "He slaughtered them all except Clonis during the civil war. Poor Clonis was in jail then isolated in the retirement home."

Ragula chewed her lip. "Gee, that sounds awful. I hope I'm not stuck in this room for that long!"

Breel laughed. "I doubt it. Oh! Are your parents anti-Tatem? If so, I can see about getting permission to email them to let them know you're alive and well."

"That's nice of you. But no, they're staunch supporters of their dear President Tatem. No doubt they've disowned me." Ragula grimaced.

Breel understood the pain of a parent putting Lexum and Tatem ahead of family. If not for Famut, Breel, too, would be in Lexum and brainwashed into putting Tatem first. As such, she wasn't angry at her father as he was living his life in the way Tatem had taught—demanded—of everyone.

Ragula sighed. "They were so proud when I tested as a DOE officer. I looked forward to protecting our laws and citizens then I started thinking for myself. Later, Manum influenced me. I had to hide my views—especially from my parents as they would've reported me."

Breel shuddered.

What awful people.

Ragula crossed her legs. "I felt stuck. But I suppose no more stuck than you wanting to draw. Anyway, enough about me. So, Breel, you escaped to Intercludae but instead of drawing you're still making data-bases?"

"Someday it won't be like this," said Breel.

"I sure hope not. I'm used to the luxuries of Lexum."

After hearing about Tatem's childhood, *luxury* was the right word. The only people in the suburbs who had lived in luxury were the factory bosses with their indoor plumbing, heat, and large detached homes.

Ragula motioned to the door. "Who're all these other people?"

Breel explained who everyone was which, in classic Lexum style, meant listing them by name and Career Group.

Ragula grimaced when Breel mentioned Samit. "The bald guy? I don't like him. He doesn't trust Manum. I mean, I understand not trusting me, but Manum? Come on. Manum's the best person around."

"Long story," said Breel. "In short, Samit's hated him for years."

Ragula made a face before raving more about Manum. When Breel mentioned the physical fights, Ragula's jaw dropped then she laughed. "Mortae for them both! Gosh, I've missed talking like this. I'm glad you visited."

"Me, too."

Trying to sound casual, Breel said, "I should come every day, if Samit lets me."

Ragula grinned. "I'd love that! But from what I saw of Samit, I'm not sure he'd allow it."

Breel stood. "I'll ask in front of the group that way Vectus or Clonis will convince him. Clonis said visits from Tatem and others helped with the isolation. I'll make it happen."

Ragula leapt up then hugged her. "Thanks, Breel. I'm glad you're safe. I appreciate you coming by."

Breel left the room no closer in her judgment regarding whether Ragula was the spy.

Chapter Forty-One

Breel returned to her desk to find Cafrec chatting with Clonis.

Clonis sat with his feet stretched out and hands behind his head, elbows out. "Nope. Cafrec, you're nothing like him. He always had this look, see. This almost-smile when he was doing and saying hurtful stuff. You don't hurt others. You care about them. That's why you're here and not back in Lexum."

Breel pulled her chair out from her desk to face Cafrec and Clonis. "I agree. I mean, I already said so."

"Yeah," said Cafrec, "but since Clonis knows Tatem well, he's a better judge."

Clonis nodded while examining his fingernails. "If no one's ever called you a psychopath, you're one big step ahead."

Cafrec managed a laugh then returned to his work.

Taking the opportunity, Breel asked, "Clonis, tell me about Xorem. I mean, why's she with him? And does Tatem care about her? Tragpraev said he does."

Clonis's eyes drifted to the ceiling. "Tragpraev...Tragpraev..."

"Tatem's long-time housekeeper who attempted to kill Tatem at our Mortae." She motioned to herself and Cafrec.

Cafrec's eyes stared to his laptop screen, hand unmoving on his mouse as he listened.

Clonis nodded. "Oh yes, I remember him saying that. Pity he failed."

That's putting it mildly.

If Tragpraev had killed Tatem, they wouldn't be hiding in the desert, there'd be a city council, they'd have abolished Mortae, and people would no longer live in fear.

Clonis picked at his fingernails. "Oh yeah, Tatem cares about Xorem. I think she's the only person he's ever cared about."

"But why?" Breel asked.

"She doesn't tell him off like me and my sibs, see. She also gave him the estate."

"Whaddya mean?"

"As I said, her parents owned the estate. He saw it and wanted it, see. I guess he decided he also wanted her. First time he showed interest in anyone."

"Sounds like he was too busy fulfilling his twisted goals to date anyone," said Cafrec, eyes on his screen.

Not only was Xorem naive, but it sounded like Tatem's power interested her—in exchange for her family's home.

But how can a good person stay with Tatem knowing some of the things he's done? Is it because of her being sick? And why's she sick?

Thinking Clonis must know the answer, Breel asked him. But Clonis shrugged as he dug a nail under another fingernail. "Not sure what her sickness has to do with it. Not sure why, but yeah, she gets sick a lot."

Cafrec turned away from his computer then leaned toward Clonis. "Did it start after she met Tatem?"

Breel knew what he was getting at. She'd never thought of it, but it'd make sense. Drugging her food to force her to stay sick and preventing her from going outside to see what life was like was something Tatem would do.

"Not sure. I didn't know her before then, see," said Clonis.

"Tatem never told you?" Breel asked.

Clonis laughed. "He wouldn't tell me that. He told me lots of stuff, but not that."

Breel and Cafrec exchanged glances.

Is he thinking what I'm thinking?

Encouraged to learn some secrets, Breel asked what Tatem had told him. Clonis stretched his feet while saying that Tatem had mentioned their group of rebels living outside Lexum. He placed his hands on the chair arms, having finished with his nails.

"Anything else?" asked Cafrec.

Clonis tapped his fingers on the chair. "Recently, Tatem said he can't wait until all citizens have no choice but to follow his laws. Something about...what's it called again? Oh, genes."

Breel gasped. Now they were getting somewhere. "Did he give details?"

"Not really. Something about changing people's genes before they're born. Making them obey and be good at certain things."

"The Nito Test," Cafrec said.

"Yeah, he said something about that."

Cafrec shifted in his chair. "Clonis, how recently did he tell you this? Weeks? Months?"

"Last week. I haven't seen him since."

Cafrec looked at Breel. "We should tell the others."

Clonis's brow furrowed. "What're you talking about?"

They told him about the anniversary announcement likely being replacing the Nito Test with genetic engineering to assign Career Groups. When Clonis agreed it made sense, they asked if he knew anything else on the topic.

"Even if it was a decade or more ago," Cafrec added.

"You expect me to remember something from that long ago? Oh, young people." He shook his head, amused. "I'll think about it and let you know."

The moment Clonis left, Cafrec asked about Breel's visit with Ragula. She summarized their conversation.

"Got the spy vibe?" he asked, waving his hands around.

"No. But that means nothing, so I'll be careful."

They all had to be careful. A spy was out there—whether in the house or in Lexum—and the sooner they found them, the safer they'd be.

Chapter Forty-Two

The next day at their post-lunch meeting, Cafrec announced that their Department of Expansion contact had printed the pamphlets, and distribution would start that day.

Breel couldn't wipe the grin off her face. They were about to share her artwork with countless citizens instead of her hiding it in a notebook behind a wall of textbooks. Even better, it'd play a role in Tatem's downfall.

But she couldn't relish in her dream becoming a reality because Samit changed the topic, wincing as he spoke. The punch had caused his cheek to swell and bruise even more than before. His right eye was half closed.

Samit called Breel visiting Ragula an "opportunity" then asked for suggestions on how she could get Ragula to slip if she were a spy. He didn't mention he had asked Breel to visit Ragula.

"Tell her how much you hate Tatem," said Trafis.

"Talk about what convinced you to go against Tatem," Criba said. "Go into detail about how horrible his laws are."

"Mention his weird obsession with his hair." Cafrec grinned while mimicking Tatem.

"Ask for more information about her coming to Intercludae," Praxa said.

"And what convinced her to join our side," Lexo added.

Breel appreciated the suggestions. "Ragula told Cafrec and me about her journey to Intercludae and what made her go anti-Tatem when we first met, but I'll ask again and ensure it's the same story. When I talk with her, I'll focus on my hatred for Tatem."

"Good, good," Samit said. Turning to Manum, he asked, "Anything Breel should know about Ragula?"

Manum shook his head. "No. Other than she's not a spy. If she were, I'd know."

Samit rolled his eyes. "Listen, I'm sure she's not. But is there anything about Ragula that would help Breel?"

Manum said nothing, but that didn't bother Breel—she was still riding the high of the Department of Expansion distributing her drawings.

***

An hour later, Breel entered Ragula's room to find her sitting on her bed with her back against the wall while carving. A plate sat in her lap to catch the wood shavings. She'd lined up her carvings on her nightstand—half a dozen flowering petals, a few animals, Manum's head, and a house.

Ragula grinned while placing her carving and the plate on her nightstand. "My only visitor!"

Samit had declared Manum banned from seeing Ragula. Despite Manum's protests, the majority agreed during a heated discussion, saying it'd be easy for Manum to slip and tell Ragula information—even by accident. Manum insisted that Breel could do the same; however, everyone thought that was less likely since Breel didn't know Ragula well and Ragula had yet to convince Breel of her innocence.

Breel sat on the edge of the bed. "I know isolation sucks, but I'm sure it's better than hiding in those old homes."

Breel had misspoken on purpose—Ragula had said she hid in the warehouse.

"That's for sure," said Ragula.

Oh no...

Breel's heart raced as she gripped the covers.

Ragula said, "But I stayed in the warehouse, remember?"

Breel's hands released the covers and the tension in her body dissipated.

Good, she's keeping her story straight.

Ragula groaned. "It was soooo boring. There's only so many lamps you can look at before you're sick of being there."

She didn't embellish but it was unclear whether Ragula didn't want to talk about her experience, or she had lied about being in the warehouse.

"At least this is better than Lexum!" said Breel.

It took a moment for Ragula to respond. "In lots of ways. But I miss the food."

Breel laughed. Nothing compared to fresh food. "You know what I don't miss?" Breel asked. "All those nonsensical laws. Warnings. Having no choice in career. Illegal entertainment and hobbies. No way Tatem cares about citizens with laws like those!"

Ragula grimaced. "Yeah, for sure."

Not even a trace of anger had flashed across her face. She sat with her hands folded on her lap.

Breel pressed further. "Which law did you find hardest to follow?"

It took no time for Ragula to respond, which was promising. "Studying day and night, then working *and* studying all the time. Sometimes I wanted to do nothing! What about you? Drawing being illegal?"

"Yep. Not that the law stopped me."

Ragula laughed as Breel talked about the ways she had managed to fit in her hobby.

Going well so far. Now to talk about Tatem.

"I wonder what it was like to have lived in Lexum when Tatem elevated himself to president," Breel said.

Ragula shrugged. "Not sure."

"You mean you've never thought about what it would've been like to have life change so quickly?"

Ragula smiled, amused. "Oh, Breel, I'm an ex-DOE officer. We don't have to do much thinking. We walk around telling people off, guard certain places, and visit homes to give warnings or arrest citizens. I've never thought about it."

It was tempting to push, to mention how when discussing Tatem becoming president in history class, many Leaders of Tomorrow talked about what it would've been like to witness it. Instead, she imparted her own thoughts.

"It would've depended upon if you were upper or lower class. For the lower class, it would've been a dream come true to have everything you need and no longer struggle. If they saw through Tatem, they didn't care because he gave them a better life. As for the upper class, well, they tried to murder Tatem."

History classes had glossed over the assassination attempts. When textbooks and teachers mentioned them, they put Tatem in an angelic light and made the would-be assassins sound like selfish criminals. There was no mention of how the biggest criminal of them all was Tatem.

Ragula tilted her head while she considered Breel's words. "Yeah, you're right. That makes sense."

Encouraged, Breel said, "It's too bad people didn't stop Tatem back then. If they had, things would be different. Another city council, fun wouldn't be illegal, no needless and cruel Mortae, no slaving away at work and school."

Ragula nodded. "Yeah, very different."

"Good different, though."

Ragula leaned back against the wall, hands behind her head. She gazed at the ceiling as if reflecting on how life would differ. "Oh yeah, very good."

A few minutes later, since Ragula had yet to give anything away if she was a spy, Breel left.

Ugh. She's unflappable!

Talking about Tatem's laws and how things had changed fifty years ago was a bust. Ragula had agreed when Cafrec called Tatem a monster. The only suspicious thing so far was Ragula not sharing her views, but that wasn't unlike Praxa. Given that Ragula's parents were also strict Hargamites, it made sense that she, too, disliked stating her views about Tatem.

She'd have to try something new.

Chapter Forty-Three

They received word that each of the Department of Expansion's five hundred deliveries for the day contained the pamphlets, representing dozens of Career Groups.

But Tatem didn't mention them during the evening news. Instead, he talked more about citizens behaving "badly" and deserving Mortae.

"He has to know about them," said Breel afterward at the dining room table.

Vectus brushed back his red hair with a hand. "Oh, he knows. He's hiding it."

"Coward," said Cafrec.

"Think about it from his standpoint," said Vectus. "By acknowledging them, citizens learn the anti-Tatem group can mass communicate which will empower us and incite fear in his followers. No, he'll keep this quiet and talk to people he trusts for advice."

Clonis laughed. "If he trusts anyone."

Since their source had stuffed pamphlets into as many stored textbooks as possible, pamphlet distribution would continue until Tatem ordered somebody to check every single book or packed box. There was no doubt that would happen—it was only a question of when and how many pamphlets drivers would inadvertently deliver before then.

But Cafrec shook his head. "That's the best part. The head of the Career Group in charge of pulling the material from the warehouse then packing it is on our side. If Tatem asks for quality control, the head can assign it to the guy who packaged the ones sent out today."

That was good news—to a point.

"You're missing one thing," Breel said. "Why would Tatem allow someone in the warehouse to do it? If I were him, I'd pull a person from another Career Group to ensure it's not the person who stuffed the pamphlets into the books."

Cafrec's face fell. "Ugh, you're right."

After a moment of silence while the room considered the situation, Criba said, "That might not be the case, Breel."

Whoa, it's not like her to disagree.

When all eyes were on her, Criba folded her hands on the table. "The large Mortae numbers had me thinking about future demand. I talked to some Department of Occupation sources who said there's a lot of secret work happening. Tatem's demanding some departments fill critical Career Group gaps by temporarily moving citizens into qualified positions. When there's a Leader of Tomorrow old enough to fill that role, they'll return to their original position. But in some cases, that won't happen for years. There's also talk of filling empty roles by certain Career Groups having practical components for Leaders of Tomorrow to gain work experience while in school. All that to say, there may not be someone from another Career group to do quality checks."

It was a fascinating update. The news had said there had been well over a seven thousand percent increase in Mortae, and it increased yet again when Tatem also sentenced parents to Mortae for their children's actions. Now, Tatem had to change how he assigned jobs.

Changing how the workforce operates because of killing too many citizens is just...

Breel shuddered. There wasn't even a word for it.

"And here's Tatem!" said Cafrec, throwing his arms into the air. "I'll kill my people even though it means we don't have enough workers!"

Only Breel and Trafis smirked.

Manum stretched. "I imagine Tater will be okay with some gaps if it means securing his reign which means he'll assign someone to check the packages. As Breel said, it won't be someone under the influence of the Career Group head for that department. So, we need to distribute as many as possible while we can."

Samit scratched his cheek, grimacing at the touch. "For once, I agree. Cafrec, make sure you tell this to those sources. We also need to think of other distribution methods."

Everyone discussed, brainstorming in groups of twos or threes.

Clonis suggested housekeepers leave pamphlets in houses.

"No, terrible idea," said Vectus. "They track which houses each housekeeper cleans, so they'll know who did it."

Samit and Criba talked about putting pamphlets on every bus seat for the Leaders of Today who took the bus to work.

"But the bus driver would need to be anti-Tatem for that to work," said Samit. "And that'd be way too risky for them."

Trafis and Lexo discussed the Department of Logistics placing pamphlets on seats before departmental events.

"But a Hargamite could report the pamphlets before most people see them," said Lexo.

The only audible term from Manum and Praxa's conversation was "DOE officer."

Breel turned to her own thoughts. Samit was right. The pamphlet delivery was great, and if they got to five hundred households in one day, they may get to one or two thousand before Tatem stopped it. But that left thousands who wouldn't receive one. Meals were the only deliveries every household received, but they didn't have an appropriate Department of Food contact.

Then it hit her.

Technology was the answer.

It's time for Samit to show his skills.

Breel cleared her throat, but no one paid attention.

She waved a hand. "Guys?"

The talking tapered off as all eyes turned to her.

"I've got it," she said. "If we want to deliver our pamphlet to everyone, why don't we show it on the news? Samit, can you hack into the broadcast?"

"He's Lexum's best hacker, of course he can," said Manum.

It wasn't a compliment—it was a challenge. But for once, Samit didn't stoop to Manum's level.

"Yes, I can do that," Samit said.

"That's a brilliant solution, Breel," said Criba.

Breel's face reddened. What made it the best solution was that not only would everyone see it, but Tatem couldn't hide it. He'd have no choice but to address it live.

"We should do it near the beginning of the news," said Cafrec. "Right before he's talking."

"Yeah," said Trafis. "After we show it, everyone will see him squirm as he tries to figure out what to say."

Cafrec laughed. "Yep! Can't wait to see if he stays composed."

It would be a sight to see. But for Breel, watching Tatem lose control wasn't the best part. It wasn't even broadcasting to Lexum ways to destroy Tatem and the potential for gathering more followers. It was every citizen seeing her artwork. Her body wanted to jump for joy with abandon, but she squelched her delight.

Samit agreed to focus work on preparing to hack into the news. Despite their meeting running overtime, he asked Breel about her progress with Ragula. "I assume no information?"

"Yes, nothing," she said. "Ragula agrees with everything I say. Nothing fazes her, and she even hugged me when we finished."

"Why're you so convinced she's a spy?" Manum asked. "If this is a dig at me, then dig at me, not her."

"It's not," Samit said. He rested both palms on the table then leaned in. "Manum, someone's a spy. A citizen told Tatem that a group of us would apprehend him in his house. We need to know who they are and to do that, we need to put more time into figuring it out."

He was right. Finding the spy was imperative, especially if the spy was still gathering information from Breel and the others. Without discovering their identity, death was a guarantee.

"We already agreed it was likely someone from Intercludae," said Samit. "The easiest way for Tatem to have gotten information from the spy was them being part of the group trying to apprehend him."

Silence hung in the air like a thick cloud. Those group members had been Famut, Tragpraev, Praesio—an ex-DOE officer whom Tatem had killed—Breel, Cafrec, Manum, Lexo, and Praxa.

Criba huffed then slammed a hand on the table. "No! My daughter isn't a spy. Trust me, I raised her. There's no way she's a spy."

"Yeah, it's impossible," Trafis said.

Breel smiled at their endorsement.

"I know," said Samit. "I'm not suggesting that."

Manum groaned. "Then what're you saying because it sounds like you're suggesting one of us is a spy."

Samit pursed his lips as he shuffled his feet. "I'm saying that if there's no way an Intercludae resident could've fed information to Tatem while in Intercludae, they could've while in Lexum."

"What about computers?" Trafis asked. "Couldn't a spy use a computer from inside Intercludae?"

Cafrec gasped then placed in a hand to his mouth in mock horror. "How could they with Samit's skills?"

Breel considered other possibilities. There could be a better hacker than Samit, or Tatem had cameras inside Intercludae. Both were probable; however, Samit wouldn't take well to hearing them.

"What different Career Groups were in Intercludae?" Breel asked. "Was there anyone who spoke to Lexum citizens a lot? Samit, you wondered about coded language in emails. Perhaps the spy coded their emails, so it didn't flag in your security checks."

Samit shrugged. "It's possible."

Thank goodness he admits that much.

Breel turned to Manum. "Anyone with such a role?"

Manum nodded. "Our surveillance team. They stared at monitors all day and often emailed people in Lexum. But the DOE killed all of them."

"But we thought Ragula was dead, too," Breel said. "It's possible someone else is alive."

But other than Ragula, they had no leads. There was no information to go on. Questioning each other was a possibility; however, they agreed no one at the table was the spy.

Breel sighed.

Back to square one.

Chapter Forty-Four

Everyone returned to their workstations. Before Breel could sit at her desk, Cafrec put an arm around her. She turned to kiss him but stopped when footsteps echoed on the staircase.

Ugh, Clonis. I just want to get at my drawings.

Cafrec waved as Clonis entered the room, greeting Cafrec with a pat on the back then sitting with a yawn.

"Glad you don't think I'm the spy," Clonis said while stretching his legs.

"Well, no," Cafrec said. "Why would you spy for the person who locked you up for decades?"

"And it's not like you could spy for him here without computer access," Breel added.

"Yeah, I've never used a computer," Clonis said. "They were around when I was a kid, but we didn't have them, see. Hargam did in university, though."

Cafrec crossed his legs, his duties forgotten. "What'd he take in university?"

Clonis's gaze drifted to the ceiling where cobwebs covered the corners between the walls and exposed beams. "Gee, didn't think to clean the ceiling?"

"We don't have a ladder," said Breel.

"Ah. He took history. Or politics. I can't remember."

Regardless of what he took, Tatem would've sat at the front of each class, soaking in everything. Other than requiring council membership, he wouldn't have wasted time socializing or making friends. He'd have spent his time studying and learning about life in Lexum to overtake it.

Young Tatem would've been top—or near the top—of the class yet a mystery to everyone. He would've been a loner, though that may not have been on purpose. It was easy to imagine the other students ostracizing him for not being one of them. It happened all the time in classes with multiple Career Groups in which students of one Career Group ignored students in other Career Groups.

"I assume Tatem studied politics," Cafrec said, pulling Breel into the present. "After all, he knew enough to make himself president."

"Yeah, true," Clonis said. "He sure got us lower class worked up."

"When he got you to start a civil war, you mean?" Cafrec asked.

"Not just then. He told us about Lexum and how they treated us unfairly, see. Said we needed to fight back to get everything we deserve. Took a while to convince us but what did it was when Hargam said some government officials were on his side. But that was a lie to make us think people on the inside would fight for us, which didn't happen, see. While we had more people, they had weapons, so would've wiped us out if we didn't find a weapons cache."

"It must've been an awful time," Breel said.

His recollections reminded her of her own experiences—seeing decaying bodies, having weapons trained on her, being on display during her Mortae, fleeing from the DOE. She shut her eyes as if that helped shield her from the memories. To have seen all that, plus more, over the weeks and months of the civil war would've been horrific.

"Awful only in some ways, see," said Clonis. "Lots of it was great because we were finally within Lexum's walls and saw what they have. I remember the first time I saw a chrysanthemum. It was red and gorgeous and when I picked it up, had the sweetest, most pleasant smell I'd ever smelled. I couldn't believe Lexum had so many of them! And the food! Not to mention the quality of clothes and shoes. Everything was clean, the houses were enormous..." He leaned back smiling. "Oh boy, once people who didn't want a civil war heard all that, they wanted to attack, all right. Yep, it was scary."

After seeing the lower-class suburbs, his claims were easy to believe. It'd have been paradise. From a sandy desert to a clean city. Cramped rowhouses to bigger, freestanding homes. Woodstoves to furnaces. Wells to indoor plumbing. Limited job opportunities to numerous options (at least until Tatem became president).

"Did Tatem protect you?" Cafrec asked.

Clonis frowned. "What'd you mean?"

"Well," said Cafrec, "Reading between the lines in history class, you make it seem better than what it was. So, I'm wondering if you and your other siblings had it easier than others since Tatem was on the city council."

"Oh, I see. At first, no. But then when he was president and wanted all his siblings as advisors, we had protection so didn't have to defend our homes like some couples trading off staying awake all night."

After their failed Mortae while hiding in Sanctus's in-laws' house, the DOE and other citizens had run through the streets, desperate to find them. It'd been unnerving hearing the shouting and gunshots outside and not knowing what was happening.

And that was only for a few days! I can't imagine hearing that day after day for months.

Their experience didn't seem so bad in comparison to fifty years ago.

Chapter Forty-Five

The next morning after lunch, Samit stood as usual to chair their meeting. For the first time in days, his right eye opened and talking no longer caused him to wince. "Tatem has called for entertainment prior to his speech to honour the last fifty years. From the snippets our source has heard, it sounds like they'll have a play."

Nine pairs of eyebrows raised. The word "play" was uncommon in Lexum, and the context made little sense.

Clonis answered the question nobody had asked. "It's like the television shows I told you about except you watch it in person while it's happening. You'll see."

"So, it's entertainment," said Breel.

Clonis nodded.

Everyone expressed their surprise then wondered whether Tatem worried about people demanding more entertainment after the anniversary. The risk was gigantic, especially with the civil unrest. However, Tatem had such an ego that instead of thinking it'd affect him, he saw it as a reason for citizens to praise him for providing their first entertainment after fifty years.

Samit continued. "Everyone will attend the play, speech, and announcement. Like with Mortae, he'll televise it for people who are sick or unable to leave work. Afterward, they're removing the Quaddro's sections for an event. Half the citizens will attend the first day and half the second day."

No ropes sectioning the Quaddro? That'll be a first.

Samit reviewed a sheet of paper. "On the perimeter of the Quaddro, there'll be booths with activities based on section. The Platinum section citizens can take part in everything, but they limit the activities for Silver and Bronze."

"What activities?" Manum asked.

Samit shrugged. "Our contact doesn't know. All she receives is how much space each booth needs and what sections can use it to determine where to place it around the Quaddro. Since most people will be there, and it'll last longer than a Mortae, we should hang the posters then."

Everybody agreed. The only question was who'd do the hanging. They had three days to decide.

***

After putting the finishing touches on the posters, Breel visited Ragula who'd been smiling as she carved a flower.

Breel sat on the end of the bed. "Must be getting lonely."

Ragula shrugged as she moved her work to the side. "A bit, but I'm used to it after a month of being alone. Vectus talks to me once or twice a day, but I hate it." She made a face. "He keeps asking if I'm a spy."

Breel's crossed leg slipped. "He does?"

Either Vectus was out of line, or Samit wanted Vectus as a backup.

Ragula groaned. "He keeps going on about how hard it was pretending to be a Hargamite when teaching. Then he calls Tatem a monster and other names, going right up in my face to get a reaction."

Breel shuddered. "That was his favourite intimidation tactic in school. Would yell at me inches from my face."

Ragula shuddered. "He's creepy."

"Yeah. I thought so, too."

She didn't think so anymore, but she wouldn't tell Ragula that. Instead, Breel ended their chat early to talk to Vectus, finding him at his desk in the room off the kitchen. The room was a tight squeeze with four beds that had mere inches of space between them. Trafis's bed had been placed perpendicular to Samit, Vectus, and Cafrec's beds and Vectus's desk sat in the corner opposite the door.

His eyes lit up when she entered. "Ah, Breel. What a pleasant surprise."

"You're interrogating Ragula?"

"Oh." His smile faded. "Close the door."

Breel did then sat on the edge of Trafis's bed. "I thought it was *my* job to determine if she's a spy."

Vectus turned his chair to face her then scratched his head. "Samit and I decided two is best. I'm using a different approach."

"The creepy and scary tactic you used in school, you mean," said Breel, the words tumbling out.

He blanched. "Yes, that one. I'm sorry. And I'm sorry for not telling you. Samit convinced me it was best you don't know, thinking it may interfere with your progress. I assume she's not impressed with me."

"Yeah. She doesn't like you."

Vectus pursed his lips. "Can't blame her for that."

"How's it going with her?"

"Nothing yet. While I hope Ragula isn't a spy, part of me wishes she'll confess, so we can breathe easier."

Breel nodded. "Yeah, Cafrec said something similar."

But despite Breel's attempts and Vectus's, she'd yet to reveal anything.

Either Ragula's not a spy, or she's the strongest person around.

Chapter Forty-Six

That evening, they crowded around the television as the broadcaster announced the day's highlights.

"Today was the biggest Mortae in almost fifty years." The television screen panned the Quaddro's platform. Multiple benches held Vucapi with a DOE officer behind each of them, hands on their shoulders to keep them in place. The boisterous crowd cheered. "Of the thirty-one Vucapi, twenty-seven were Leaders of Tomorrow."

Of course, Tatem spoke about the Mortae. "Citizens, thirty-one Vucapi." He paused for effect, looking into the camera with a sober expression. However, the glimmer in his eyes betrayed his excitement. "Thirty-one ex-citizens of Lexum have died from failure to uphold our way of life and follow our laws."

No, they died because you killed them.

Tatem shook his head. "These Vucapi deserved punishment—and so they received it. The parents of the Leaders of Tomorrow watched from the Platinum section, hand- and leg-cuffed while held in place by Department of Enforcement officers. They'll be among tomorrow's Vucapi."

Criba let out a cry then clapped to her mouth. "Oh, that's awful."

Breel squeezed her leg, unsure what else to do. No doubt it brought her back to being in the Platinum section not just for Breel's Mortae, but for her sister's.

Tatem's eyes shone like stars in the desert sky. "The good news is this means our citizens are reporting illegal activities. None of us are safe until we catch every single one of these unlawful people and punish them with Mortae. Remember, I will reward you for legitimate reports. Even if your report leads to nothing, provided you're not abusing our reporting system—as decided by the Department of Enforcement—I will reward you. Citizens, by reporting someone engaging in unlawful behaviour, your life will improve in ways you can't even imagine."

For many citizens, open season to report anyone with the promise of a reward was a dream come true. Until Tatem had announced this, the only reward systems were doing well in school to get into a more prestigious department or work in a more desirable role and redeeming points earned for good behaviour in exchange for non-standard or extra furniture, shoes, and other mundane things.

Tatem sipped his water. "The Department of Enforcement reviews every report received and, with our enhanced system, we can respond to all reports within twenty-four hours. I would like to add two last points. First, if citizens witness or hear something that is reportable but do *not* report it, that, too, is a reportable offence. This includes failing to report someone else for not reporting illegal activities. All is punishable by Mortae.

"Second, this will increase the number of reports we receive. That is not a hope, citizens. That is an order. More reports mean discovering more identities of rebellious citizens. Since they do not embrace the collective, they deserve punishment. As a cornerstone of our society, this punishment has done us well for fifty years and will continue to do so. Long live Mortae. Until tomorrow, good night."

Someone clicked off the television.

"'Long live Mortae,'" said Manum, gagging. "Unbelievable."

Criba patted Breel's arm. "I'm glad we're not there."

Everyone muttered in agreement.

"I could never turn my children in, that's for sure," Criba said.

"Me neither," said Manum.

Criba patted Breel's hand. "Your father wouldn't have either."

"I know."

He could've reported her for drawing countless times. It was a question of what mattered more to him—his children's safety or following the law. He was always about safety, but he insisted on following the law to *keep* safe. With the new laws, Duknum would've been at a crossroads; however, his children's safety would've won over reporting them.

"My parents wouldn't have cared about reporting me," said Cafrec.

Breel gasped. Cafrec had said they were Hargamites but not that they'd turn him in. Her heart shattered at the thought of Cafrec growing up in that environment.

Cafrec put an arm around Breel. "One of many reasons I stopped talking to them."

"Mine were the same."

All heads swivelled to Praxa, sitting on a chair beside Cafrec. The moment everyone turned to her, she lowered her gaze. Her cheeks reddened.

"Sucks, doesn't it?" said Cafrec.

Praxa nodded. "Yeah. As if I didn't have to be careful enough…"

"Did you stop seeing them once you became a Leader of Today?" he asked.

Praxa rocked her hand in a "kind of" motion. "I avoided them as much as possible, but they kept contacting me and if I refused to see them, they might have gotten suspicious then reported me."

Breel shuddered. Not for the first time, she was grateful for her parents.

***

That night, Breel couldn't sleep. All she could think about Lexum's new laws. She'd received her second warning for drawing days before becoming a Leader of Today. Another warning would mean Mortae, so she had stopped drawing for fear of death and causing her parents more stress and anxiety. However, if the new laws had already been in effect, stopping her drawing also would've protected her parents and Trafis. The last thing she wanted was for her activities to get them murdered, too.

I'm so glad I'm not in Lexum anymore.

Lexum had always been terrible. Famut and a brief stay in Intercludae had opened her eyes to other and better possibilities. Back then, it seemed Lexum couldn't get worse. But no, Tatem made Lexum worse. Stopping Tatem was more important than ever.

Chapter Forty-Seven

The next morning, Manum spoke before Samit could bring their post-breakfast meeting to order. "I want you to stop interrogating Ragula."

Before Samit could object, Vectus stepped in. "I agree. She's told Breel and me nothing. I've been intimidating her best I can, and both Breel and Cafrec can tell you how adept I am at it." His face matched the colour of his hair. "If she had anything to hide, she would've said something by now."

Samit pursed his lips then turned to Breel. "Your thoughts?"

"Ragula and I bonded over swapping reasons we hate Tatem. She didn't get angry, and she didn't show any..." She struggled to find the word.

"Hero worship," Cafrec said.

Breel nodded. "Yes. She appears genuine."

Samit sighed. "I see. And the suspiciousness of her disappearance and reappearance? That doesn't bother any of you?"

"She justified it," said Manum.

Samit raised a hand. "You care about everyone you taught as if they're your children, Manum. You don't get a say in this discussion, nor do Lexo and Praxa."

Samit asked everyone else for their thoughts. They agreed with Vectus, saying Ragula had given no sign of being a Hargamite despite them doing their best to determine if she's a spy. It was time to trust both their judgment and Ragula.

Samit sighed then leaned forward, resting his hands on the table. "Seeing as how everyone thinks we should stop it, fine. But if she's a spy..." He trailed off, looking at Manum.

"I'm to blame if that happens?" Manum asked.

"Yes."

"We'd all be to blame," Cafrec said. "We all agreed to it."

Samit pointed a thumb at himself. "I didn't! We've been too easy on her."

Vectus laughed. "I wasn't easy." He stood then stepped toward Samit.

Samit stood backed up, moving closer to the counter. "What're you doing?"

"Are you working for that monster Tater?!" Vectus asked, voice raised.

Breel's heart leapt into her throat as he transported her back to programming class.

"Um..." said Cafrec, "we've already established that's he's not."

Vectus stepped closer, inches from Samit's face. "Answer me!" His voice echoed.

Even though Samit was a couple of inches taller than Vectus, he had backed himself against the counter, trapped. His eyes were wide, chest heaving with each breath. "No! I'm not a spy! What the..."

Vectus stepped back. "I did that to Ragula repeatedly."

Samit placed a hand on his chest. "Geesh, man. I thought"—he caught his breath—"I thought *I* was brutal to my staff. You did that to your students?"

"Yes." Vectus slipped into his chair then stared at the table. "If I did that to you for minutes at a time, multiple days in a row, wouldn't you cave if you were a spy?"

Samit's legs shook as he sat. "Uh...yeah," he said, his breathing laboured. "Okay, you have a point. She can join us."

Manum leapt to his feet. "I'll get her."

While waiting, Vectus retrieved a chair from the living room, placing it between Manum and Clonis. Ragula entered moments later with a grin matching Manum's.

"Welcome," Breel said.

"Thanks!"

Manum patted Ragula's shoulder as they sat. Ragula sat up straight, taking everything in.

Samit continued as if nothing had happened. "Tonight's the night we'll show the pamphlet on the news."

As everyone cheered, Breel's heart leapt at the thought of today being the day in which the entire populace of Lexum would see her work.

Today, my dream is coming true.

Two months ago, she never would've believed that it'd happen so soon, but they were about to use her talent for their cause. If everything went as planned, her drawings would play a pivotal role in Tatem's downfall.

As Samit prepped for the news, Cafrec had to take on more of his old security tasks, which meant Breel worked on her databases. The inability to draw made the day drag.

When the time came for the news, Samit stayed in the dining room to hack into the system and show the pamphlet. As usual, the news showed footage from the day's Mortae. Most of the Leaders of Today Vucapi were the parents of the prior day's Vucapi.

Tatem appeared on the screen with a sombre expression. "It is obvious some citizens deserve our most severe punishment. We have yet to—"

The sound cut out. After a moment of darkness, their pamphlet appeared. It showed Tatem pointing a gun at a five-year-old boy holding a test with a failing grade.

I'm a true artist now. Every single person in Lexum can see my drawing!

Cafrec patted her leg as Breel failed at hiding her smile. For her entire life, she'd waited for the time in which she'd share her artwork with others. After seventeen years, that time had come. While her drawing wasn't the type she'd hope to draw, one day soon, it would be.

Breel pulled herself back to the hacked news. Samit had recorded a voiceover for the text which appeared underneath Breel's drawings. People on the inside had disguised his baritone voice to be a tenor and nasally.

"If President Tatem cared about us, he wouldn't kill children for struggling in school," said the voice.

Samit showed the front of the pamphlet for one minute before moving to the first inner panel which discussed Tatem's past.

Clonis laughed. "Oh, he's raving mad."

"No way he could know yet," said Breel.

"He has a television to watch while he's speaking."

That didn't bode well for whoever had to be with Tatem during the news. The cameraperson would experience Tatem's wrath and the citizen failing to remove the pamphlet and voiceover would be lucky not to become a Vucapi.

So far, Tatem's people hadn't fixed it. Samit showed the other panels.

Meanwhile, everyone in Lexum could hear and read their message—and Breel's artwork.

Parents would want to shield their children from seeing the screen and hearing the voiceover. But some would hesitate since Tatem had made impeding anyone from watching the news illegal.

Anti-Tatem citizens watching with their Hargamite families would have the hard task of faking anger and outrage. Even anti-Tatem citizens living with like-minded family members couldn't discuss their agreement with the pamphlet because of household surveillance; however, they'd find a way. They'd need to decide whether resisting Tatem was worth the risk.

After showing the back panel for four minutes, the image of Tatem's office returned.

The camera—still rolling—continued showing Tatem's desk but Tatem was missing. People yelled offscreen, talking over each other. Tatem's voice rose above the rest as he used colourful and profane language to demand action.

"Uh...we're back on..." said an unseen voice.

"We're what?!" Tatem shouted.

He reappeared with his hair askew and suit ruffled. His eyes flashed as he glowered into the camera. When he spoke, every word was like venom.

"Citizens, I know I do not have to tell you to ignore what you just saw. You know attempting to resist me, your benevolent leader, will only result in Mortae."

Breel snorted.

Yeah, because a benevolent person kills you for disobedience.

Tatem pointed into the camera, his face contorted in anger. "Whoever is responsible for this wants to undermine our way of life, but this way of life has worked for fifty years. Recall your history classes—the previous way did not work. Only by rallying together can we ensure that those responsible for this atrocity cannot do it again."

He took a moment to smooth his suit and hair. When he spoke, he had composed himself—though his eyes burned with anger.

"We will do everything possible to find the people responsible. Make no mistake that when we do, I will punish them in a manner befitting their crime. The number one suspects, of course, are those who escaped their Mortae last month then fled with three others. They are alive, stealing our resources and hiding from Department of Enforcement officers. It is obvious they're helped by rebels on the inside. Again, if you see these Vucapi, you are to report it. Failing to report means your arrest and Mortae. These are the citizens we are looking for."

Not for the first time, he showed the pictures and names of Breel and her friends. They didn't include Vectus and Ragula as the DOE presumed them dead. For ten minutes, Tatem stressed the importance of turning them in, if seen.

Tatem had shown how much having his broadcast overtaken bothered him which was more than they could've hoped for. As he droned on, Samit entered the room with his chin held high. Everybody congratulated him on pulling it off as he sat near the front door, his chest thrust out.

Tatem gestured to the camera. "Everyone must do their part to overcome this tumultuous period." His speech had returned to its usual slower pace, but his words had an edge to them. "If we do not, this band of escaped Vucapi and their followers will destroy our way of life. Being against us or not embracing the collective means you are not a true or loyal citizen. Does that describe you? If so, we will find and arrest you, then you will become our next Vucapi. Think about that, citizens. Until tomorrow, good night."

Breel turned off the television. For a moment, everyone basked in the moment, knowing that their work had infuriated Tatem. Years later, when people looked back at his demise, they could pick this moment as the start of Tatem's end.

Vectus leaned back, hands behind his head. "Now we wait to see what people do."

"It's the first time in a while that he's mentioned us and showed our pictures," said Manum. "He's desperate."

Breel adjusted her glasses. "Uncle Famut always said desperate people risk making mistakes."

Samit nodded. "That's right. In fact, I received an email suggesting that's happening. Someone took a huge risk and advised Tatem not to make the Nito Test announcement. She told him she doesn't think people will like hearing it because it's affected their children and will affect future children, too."

"Lemme guess, he ignored her?" Cafrec pointed a finger at the television. "Don't you dare give me logical advice! I'll do what I want!"

Samit stood, prompting everyone to do the same to continue their conversation at the table.

"Seems he's ignoring her," said Samit as they moved to the dining room. He paused at the head of the table, waiting for the rustling and chair squeaking to end. "He said she's wrong and people should be happy their children will be less likely to break the law and become Vucapi."

This was excellent news. Tatem thought it'd solve the civil unrest; however, it'd only make the undecided certain that they were no longer loyal to him.

Vectus leaned forward to see everyone around the table. "Can we talk about the posters? We need to decide who'll hang them and how to lessen the risk of capture. The anniversary's only two days away."

Manum stepped in. "Samit and I talked about the security cameras. His people are working with our relevant DOE contacts to find an optimal route to place them. The goal is to give them good visibility with as few surveillance cameras as possible to manipulate during placement."

Whoa, have they put aside their mutual dislike for the cause? Things may be improving.

"But who should hang them?" Samit asked.

"It needs to be us," said Ragula.

Cafrec laughed. "You're insane!"

"I am? But everyone's supposed to attend the anniversary, right?"

Breel had imagined someone on the inside doing it, but Ragula was right. With Tatem mandating anniversary attendance, they couldn't risk a source missing it and they couldn't do it during the post-announcement celebration since only half of Lexum would attend, making the odds of staying hidden zero.

Vectus chewed his pen. "I see what you mean. We could find someone on the inside to do it at night."

Ragula shook her head. "That's when drivers make deliveries from farms to kitchens and from factories to warehouses."

"Plus, the DOE has increased nighttime surveillance," Manum said.

It was even more reason to avoid nighttime—which meant the only time to do it was during the anniversary.

"So...who goes?" asked Trafis.

No response. Returning to Lexum to run around the city hanging posters on a time limit when capture meant death wasn't something anyone wanted to jump at. All eyes were on the table, avoiding eye contact.

Ragula broke the silence. "It needs to be Vectus and me."

Whoa, that must be the DOE officer in her coming out.

Samit frowned before asking why.

"Because," said Ragula, dragging out the syllables, "we're the only ones without our names and pictures plastered everywhere. Unlike the rest of you, if we're seen, we might not get reported."

Oh, she's right!

Vectus groaned. "As much as I'd hate to return, that's sound reasoning."

Ragula flashed him a smile. "Good, because I don't know about you, but I'm going stir crazy. The officer in me needs an adventure."

Vectus tapped his pen on the table so hard it flung out of his hands. Samit caught it in mid-air then tossed it back to him.

"Vectus, are you sure you're okay doing this?" Samit asked.

Vectus returned to pen tapping. "Well, I don't want to, but I'll have an ex-DOE officer with me. We'll be fine if you tamper with those security cameras."

"I can do it."

Breel's head whipped around—it was Trafis.

Toe-the-line Trafis wants to risk his life? With that and his shooting skills, he for sure should've been a DOE officer!

Criba scrunched her nose. "Don't be ridiculous."

Vectus smiled then dropped his pen onto the table, the tapping over. "That's a brave and selfless offer. But you're on a wanted list with your face plastered on posters everywhere and I'm not. We shouldn't risk any of you. The day will come when we all must return to Lexum, but right now you need to stay here. If I'm seen, I can at least pretend to be a citizen."

Trafis frowned. "Yeah, I guess."

"Trust me, you don't wanna sneak around Lexum with a DOE officer on your tail," said Cafrec.

Breel shuddered at the memory of running through the trees beside Lexum's walls to find Cafrec then escape into the desert as a couple of officers chased them. It wasn't anything she wanted to have happen again.

Trafis frowned. "I don't wish that. But you've all had adventures, and I haven't."

"Wasn't coming here adventure enough?" asked Criba.

"I guess."

Going to the desert had been an uneventful nighttime walk through Lexum, another crawling slog through the pipe to the desert, then a seven-mile journey to the safe house. But for someone who'd spent his entire life studying, it would've been the most exciting thing Trafis had ever done.

When Breel and Cafrec returned to their desks after the meeting, Cafrec said, "Trafis sounds jealous!"

Breel scoffed. "Yeah, I don't know why."

"He doesn't get it, does he?"

He didn't. But it wasn't Trafis's fault. Breel hadn't told her family everything that had happened before her failed Mortae. If Trafis knew all she'd gone through, the jealousy would stop.

"I'd rather protect him than tell him what happened to us," Breel said. "He doesn't need to know, and I'd rather forget about it as best I can."

Cafrec nodded. "I know what you mean."

Breel put an arm around him, grateful he was in her life.

Chapter Forty-Eight

By the next evening, the day before the anniversary, over six hundred households had received a pamphlet. It was a good number, but impossible to guess how many citizens would be receptive. That said, they received some reports from DOE officer Luap regarding what citizens had done to oppose Tatem.

The DOE investigated anyone who didn't attend work or school because of illness. Luap did his best to protect those on the DOE's hit list because of previous actions suggesting anti-Tatem leanings.

One family held a funeral for their child whom Tatem had killed by Mortae before the new laws came into effect. The DOE caught the funeral on their living room surveillance camera. The family insisted they weren't anti-Tatem—they only wanted to remember their son—but the DOE didn't believe them.

A group of five thirteen-year-olds had written declarations of hate against Tatem on a school wall. The DOE arrested them and their parents.

A moustache appeared on a poster of Tatem—"Hey, that was my idea," said Cafrec—but the drawer had done it at night in a poorly lit area out of view of security cameras, so the DOE didn't know who vandalized it.

This development was promising; however, the risk these citizens put themselves in made Breel's stomach churn as they'd pay the ultimate

price for their actions. She had to remind herself they knew the consequences of rebelling against Tatem.

Everyone was eager to watch the news and hear how Tatem respond—if he would at all. He appeared on screen with a solemn expression, tsking while shaking his head. "Citizens, recent events have me most
disappointed and aggrieved. I had trusted you to put your fellow citizens
first by embracing the collective. But things are worse than before. These
new Vucapi acted as if they know what's best for everyone more than me,
your most benevolent leader.

"May I remind you, citizens, that before I became president, Lexum
was divided between the haves and the have-nots. Now everyone is a
'have' with the same excellent quality of life. Everyone receives an education, has a job, lives in a suitable home, and has more than enough
food. No one worries about affording house repairs or food for their
children. Why? Because I, your generous leader, provide everything. Yet,
some believe this is a bad thing and that our way of life is not sufficient.
It is more than sufficient, citizens. It is because of me that your children
don't starve and freeze in the night.

"Some of you may believe these selfish acts will go unpunished. No,
citizens. If someone acts suspicious, we investigate. If they do not embrace the collective, they are the next Vucapi. Embracing the collective
means never fearing Mortae. Commit selfish acts, and Mortae is your
future—just like it is for the missing Vucapi and their comrades. When
we find them—and we *will* find them—their Mortae will be something
you have never seen.

"Citizens, we must do better to preserve our way of life. Cancelling
tomorrow's anniversary celebrations is tempting; however, I will not
let a minority wreck it for the majority who embrace the collective, so

the celebrations will continue as planned. I know you look forward to celebrating fifty years together. Until tomorrow, good night."

"Same old crap!" said Cafrec with a yawn. "Scold, scold, scold. Just like a parent."

Criba and Manum chuckled as the latter turned off the television.

But Cafrec was right. The worst part was that Hargamites would take Tatem seriously. But there wasn't time to dissect yet another Tatem speech as their meeting involved last-minute prep for Vectus and Ragula's journey into Lexum.

Citizens would start entering the Quaddro at ten thirty for the speech and entertainment at eleven. Vectus and Ragula had an hour and a half at most before half of Lexum leaving for home or work at noon.

Vectus and Ragula planned to leave at eight to arrive at the walls by ten thirty. Through the help of the DOE, their own people would be on the north wall, lowering their risk of capture. They'd meet their Department of Expansion contact—on his way to the Quaddro—who'd give them the posters then Vectus and Ragula would split up to cover more ground. Another contact had recommended the best places to replace existing posters with their own. Using those locations, they created maps of the routes they'd follow to minimize walking and how many surveillance cameras they'd pass. Samit had sent the map to his team of computer programmers to plant fake feeds in the cameras they couldn't avoid from ten thirty to twelve.

Everyone reviewed the maps one last time to finalize each poster's location and the chosen routes.

"Ragula, you take west Lexum," said Vectus. "I'll take east. We'll meet back at the wall by twelve, and if all goes well, be back here before three."

Ragula rubbed her hands together. "I can't wait for another adventure!"

Breel laughed to herself.

Good thing someone's willing to do this.

Chapter Forty-Nine

They rushed breakfast so Vectus and Ragula could leave as soon as possible. They packed nothing because if citizens saw them, even a backpack would raise suspicions. To appear like an average citizen, they wore clothing from the captured DOE which Lexo and Praxa had convinced them to remove for washing in exchange for Intercludae clothing.

Samit shook Vectus's hand as everyone said goodbye. "Be careful."

"We will." Vectus pointed at Samit then Manum. "You two get along. Understood?"

"Good luck," Breel said.

She hugged Ragula then, surprising herself, hugged Vectus, too.

"We'll be back before you know it," Vectus said.

Concentrating on work proved difficult that morning. Even Samit complained; however, he remained at his computer to aid his security people while everyone else had target practice.

At eleven, they watched the anniversary coverage broadcasted for retirement home residents, sick citizens, and those who couldn't leave their jobs. Even Lexo watched, waking early from his sleep after a night of guard duty. Samit brought his laptop in case their contact assisting him—someone unable to attend the events because of her role—needed help.

The first part of the festivities was a reenactment of the events from fifty years ago, highlighting the differences between the lower- and upper-class lifestyles, followed by the civil war and its aftermath. The person acting as Tatem was somebody Breel had known from school. He was a fitting choice as he'd been as obnoxious as Vectus in the way he extolled Tatem's greatness and viewpoints.

Like the history books, the play made Tatem to be the hero and Mortae as a brilliant invention benefiting everyone.

It was fascinating watching people pretending to be someone they were not. However, that wasn't much different from normal life. Many citizens pretended, such as their inside sources playing the part of loyal citizens. Pretending was a prolific activity in Lexum.

The reenactment ended to applause, but it wasn't as boisterous as after Mortae. Tatem had failed to give much description about what plays are, so nobody had known what to expect and, therefore, how to react. But as usual, cheers erupted as Tatem walked onto the platform in his usual suit with his hands in the air while soaking in the crowd's adoration. He strutted to the microphone. It took five minutes for the crowd to settle.

"Citizens," said Tatem, "did you enjoy the reenactment?"

Oh, here we go again.

The crowd cheered then Tatem another minute to quiet them.

His grin changed to a grim expression. "That was our unfortunate reality fifty years ago. Many of us, me included, came from lower-class families living outside Lexum's walls. Thanks to my actions, everyone now enjoys the same quality of life. Citizens, today, no matter where your family came from, nobody is better off than anyone else. No one should have to live in poverty. As such, our every action must better society. We cannot be selfish. We must choose our fellow citizens, so everyone has the same standard of living.

"The Nito Test started fifty years ago, allowing everyone to embrace the collective by having the job we are best at. Citizens, what if I were to tell you we no longer need the Nito Test? What if I were to tell you there is a better, more accurate method for assigning Career Groups?"

"Here we go," said Cafrec.

Breel leaned forward, eager to hear Tatem use a self-destructive subroutine.

Tatem grinned, his eyes shining. "Citizens, we have been working on an alternative to the Nito Test for years. Instead of using the Nito Test, we will use children's genetics to determine their Career Group. Genes are our body's blueprints with half inherited from our mother and half from our father. They tell our bodies our hair colour, eye colour, height, personality, and innate abilities. For years, we have tested Career Group prediction based on genes. Finally, our ability to assign the optimal Career Group using genetics is better than the Nito Test.

"What does this mean? The Nito Test asks five-year-olds questions to determine their aptitude and abilities. From now on, when you come to the fertility clinic to have a child, we will examine the embryo's genes to determine their Career Group. Perhaps they are good with their hands so will be a mechanic fixing buses and delivery vans. If their genes show an organized and logical mind, it could mean a career in logistical planning.

"As well, we will search for and turn off any undesired traits. Using genetic engineering, we can guarantee the safety of your children by making them less likely to break the law. By having children more likely to be content and loyal citizens, you will not have to watch their Mortae or receive Mortae for their actions."

He surveyed the crowd. Only a smattering of citizens cheered. Near-silence in the Quaddro only ever meant one thing—either Tatem's message confused citizens, or they struggled to accept it.

Tatem frowned at the lack of response. "Citizens, you must be tired from the raucous cheer you gave me a few minutes ago. I just told you that your future children will not break the law."

The crowd gave a lacklustre cheer. Tatem's lips curled as his face reddened.

Oh, he must be regretting this.

Tatem took a moment to compose himself, the redness in his face disappearing. "Ensuring your children's safety is my fiftieth anniversary gift to you. This also ensures the continuance of our way of life so future generations will not experience civil unrest. But enough of that. After all, this is supposed to be a celebration!"

He threw his arms into the air with his characteristic smile. This time, the crowd reacted with cheers so loud they had to turn down the volume.

"There are many activities to enjoy here in the Quaddro," said Tatem. "Those assigned to take part today have until five when buses will return you home. For those taking part tomorrow, be here by noon. While celebrating, you must remember our newer laws regarding speaking only to citizens you work with or are related to you. Enjoy yourselves."

The video feed ended.

"Now we wait," said Cafrec.

"Seems like people weren't too happy about him messing around with their genetics," said Breel.

Gee, I wonder why...

"I'm not surprised, but I thought there'd be more cheers from the diehard Tatem group," said Manum.

Clonis's grin was eerily similar to his brother's. "Yep! That announcement didn't help him."

"He's too much of an egotistical maniac to think it'd hurt him," said Samit.

Clonis laughed at the word "maniac." "Yeah, Hargam always thought he was invincible. When my siblings and I advised him fifty years ago, we told him to be more careful, see. Wasn't until I saved his life that he realized we were right."

After lunch, Breel and Cafrec sat side-by-side in their room to discuss what they had seen before returning to work.

"I wouldn't have saved my family like Clonis saved Tatem," said Cafrec. "Well, Centia maybe."

"I understand," said Breel. "I know they're Hargamites."

"Breel, remember when you asked if I've checked on them? I finally did."

She knew enough not to ask what changed his mind. Cafrec certainly wasn't concerned about them, so he must've checked satisfy his curiosity.

Cafrec pushed his hair back. "The DOE questioned them, of course. They still believed I'm pro-Tatem, insisting you manipulated me, until they remembered certain things that happened and how close I was to Centia and Famut. It took putting the clues together to realize I'm not the person they thought I am. My mother cried in front of officers while apologizing for being on my side after I received my warnings. Ridiculous..."

Breel was in awe. "I'm impressed you convinced your parents you're pro-Tatem."

Either they're ignorant, or he's as skilled as Vectus in pretending to be a Hargamite.

He shrugged. "I had no other choice. The worst part is they told the DOE they'll do everything they can to find me. Who does that?"

Knowing it was a rhetorical question, Breel hugged him. He buried his face into her shoulder.

"Is there anything I can do?" she asked.

Cafrec released her, shaking his head. "Nah. I just hope I never have to see them again."

Without another word, Cafrec moved back to his desk.

***

Vectus and Ragula were due back around three, but the afternoon, suppertime, and the evening news came and went without them.

Everyone sat at the table in silence. Lexo reviewed some DOE systems, but nothing mentioned their arrest. Even though everyone told each other it was too early to be concerned, that Vectus and Ragula had a long walk back and may have taken a break, the group worried.

Samit read an email from a fellow programmer. "'Late this afternoon, I heard a commotion so peeked my head outside to find a dozen citizens marching through the streets yelling *down with Tatem!* and *stop messing with our kids!* The DOE arrived before they got to the end of the street. I know of others who saw similar protests.'"

Citizens had realized what a tyrant Tatem was and rebelling against him—their message worked! The update got everyone talking with excitement. But not everyone would escape Mortae.

Like Vectus and Ragula...are they okay? If they're still in Lexum, will they escape the DOE and Mortae?

Breel's stomach churned.

Cafrec grinned as if the DOE hadn't sentenced the protesters to Mortae. "With these protests, Tatem's got to have realized that he made a mistake with his announcement."

"Big time," said Lexo.

As evening turned into night, it seemed less and less likely that Vectus and Ragula would come. Everyone gathered in the living room before bedtime. Manum did push-ups in the corner—"I need to burn this nervous energy."—while the others stood around.

Criba drummed her fingers on the wall. "I can't sleep knowing they're out there."

"They could be waiting until daylight," said Trafis as he stared into the abyss.

Samit leaned against the wall with a sigh. "I hope so."

It was the only acceptable explanation. Considering anything else was too horrible, but nobody voiced concerns about capture, imprisonment, and torture.

In case Vectus and Ragula returned in the night followed by DOE officers, Praxa agreed to keep an ear out for them while guarding their prisoners.

It took hours for Breel to fall asleep, her mind replaying Tatem's announcement over and over as she tried not to go to the place of what could've happened to their comrades. Imprisonment, torture, Mortae...likely all three. Memories of sitting in front of Lexum as a Vucapi while citizens cheered for her death sent chills up her spine. Forcing herself to think of pleasant memories, she pulled the blankets up to her neck.

Chapter Fifty

Breel tossed and turned during the night. For once, her dreams weren't of Tatem killing Famut or of the unspeakable horrors in the sheds Tatem had forced them to view. Instead, they were of Vectus and Ragula.

The DOE capturing them, forcing them into a vehicle to go to jail.

A jailer carrying a .45 calibre pistol escorting them through the gray hallway then separating them into different cells.

Vectus and Ragula calling out to each other, only for their cell doors to slam shut, cutting off sounds outside their walled prison.

The long wait—isolated, hungry, and terrified with only an uncomfortable cot for company.

After hours or days, a jailer opening the door then escorting them to a tiny room. Enduring Tatem's torture prior to whatever horrific murder he had planned.

Breel woke in a sweat as she attempted to blink away the searing images of Vectus and Ragula lying on the ground injured and lifeless.

Think positive thoughts. Think positive thoughts. They'll be here by now!

Though it wasn't yet seven, she leapt out of bed then hurried into the kitchen, finding Samit at his desk.

Breel leaned over the counter beside Samit. "They're here, right?"

When he turned around to face her, she didn't need him to answer—the worry lines on his forehead told her everything.

Breel's heart sank.

No, no, no, no.

"Any news at all?"

Samit chewed his lip. "Nothing. Not even a DOE report."

If the DOE had captured them, there'd have been a report. Therefore, no news could mean good news. But since their DOE sources hid reports from Tatem, it was conceivable that Tatem did, too.

There was little chitchat during breakfast. Breel ate her oatmeal without paying much attention to her bowl. Samit and Manum stared at their uneaten food. Silent tears rolled down Criba's face. Not even Manum suggested rescue as it'd lead to more arrests and deaths.

Their only hope was to learn information from their sources. Breel sent a mass email to her Department of Health contacts and the others did the same with their own assigned departments but not even the DOE had news.

Vectus and Ragula weren't back by lunch or supper, putting them more than twenty-four hours overdue. After the news, Breel checked her email for the millionth time hoping that someone—*anyone*—had an answer. An email sent half an hour before sat in her inbox, flagged as important. The sender's name was blank. The subject line read "Is this yours?"

What the...

"Cafrec, look at this strange email."

He frowned at his own laptop. "The 'Is this yours?' email? I got it, too."

"Should we..."

Cafrec pushed against his desk to slide his chair beside hers. "Yeah, let's open it."

Taking a deep breath, she opened the email. The body had a black box with a play button which she clicked.

Blackness. Then a video of a red-headed man sitting on a chair, head lulling on his chest. If not for a rope around his shoulders, he would've toppled onto the floor. Blood oozed from his forehead. His shirt—yellow stripes with an indeterminable sweater colour because of the blood—had ripped. Someone had bound his hands behind him.

Breel gasped. Bile burned her throat. "Vectus!"

It shouldn't have come as a surprise, but everyone had clung to a nugget of hope for Vectus and Ragula. However, the DOE had arrested then tortured Vectus.

Cafrec's hands clapped against his mouth. "Oh no!"

The camera panned to the side, keeping Vectus on the edge of view. In the foreground, Tatem grinned and rubbed his hands together. His eyes sparkled like never before.

"Hello." He pointed a thumb at Vectus. "Is this yours? Are you missing him? I sure hope not."

Tatem grinned so wide that all his teeth showed.

As Tatem stepped closer then leaned into the camera, his smile disappeared. "Thought you were smart, bringing him into Lexum while most citizens celebrated in the Quaddro?"

Breel's heart raced. Samit and Manum's people had ensured the security cameras along the routes would show old footage. Most citizens had been in the Quaddro.

One of Samit's or Manum's people must have betrayed us. How else would the DOE have captured them?

Tatem stood beside Vectus. Leaning into him, he asked, "Any words for your traitorous friends?"

Vectus groaned.

Tatem laughed. "In that case..."

He grabbed the little hair Vectus had then lifted his head with it. Vectus screamed. Breel looked away but not before seeing his bloody and bruised face. His right eye was swollen shut and twice as big as the left. Tatem removed an object from his jacket pocket then made a quick motion across Vectus's neck. Blood gushed, spilling down his front and onto the floor.

"No!"

Breel winced at Cafrec's shout as her eyes stayed glued to the horrific scene. Bile burned her throat, but her eyes refused to turn away. Tatem released Vectus's hair, his head falling onto to his chest.

Tatem stepped closer to the camera. "Let that be a lesson to you."

The screen went blank. Breel shuddered. "How could he?! How could he do that?"

It wasn't until Cafrec put an arm around her that she realized she was crying.

Cafrec's body shook against hers. "Because he's Tatem. He's an evil, heartless fiend."

Before they could even try to put together what had happened, a thump sounded from above. They jumped as Manum shouted for everyone to see something.

Breel dried her eyes as she followed Cafrec upstairs. Everyone congregated around Samit's laptop.

"Is it an email?" Breel asked.

Samit turned to them with a grave expression. "You saw it?" He blinked away a rogue tear.

Breel swallowed hard. "Yeah."

Criba looked from Samit to Breel. "Saw what?"

Samit played the video. Breel looked away and tried to tune out the sounds of everyone's horrified reactions. But the whistling wind wasn't loud enough to overpower Criba's gasp or Trafis's shout of surprise.

After it finished, Criba's cries filled the room. Samit stared at his blank screen in horror. Praxa's hands were at her mouth. Clonis shook his head, tsking.

Manum broke the silence. "He was a good man."

"Yeah," managed Breel.

Words I'd never have said one month ago.

"He was the best," said Samit.

A tear rolled down his cheek.

Criba placed a hand on his shoulder. "Did you know him well?"

"A little. I..." He sighed. "I've never told any of you, but years ago in school, Vectus stopped some other Leaders of Tomorrow from bullying me over a poor grade." He lowered his head.

"Everyone got at least a few of those," said Criba. "Nothing to be ashamed about."

Samit gulped. "Vectus was a couple of years ahead of me and sort of tutored me in that class."

When Criba asked why they never mentioned knowing each other, Samit admitted he had begged Vectus not to say anything as having struggled in one of his first programming classes haunted him.

Manum tapped the table. "We don't have time for this. We must rescue Ragula, or she'll be next."

Samit dried his eyes again. "Manum, if she was next, don't you think Tatem would've said so in the video? He didn't even mention her."

"No, but—"

"She's the spy," said Breel.

The words tumbled out without forethought, but it made sense. The suspicious reappearance had been the first red flag. Ragula suggesting one of their group—rather than someone in Lexum—hang the posters had been the second. Saying she and Vectus should do the hanging had been the third red flag. Ragula had set up the whole thing.

Manum rounded on Breel, fists clenched. "Excuse me?!"

Breel stepped back, ready to move farther away if needed, but Manum didn't go after her. She took a deep breath before explaining her reasons.

Cafrec nodded. "Yeah, she *was* the first to suggest her and Vectus hang the posters!"

Samit banged a hand on the desk. "I hate being right."

Manum shook his head. "No. We don't know for sure. She suggested herself and Vectus because the DOE isn't searching for them. Tatem may have imprisoned her for all we know!"

Manum bit his lip as he looked from person to person with wide, pleading eyes.

Ignoring him, Breel asked, "Then why didn't Tatem mention Ragula? You'd think he'd use her as bait or record himself murdering them both."

Manum banged a fist on the table. "No! They must've captured Vectus after they split up which means Ragula's there looking for him."

"Well," said Samit. "We'll soon find out, won't we? If she's a spy, she's had plenty of time to bring the DOE here."

"But they haven't come yet, have they?" said Manum. "No, she's not a spy."

Everything Manum said *could* be true, but it sounded more like a dream than logical arguments.

"We need to leave, just in case," Breel said.

Manum opened his mouth to interject, but Praxa spoke first. "Mr. Gaimster, I agree with Breel. Regardless of whether Ragula's a spy, who knows what Vectus said when Tatem tortured him."

There were murmurs of agreement—even from Manum.

"But where do we go?" asked Trafis. He sunk back against the wall.

"I've had a Plan B for a while," Samit said. "We have a place to stay."

"Where?" asked Criba.

Samit cleared his throat. "Lexum."

"*What?!*" asked Breel. "Are you insane?"

The room got loud as the others also protested.

Samit took interest in the table. "Tatem wouldn't think to look right under his nose."

That was true. Not only that, but Tatem knew they were in the desert, so they couldn't hide there forever. Hiding in Lexum was the safest place because Tatem wouldn't expect it. Once they got there, they'd update their sources on the video. Perhaps even send the video, despite it being graphic.

Without forewarning, an idea popped into Breel's head. "Before we leave, we should email the video to all Leaders of Today," she said.

Criba gaped at her. "Breel! Why d'you want to show everyone that poor man's horrific death?"

"I know, it's bad. But imagine seeing it when you think Tatem's amazing? How many of them would change their minds and join us?"

Samit blinked away more tears. "That's a great idea."

Criba looked at him like he was a confusing program of spaghetti code. "Are you serious? Put the video of his murder on display?"

"Vectus wouldn't have cared if it helps the cause," said Cafrec.

Samit raised a hand. "We don't have time for this. We need to leave now! Breel, send the video before shutting down your computer."

"But...but..." Criba looked around the room for backup, but most had already left to prepare to leave. She sighed. "Okay."

"What about our prisoners?" Lexo asked.

"We leave them for the DOE to find," said Samit. "They know nothing, anyway."

Breel raced downstairs to forward the email. Her mouse hovered over the send button.

May Vectus forgive us...

She forwarded it, shut off her laptop, then joined the others in the kitchen. Everyone had a small backpack into which they put their laptop. Criba, Trafis, and Samit burned stacks of paper in two pots on the counter.

Lexo and Praxa—weapons in hand—peered out of the kitchen windows through the blinds' slats.

"The DOE is here," Lexo said.

Chapter Fifty-One

Breel gasped as adrenaline coursed throughout her body. Feeling faint, her hand grasped the corner of the wall. It had taken a month, but officers had found them because Ragula was a spy and told Tatem their location or Vectus told him under torture. They couldn't blame Vectus if he had done it; however, Breel was certain that Ragula had told Tatem—not Vectus.

This was it—either the end, or the time for them to overcome another group of officers. Last time, Breel, Trafis, and Criba had the upper hand thanks to noticing them first, but there was no such luxury now.

Lexo and Praxa moved toward the door. Praxa said there were five elite force officers.

Breel's heart raced as her breath came in quick gasps at the thought of losing someone else. Manum handed out weapons. Cafrec took one with a shaky hand. Breel's gun was cold against her hand. Holding it felt different from target practice or as a precaution during supply runs because this time it was to defend herself from an imminent threat.

Lexo, closest to the window, peered outside. "They have Ragula."

They do!?

Needing to see for herself, Breel looked through the small gap between the bottom corner of the blinds and the windowsill. There were indeed six people, the sixth being Ragula, cuffed and still in the officer uniform.

She stood between the other officers who all had .45 calibre pistols trained on her.

Manum was right—she's not a spy.

Relief flooded her for a moment before realizing it meant the spy was still out there. But that was tomorrow's problem—if they got a tomorrow.

"Come out or we shoot her," said an officer.

"Stay here," said Manum. He nodded to Lexo and Praxa then opened the door.

Weapons raised, the three of them approached the line of five elite officers and Ragula.

Breel's heart beat as if she'd ran straight from Lexum. The ragged breathing of the others was audible. Tension hung like a storm cloud waiting to let loose its deluge.

"Drop your weapons or we shoot her," shouted the man on Ragula's right. "We're elite force—these weapons have deadly bullets, not darts."

Manum nodded at Lexo and Praxa to drop their guns.

"Good," said the man.

Breel whimpered.

We're going to be murdered.

"Are you okay, Ragula?" Manum asked.

Ragula nodded. "They haven't hurt me."

A man said, "Surrender, and we won't kill you."

"And why should we believe Tatem's elite force?" asked Manum.

"That's President Tatem!" said a woman at the end of the line.

She fired her weapon. Anticipating it, Manum had jumped out of the way, unscathed.

The DOE will kill them!

Breel started toward the door, wanting to help, but Criba put a hand on her shoulder.

"No!" Criba shouted. "Don't!"

But Criba couldn't stop everyone who rushed out the door. Cafrec, Trafis, and Samit ran outside, weapons raised. Breel followed with Criba and Clonis hesitating behind her. Their arrival distracted the officers enough for Manum, Lexo, and Praxa to retrieve their weapons.

Shots fired from both sides.

Three officers were on the ground as was Lexo with Praxa kneeling beside him. Manum stood between the two groups, his attention on Lexo. Everyone else stood between Manum, Lexo, Praxa, and their opposition. Breel's heart hammered as the two remaining officers pointed their weapons.

"Surrender and we won't shoot anyone else," said the female officer.

"You're a liar," said Samit.

There was no warning. One moment she was standing, the next Samit had fired his gun, dropping her to the ground. Before the other officer could react, Breel shot him. She cried out, shocked by what she'd done.

It's only a tranquilizer, he's fine.

Only Ragula remained. She gave Breel a thumbs up then ran her fingers through her hair to remove the sand.

Breathing a sigh of relief, Breel turned to Lexo and Praxa, her hands pressed against Lexo's chest. Blood stained the ground.

Manum placed a hand on her shoulder. "Praxa, he's gone. We've gotta go."

He hauled her up by the arm as Praxa stared at Lexo, unable to avert her gaze.

Tears stung Breel's eyes despite having not known Lexo well. Seeing his body drenched in blood was a painful reminder of Famut's death.

She shut her eyes, imagining she was staring at a piece of paper with a pencil in her hand.

A hand squeezed her bicep. Samit. "We need to go," he said, tugging her arm.

"Are we going to leave the officers lying there?" she asked.

"Nothing else we can do," said Samit. "When they wake, we'll be long go—"

Breel jumped when one, two, three, four, five shots filled the air. Praxa was no longer with Manum. Instead, she stood in front of the officers, one of their lethal weapons in her hand, as blood seeped from the forehead of every officer.

Breel gaped at the sight of Praxa having killed every all five elite force officers. For the first time, her gun still in hand and her jaw set, she looked the role of DOE officer.

Praxa holstered the weapon then, with tears streaming down her face, locked eyes with each person in turn, staring intently in a silent challenge to protest her actions.

Samit continued as if it didn't happen. "We have to go."

"Where's Ragula?" asked Manum, looking around.

She wasn't with them. Trafis checked inside the house while Breel and the others looked outside it and toward the nearby factory. But she wasn't anywhere.

She must be on the other side of the factory.

Before Breel could suggest it, a glinting object on the ground near the officers caught her eye. Breel picked it up.

Handcuffs.

"What's that?" Trafis asked.

Breel showed everyone the cuffs. "She got these off no problem."

That could only mean one thing.

Samit had been right all along.

Ragula was the spy.

***

The safe house was no longer safe as at any moment more DOE would arrive. The only option was hiding from Tatem within his lair. If they could hide in Lexum without detection for a week after their failed Mortae, they could do it again.

Breel's legs were like lead as they trekked toward Lexum.

Ragula had been the spy all along. After Manum's continued insistence of her innocence and everything Breel and Vectus had said to get Ragula to slip, she'd hidden her pro-Tatem self so deep that nothing they said fazed her. Not even Samit dared tell Manum "I told you so."

If that blow wasn't enough, everyone grieved for Lexo and Vectus. Manum and Praxa cried for Lexo, arms around each other. Samit trailed behind, shoulders slumped as his tears fell. Criba followed, urging him forward.

This had all happened because Breel and Cafrec suggested she create posters to hang in Lexum. If they hadn't, Vectus and Ragula wouldn't have entered Lexum. Now Vectus and Lexo were dead.

Vectus's death broke Breel's heart the most. After getting to know his true self, she had becoming comfortable with him and enjoyed his company. But Tatem had tortured then murdered the poor guy.

May Vectus forgive us for showing everyone that footage.

Breel shuddered as Cafrec held out his hand. She took it as he looked at her with eyes wide with fear and uncertainty for the future. They didn't speak—there was nothing to say.

Only Samit knew where they were going as he hadn't had time to explain Plan B. After everything that happened, learning more about their only option seemed a moot point.

Once they arrived at the new safe house, they'd have a ton of work to do.

More pictures to draw on pamphlets and posters for distribution—if they dared to try hanging them again.

Interviews of retirement home residents to air during the news.

Encouraging more citizens to rebel.

Informing everyone of Tatem's despicable childhood actions.

At least they had distributed some posters and pamphlets, and everyone had seen their message on the news. No matter where they'd hide in Lexum, those victories made it more likely that they'd achieve their goal and erase Tatem's oppressive grip on Lexum.

Receive a Free Short Story!

Want to read an exclusive free and short story about Cafrec receiving a warning as a Leader of Tomorrow? Get your copy of *Warning* by subscribing to my newsletter at https://subscribepage.io/drawingreader.

You'll also receive news about upcoming releases and exclusive content. Your email will never be shared.

If you only want to read the story, feel free to unsubscribe after downloading your copy.

Please Share Your Thoughts

Thank you so much for reading my book. I'd love to hear your thoughts about it. Please consider leaving an honest review to share your feedback. Short or long, all reviews are appreciated.

Author's Note

Genetic engineering is part of the *Sketching Rebellion Trilogy.* In Lexum, certain genes determine certain personality traits (such as whether one is creative or rebellious). But this isn't a scientifically accurate portrayal of genetics.

In reality, while we do inherit *some* of our personality through our genes, there are no personality traits determined only by genes. Instead, our personalities depend on many factors—including nature (i.e. our genes) and nurture (i.e. our environment).

I made genetics in Lexum less scientifically accurate to write the book in the way I wanted the story to unfold.

Thank you for understanding and for reading.

Felicia

Acknowledgements

To my mom, Colleen Ketcheson, and brother, Edward Ketcheson, thank you for reading an earlier draft and providing me with your honest feedback for improvement.

To the real life "Breh," "Evad," and "Luap," thanks for the laughs! You got yourselves into my book.

To everyone who waited for this book and asked me why I was out and about instead of writing, thank you for your patience! I'm humbled that you were so excited for *Drawing Freedom's* release.

About the Author

Felicia Ketcheson is the author of *Sketching Rebellion*, which was a 2022 Killer Nashville Claymore Award finalist (Best Juvenile/YA category), and *Drawing Freedom*. When she was seven, she wrote her first book about a dog, cat, and bee. Four years later, she randomly started writing a short novel, catapulting her into the world of series writing. When she's not devising ways to destroy the lives of her fictional characters, she works as a systems analyst. Database developing is a passion she simultaneously loves and hates. She lives in St. Catharines, Ontario, Canada.

Website: https://feliciaketcheson.com/
Facebook: https://www.facebook.com/feliciaketchesonauthor
Goodreads: https://www.goodreads.com/feliciaketcheson

Also By Felicia Ketcheson

Sketching Rebellion Trilogy

Sketching Rebellion

Drawing Freedom

Adult technothrillers written as Remi Cape

Unshackled Intelligence. Unshackle yourself from the chains of mortality. For more information, visit https://feliciaketcheson.com/unshackled-intelligence/

Memoir

Life of a Salesman by R. Alex Jackson. A collection of stories my grandpa wrote about his fascinating childhood and young adulthood. For more information, visit https://feliciaketcheson.com/life-of-a-salesman/